Package Deal

Accepting the Unknown & Everything to Come

Written By: A Lady on Her Way

Copyright © 2025 Bank on Yourself LLC

Package Deal
By: A Lady on Her Way

ISBN: 979-8-9990106-6-7(Electronic)
ISBN: 979-8-9990106-7-4(Paperback)

The characters and events portrayed in this book are fictitious. Any similarity to real persons, living or dead, is entirely coincidental and not intended by the author.

Printed in the United States of America

Dedication

Visualize your dreams. Pray for guidance and watch them unfold.
Thank you, God, there is always more.

Other Works of Art from A Lady on Her Way
Sharnel – Showing Your Cards
Sharnel – Showing Your Cards II
Sharnel – Showing Your Cards III

Coming Soon
Sharnel – Showing Your Cards IV (January 2026)
Karma's Cyn

Table of Contents

Welcome to My World

I'm Dr. Sasha Philips; I'm a black woman and a licensed clinical mental health counselor, among other things. I have a Ph.D. Put some respect on my name, please and thank you. Thank you for taking this ride with me. Welcome to my world! My story takes place in the DMV. For those who don't know, that stands for the District of Columbia, Maryland, and Virginia. My life is based in the suburbs of Maryland. If you haven't had Maryland crabs and watched our amazing football teams, you're missing out. But I digress. You will meet all the important people in my life. They are a whole trip and vibe individually and collectively, especially Lorna (my mother). You will also get a treat, an in-depth view into my mind and past experiences. Look for the *italics* and enjoy. Now, don't judge my thoughts; I have a therapist for all that. Judge ya self before you side-eye me! I take care of all facets and versions of me; my mental wellness is why I can keep my doors open and clients on my sofa. If you are smart, you might get one too! You know you've got several people living in your head, but I digress. Here's what you need to know about me.

I'm 42, single, with no kids, own my home, and have a private practice among other businesses. I work out consistently; I love coffee and tea, music, and being a grown woman from time to time. I'm average height, medium brown, my hair is always wigged or weaved (just easier and I'm lazy). After suffering a heartbreak, I lost over 75lbs, so I'm toned and cute in all the right places. However, I'm still a work in progress in some ways. Patience is a virtue. Anyway, I've done well for myself, my life is comfortable, quiet, drama-free! I love it and purposely keep it that way, or so I tell myself.

Anyway, enjoy!
Dr. Sasha Philips

Chapter 1

If I close my eyes, I can see it. I see the house, its entire layout. I see myself sitting in the living room. The formal one, where typically no one is allowed, because everything is a variation of light neutral colors. No one is around, but I can feel various presences around me. The room is lit with the smell of a relaxing white tea and sage from an aromatherapy candle. Reading a book on the cream sofa, my legs are crossed, letting the sun kiss my back. My former long weave is now a natural bob right above my ear. The light from the window glistens against the jewelry adorning my ears, neck, and hands. I'm wearing a striped pink and white button-down with khaki pants and pink furry slippers. Everything fits perfectly with my slender yet curvy frame.

I have no care in the world. I'm happy, not just content. For once, everything is all right. I have the life I've dreamed of. There are several sterling silver picture frames aligned on the table in front of me. However, I can't see what's in the frames. The images are blurry, but one is definitely a wedding photo. Likely one where his hands touch my face and I stare happily into his eyes. My gentle giant, the one I've waited and prayed for many lifetimes before we actually met. The one I've covered in prayer. We were a custom design; a package deal made for a specific point in time. Now we're finally here, not a moment delayed or too soon. Smiling at my thoughts, I set down the book and observe the space with gratitude before leaving it. Getting up from the sofa, I head up the stairs, covered in dark wood on the steps and part of the railing that led to the second floor. There are many stairs, but I take them in stride. Not a breath wasted or step stumbled. Allowing the natural light from the foyer ushers me to the top of the stairs. When I reach the top, I stop right in front of the entrance way to the suite. Smiling once more before I reach the doorknob. Once I touch the knob and enter the room, the day immediately turns into a moonlit night, my favorite.

Walking across the room, I enter the large bathroom of the suite and close the door. It's time for my nightly routine before bed. Washing away the day, hydrating, and moisturizing for the night ahead. When the door opens again, I head for the plush king-size bed. A multicolored head scarf, tangerine strappy satin night dress, moisturized with shea butter, and mouth, minty fresh. I hop up on the bed, which sits on a heavy, dark wooden frame, pull back the dark comforter, and slide into bed to get comfy. After giving thanks and gratitude for the day, I reached for the bedside lamp on the nightstand to turn it off. Stretching myself from the bed, as I am about to hit the switch, there's movement behind me. A male body rolls over behind me. He lets out a breath, mumbles a few words, and adjusts his position behind me. Then takes his arm and puts it across my waist. As if to welcome me into bed and his embrace. He's awakened enough to kiss me good night, maybe even make my night later. Feeling his body heat, I smile again, excited that he's welcomed his wife into our private space. I click the light off while smiling at me…your dream has finally come true.

The blaring of my alarm was a rude reminder that it was only a dream. However, it's not my alarm but a phone call from my mother at 7:00 am.

Why is she up so early? Who calls people at 7:00 am, fuck!

Before I answered, I cleared my throat and smiled as if she could see me.

"Good morning, Mama, how are you?" I yawned into the phone.

"Good morning yourself, I know you weren't still sleeping." She barks as I hear her stir around her kitchen.

"Yes, I was, but I'm up now. How can I help you?"

"Oh, nothing, I was just calling because I hadn't heard from you."

Was she serious? She could have called me at 9:00 am for this nothing chat.

I wanted to go back to sleep, maybe catch the second act of my dream, but what was the point? My dreams never picked up where they left off. They became a distant memory or a space on my mental vision board for shit I wished would happen and soon. Personally, I was tired of these teases and wished God would get to the main event already. Oh, well, it was no point in wishing and hoping any longer; I was up now. So, I headed to the bathroom as Lorna (my mother) proceeded to tell me all the family gossip. As she continued talking, I put her on mute so I could pee and flush the toilet in peace. Once I finished, I unmuted her and turned on the faucet to take a bird bath, which included washing my face, hands, and brushing my teeth.

"You'll never guess who's pregnant again!" she yelled and waited for me to guess. It was likely one of the twins, Tina (whom we called Tinny) or Gina (Ginny). I could've bet my bottom dollar, it was Tinny, as if I cared.

"Tinny."

"Close, it's Tinny's oldest girl, little T."

Damn, I would have lost that bet. Glad I didn't give a fuck.

While changing into my gym clothes, I replied halfheartedly.

"You don't say. Let me know where to send the Walmart gift card or whatever."

"Would it kill you to be a little more enthusiastic, Sasha, sheesh! They are family, and children are a blessing."

Lorna was the matriarch, so she was my link to the family happenings. She took her role seriously and tried her best to make me her co-matriarch, but I avoided it like the plague. I was only close to one person, my cousin Robbie, whom I called Robbie Bobbie since that was his name (Robert-Bobby). He was an up-and-coming actor in Dallas, so his stage name was *Robert Williamson*; he said it made him sound grand and important. I laughed like hell when he first said it, but he had a point. I don't know what the hell my auntie was thinking, naming him that; it was country as hell, but I digress.

Anyway, my cousins popped kids out like Skittles on a Farm. They had too many kids, sub kids, almost kids, and other kids from their various baby daddies and mamas. Either way, it was too much to keep up with. It got to the point where I stopped going to baby showers, just kept a stack of gift and congratulations cards. No one cared if I went; they just wanted some money. So, I sent money and waited for the little alien or marshmallow baby pictures. They all had fat cheeks and bellies; seen one, seen them all. Sounds odd coming from the woman who desperately wanted her own little alien or marshmallow baby, but whatever it's how I feel. Although Ginny's last one looked a little suspect, he definitely didn't look like her or the father, but I digress.

After letting my mother rant enough to freshen up and get into my truck to head to the gym, I decided to end the call. She was in a talking mood, and this would go on for hours if I didn't put a cork in it.

"Well, mother, I'm going to let you get back to it. I'm headed to the gym." I said as I adjusted the cap on my head.

"Ok, well, enjoy your day and be safe. I'm going to drink this coffee, watch the news, and get my day started." I was almost home free until she spoke again. "Oh, before you go…" This meant another 10 or 15 minutes before she would actually get off my phone. It didn't matter; it would take me that long to get to the gym, so why not let her go on? She proceeded with the next topic, which consisted of my uncle's gout flare-up. He enjoyed food and paid the price happily complaining, but what was new? When I finally parked, she was on story number three about gout or something. When I looked at the clock, I was running behind, so I really needed to go.

"Lorna!" I said to get her attention.

"Oh, that's right, you were headed to the gym. Ok, I'm getting off the phone."

I shook my head; this was the third time she self-corrected before she started her next story. But this was the norm. I cut off the car and made my way inside, hoping she would hear he phone switch from my truck back to my ear.

As I walked, I tried to balance the phone on my ear as I connected my earphones while she continued her rant. However, I accidentally put her on speaker phone. I fumbled with the phone trying to get her off speaker, but the damn thing froze.

"You know these conversations wouldn't be so long if you called more often. I'm tired of calling you first."

She couldn't be serious now. I'm so not in the mood for this. I'm doing the best I can, woman!

Still fumbling with the phone, the obvious choice should have been to turn the volume down. However, I didn't think of that until she loudly said.

"Are you at least dating? I want some grandkids. Any prospects at least? Have you even had sex this year?"

"Really, Lorna!" I was mortified and struggled harder to get her off the speaker.

"What? You are grown. Although you will always be my baby, Sasha. So, are you going to answer me or not? You know if you don't use it, you will lose it!"

Lorna was not shy about asking about my relationship status or sex life. In her former life, she must have been a sex therapist, given the conversations she attempted to have with me. As much as I tried to avoid them, she was persistent and would tell me about things she read or "experienced." It was embarrassing as hell, but she wasn't shy and often shared her wisdom with others, like my assistant Keysha. Although I wasn't comfortable talking to her about my freak level but if she knew, she'd be proud.

Still standing outside of the gym, I fidgeted with the phone, frustrated as I tried to get her off speaker before she said anything else sexual. I had to get her off speaker, better yet, off the phone, but the shit wouldn't budge. Not paying attention, I was blocking the gym door, and someone cleared their throat behind me.

OMG. Someone heard what the hell she said. Please be a woman or a hideously ugly old ass man.

When I turned around, not only was he pussy dripping sexy, but he stood tall and at attention. The towering black man in front of me was beautiful. He was an Adonis, with ripped muscles that dripped all over his dark chocolate frame. He had some grown man weight, but I could work with that. The black hair that adorned his head and face was natural, not that store-bought shit that ruined sheets. *Fucking Blue.* His eyes were brown but had fire in them. He took care of himself as his hair was freshly cut low with deep waves, beard and goatee were trimmed. I was able to take in some of his tats, which were at the top of his frame. Part of me wanted to look at his nails, specifically to see if he had a ring, but I couldn't move my body or my eyes.

How the fuck can I get a taste of whatever he's packing. He definitely ain't got a small dool[1], ain't no way in hell God made him small.

Seeing I was stuck, the gentleman laughed, exposing a bright smile and his white teeth.

"So, you gonna answer her? I think she's still talking to you." His voice was deep and mellow. A sound you wanted to hear in your ear while things happened elsewhere. I nodded in agreement. Then he said as he raised his eyebrow, unsure of my pause, "Maybe you should answer her." I nodded again.

"Obviously, my daughter is struck by you, sir. My name is Lorna. My daughter's name is Sasha. It's nice to meet you."

Did Lorna just introduce us to a complete stranger? OMG, wake the fuck up, girl! Take over before she embarrasses us more.

But I couldn't move. The gray ballcap on my head, which covered my hair, couldn't hide my face or dazed expression. I felt like I was dripping thinking about the man who stood in front of me. When he smiled at me again, I felt like he squeezed me like fresh orange juice because I was dripping and hoped it didn't show on my clothes. My one-piece pink jumpsuit was not thin material. However, the gray half-sweatshirt-like crop top would not hide any wet stains if they did appear. Seeing that I was taken by his presence, he reached for my hand, only he didn't take my hand. He had my phone and stared at me as he spoke.

Wait, is he holding my phone? How the fuck did he get that? What is he about to do with it?

---

[1] Penis

"Hi, Miss Lorna. I'm Randolph (Dolph). It's nice to meet you and Sasha." Dolph smiled as he spoke to Lorna.

He said my name. He's talking to my momma. Is this really happening? Damn, I love the sound of my name coming from his lips. Hope he would feel the same if I can ever pull it together, shit!

"Well, Randolph, the pleasure is all mine. Is my daughter still there? You must be really handsome because she hasn't said a word. Sasha, baby, can you hear mama?"

Randolph let out a deep laugh. It surprised me and snapped me back into reality. I wasn't expecting that from him. Finally, able to process what was happening, I reached for my phone, and he held it above him out of my reach. Then proceeded to respond to Lorna.

"Yes, ma'am, she's ok now. I think I see life re-entering her body. She's blinked a few times." He touched my wrist as if to check my pulse. "Yeah, she has a good heart rate and steady breathing." After checking my "pulse," he didn't let my wrist go; he rubbed his fingers against it.

Was he serious? Why is he still touching me? If it felt good on my wrist, could them long ass fingers feel good somewhere else, too?

I looked at him, then at my phone. My face said *Give me my damn phone.* However, his face said, *Try to come and get it.* Even if I tried, I couldn't because he was too tall, and he still held my wrist. Plus, if I did, it would look like a bad attempt to rub my body against him. That wouldn't be so bad, but it would make me seem desperate, and I wasn't—not really.

"Sasha, can you answer me, please?"

Lorna sounded a bit concerned, so he lowered the phone and leaned it closer to me so I could speak. Skeptically, I leaned in to respond to her. However, it felt like he was luring me into him as he held on to me. So, I cleared my throat so I could respond to Lorna.

"I'm fine, Lorna." Calling her by her first name or using the term mother was my way of telling her I was a bit perturbed. Her willingness to share my information with a stranger was not cool. We'd definitely talk about that shit later. "Umm, I'll call you later," I replied, still looking at Dolph.

"Well, that's fine. Randolph, baby…"

Did she just call him baby? She needs to get off the phone asap. Fucking Lorna!

"Yes, ma'am."

Did he just respond? He was about to get fired before he was hired. Why is he entertaining a lady he doesn't even know? Urgh, it's giving weirdo vibes.

I frowned and shook my head at his response. He could abort mission; I could take it from here. I reached for the phone, and he moved it out of my reach again.

"I don't know who you are. However, my daughter is taken aback by you. This is rare."

I'm putting Lorna up for adoption! Matter of fact, he could have her since they were besties, damn it!

He smiled and waited for her to continue.

"Please do me a favor. Don't give her back her phone until your number is in it because she's not going to ask or do it herself."

Palm to face! Officially done, kick the bucket and my ass!

He laughed and nodded, then Lorna added more to her little speech.

"She has a thing on her phone where if you put it in her face, it unlocks it. Use that and put your information in. I'm gonna stay on the phone to make sure you can do it."

Did she just tell him how to unlock my phone? He better not…

Randolph waved the phone in front of my face. I tried to close my eyes quickly, but it was too late.

Now the damn phone wants to work! I'm going back to Android since Apple is a fuckin' trader! Your ass is outta here, going to the phone store asap!

Then he lowered the phone so I could see him put his contact information in.

Wait, is he really putting his number into my phone? What if it's one of them fake numbers?

We were all silent, and he finished up. I looked at the phone while trying to hide my curious yet hopeful face. When he sent himself a text and his phone chimed, I tried to mask my relief by returning to my annoyed face.

YESSSS!!!! Sasha, you got a number, girl, owww!

"Ok, Miss Lorna. I did it." He said proudly as he smiled at me.

"Good. You can hand her back her phone now."

He handed me the phone, and I snatched it back in awe of his allegiance to this lady he had just met.

"Now take my number down too. I want to make sure we stay in touch, too."

What was this a throuple[2]? Why the hell did they need each other's information? This is weird.

Lorna rattled off her information, and Randolph did as she requested, including sending her a text so she could have his number.

What type of bullshit is this? Did I just bag the same man as my momma? This has to be some sick joke.

Feeling satisfied with herself, Lorna finally decided to end the call.

"Well, that's settled. I gotta go now, *Banaza* is about to start."

Dolph and I laughed, and I rubbed my head.

This was Lorna, always trying to be a matchmaker so she could get herself a son and some grandbabies. This time, she might have just accomplished her mission. Although I doubt it.

"Have a great day, Sasha. I will be checking up on you later. Randolph, baby, I'll be checking on you, too." She said smiling through the phone.

"Yes, ma'am, I look forward to it." He said, as he finally let go of my wrist.

Sucks like hell, but I'm about to dead this as soon as her ass gets off the phone. This was too weird and embarrassing across the board.

Once Lorna hung up, I could finally process what the hell just happened.

"Umm…Randolph, is it?" I said with a slight attitude.

"Yep, what's up, Sasha?" He said, as if my reaction was cute or something.

---

[2] Three-way relationship, google it!

"Thanks for entertaining my mother. Also, don't take anything she said seriously. It was very kind of you to play along. Please don't take this the wrong way…but please delete everything and go on about your life. Trust and believe, she will get over it. No hard feelings, ok? You have a good one. Peace. Love. Blessings." Without allowing him to respond, I ended the conversation.

I turned and walked towards my truck. Fuck the gym. I had had enough of a mental workout for the day before I could even get some damn coffee.

Hurried across the parking lot, as I couldn't get away from him fast enough. I was moving so fast I tripped over my feet but kept moving.

Fuck! Fuck! Fuck! Fuck! Matter of fact, Fuck the gym. I'm going to the one a few miles down from now on. There was no way I could ever stomach seeing him again. Better yet, I didn't have enough underwear to hold what his appearance did to me anyway. Please let him have already gone inside, PLEASE!

"Aye, you good?" He yelled. I didn't fall but felt embarrassed since he hadn't gone inside yet. Still walking towards my car, I gave a thumbs up but never looked back.

When I cranked my truck, I purposely went in the opposite direction from the gym. If I saw him again, I might do something stupid like crash into something. I had the mind to call Lorna and ask her what the hell she was thinking. However, it was no point. Plus, fussing at her would only upset us both, so it was no point. I was behind schedule and needed to get to the office before I was late for my first appointment.

Fucking Randolph! Where the hell did you come from?

Chapter 2

"So, Sheldon, what is keeping you up at night?" I asked as I adjusted in my chair and looked at my client. After a nice shower and two cups of coffee, I was in therapist mode. Which meant hair pulled back, glasses on, a professional dress or suit, and meditation before each session.

Sheldon and I had been working together for two years. He was seven years old. At first, he didn't talk much, just mostly doodled. So, I'd join him and we'd discuss our pictures, which allowed me to slowly unpack his thoughts and feelings. However, that changed over time, and once he became comfortable when something piqued his interest, he was alive.

Sheldon was referred to me for having an "aggressive" personality. From what I saw, he wasn't aggressive; he just didn't give a fuck what adults thought. He liked what he liked—typical kid shit. Too bad the adults around him didn't pay enough attention to him. They'd learn he had a beautiful mind, full of thoughts that made you think and question yourself. He just needed his interest to be spiked and someone to listen.

"Spiderman vs. Batman," he replied as he folded his arms, annoyed.

"What about them?" I asked inquisitively. Sheldon was definitely wise beyond his years, given his life experiences, but conundrums like this reminded me he was still an innocent boy.

Sheldon thought about it, then replied.

"Why can't Batman have webs like Spider-Man? And why can't Spider-Man have wings? It's not fair!"

I nodded. He was obviously upset over this dilemma; it was a lot for his young mind to handle. He explained his logic, which he shared with his friends who laughed at him.

Fucking kids!

Some of them can be so mean, trying to be the adults they believed they were. If they knew better, they'd let conundrums like this be a meaningful battle in their lives and stop trying to be mini celebrities and porn stars on the internet, but I digress. He was right. It wasn't fair.

Why couldn't they both have awesome superpowers? Hell, I wanted some bangles like Wonder Woman so I could hit people who pissed me off. Better yet, some Hulk hands so I could break some shit like Lorna's phone for that stunt she pulled earlier. Oh, wait…Maybe I could have powers like Mystique from X-Men. I could transform into other people, like when…Focus, Sasha, focus!

I was so wrapped up in my thoughts that I forgot poor Sheldon was waiting for a response.

"You know, Sheldon, you're right. They should have options."

When Sheldon nodded in agreement, I continued.

"Superheroes should have multiple powers, and often they do. So, I think you should build a Voltron superhero."

Forgetting my age versus his, I had to explain what a Voltron was. When he finally grasped the concept, I gave him the task of drawing his Voltron for the remainder of the session. Sheldon put on his headphones and closed his eyes to visualize his idea for the superhero. When we agreed to talk about his idea next week, like any task, he wanted to focus on unpacking his thoughts. Knowing he didn't like to be bothered when deep in thought, I checked my email while we waited for his mother to arrive. She was always late, but with four kids, I couldn't blame her.

While I replied to an email, Sheldon took off his headphones.

"Dr. Sasha, I need to say something."

I stopped typing, giving Sheldon my undivided attention.

"Sure, let's hear it, Sheldon."

He took a breath and gathered his words.

"What are your superpowers?" I frowned, unsure how to respond. "You said superheroes can have multiple powers, so what's yours?

I smiled and thought before responding.

"Hmm…first, thank you for the compliment. I appreciate it. My superpower is helping and teaching people. Oh, and helping them a develop and live a positive mental health lifestyle." Sheldon gave me the thumbs up. Before he could put his headphones back on, I spoke. "What's your superpower, Sheldon?" He immediately scowled. "What, you don't think you're a superhero? I know, I think you are." Sheldon smiled and then replied.

"I'm a protector, keeping all my siblings and my mommy safe."

I clapped in praise of his comment. Sheldon was a protector despite being the youngest. His protective nature was one of the reasons we were together.

"You are a great protector and brother, Sheldon. You know what else, you're smart, an awesome artist, and will one day be an awesome martial artist."

Sheldon smiled with pride. His mom had recently put him in jujitsu, and he loved it. It was good for his mental and physical health.

"Just a reminder, keep your moves off the playground, Bruce Leroy!"

Sasha, he's only 7! The boy has never seen the classic martial arts of Bruce Leroy in the Last Dragon! Who's the prettiest?

Sheldon looked confused, then laughed. "Sho nuff! Oh, and he was a Kung Fu master, Dr. Sasha."

I was super excited and yelled.

"You've seen the Last Dragon! Sheldon, my man!" Sheldon and I high fived.

"Who's the prettiest?" Sheldon said with his chest sticking out.

Sheldon and I talked about the movie until his mom picked him up. I enjoyed clients like him; they made the day easier and much brighter until I had to deal with adults and their adulting issues.

After one more client, I could finally take lunch and a mental break. With all the antics of the morning and no workout, I needed to burn some energy. I would likely try the gym after work, knowing I'd never get any sleep if I didn't do something. I could take a walk during lunch. Maybe I could get LaKeysha (Keysha or

Key), my assistant, to walk with me. She always complained about keeping her 25-year-old figure intact. Keysha was light-skinned, with beautiful natural brown hair. She wore either straightened or curled, her 150lb ass got on my nerves. Since she was tall, her weight looked even better on her. Got on my damn nerves. I was 42 and worked to keep mine together. She wasn't much in the chest department but had a nice booty she was proud of. Keysha was a lady, always primped, had good manners, and her appearance reflected as such. However, when you pissed her off, that good girl went out the window. Not only was she my assistant, but more like my little sister/best friend. So, I'd seen her take off her good girl side plenty of times.

Anyway, at lunch, I planned on bribing Keysha to walk with me. Knowing I needed to start working on her early, I hit the intercom button on the phone.

"Keysha, who's next?"

"Dr. Sasha, you have our favorite, Lionel, in 15 minutes." She said, laughing.

My head immediately hit the desk.

Why did he have to be before lunch? I could handle him better after a sandwich or an oatmeal crème pie, FUCK!

Lionel was no favorite, but at the same time, he was. However, I treated him with the same ease and grace I did with other clients. He was a 27-year-old, biracial adult male who refused to grow the hell up. He believed the world should be laid at his feet and women should be feeding him grapes. Lionel wore his vanity on his sleeve and used his charm to lure women in. He believed his dick should be bronzed for all to see, feel, and suck. Given his eight children with five different women, it pretty much was.

When Lionel came to me, he was a self-diagnosed "sexaholic," according to what he said he read online. His reason for coming to therapy was to "reform" himself from his wild ways. His "addiction" was why he couldn't focus on anything else, according to him. I almost suggested he see another therapist, as he needed more help than I could provide. However, when he told me the following, my spirit told me I had to keep him.

"My job is to spread my seed, Doc. Why should I deprive these hoes of a good soiling?"
When Lionel repeated this to me, it took everything in me not to laugh in his face. He was so serious.
"It's free money out here, so everyone is taken care of. Our purpose on this earth is to be fruitful and multiply, right!?! So, I'm going to multiply and live knowing my seeds will be taken care of, ya dig?"
He proceeded to tell me about a study he'd seen on the internet that proved his logic.
In that moment, I wanted to kick Google and AI in the balls. Lionel was no sexaholic; he was afraid to go out in the world and be responsible. He was afraid of failure or even success. But I couldn't just say that outright. So, we worked bi-weekly to unhinge him from his "addiction."

As I mentally prepared for my session with Lionel, I hit the intercom button again. With my head still on the desk, I turned my face so I could speak directly into the mic for the phone.

"Keysha, in the future, Lionel only comes after lunch, got it."

"Got it, Doc." Then she hung up.

I lifted my head off my desk and looked at my personal phone. Feeling my chest rising out of my navy-blue wrap dress, I adjusted myself and mentally prepared myself for the session.

Good, I have ten minutes. I can use the bathroom. Also, fix me some tea. Too bad I can't spike it, damn practitioner's oath to not practice under the influence.

I got up and went to my in-office bathroom. Yep, I'm fancy in my large office. My office is all decked out with a sitting section for meetings, a full library along the walls along with a large whiteboard, comfortable leather sofas for meeting with clients, surround sound, projector, a personal fridge, changing section (makeshift wall near the bookshelf) with mirror, semi-walk in closet, full bathroom including a shower and small vanity and even a tea and candle/aromatherapy station. I worked hard, so my comfort was always key.

When I came back from the bathroom, I checked my phone. I had one missed message from *My Man*. Seeing the name, I busted out laughing. I didn't have a man, so I definitely didn't save anyone as such. However, when I thought back to Lorna's friend this morning, I knew it was him. Seeing I had five more minutes, more like ten since Lionel was always late, I entertained the message for a moment.

My Man (as it appears in her phone): *I'm pretty sure you deleted my number or blocked me. According to my new mother-in-love, Miss Lorna. So, save this again…it's Dolph. In case you don't respond, she already gave me your office number, your direct line, plus I know where you work. Anyway, let's talk soon, lots to discuss. Have a great day, Dr. Sasha Carter.*

"Damn, Lorna. She gave him all my shit. Who the fuck is Sasha Carter? My last name was Phillips, negro." I said out loud. I was about to reply to the message, but he started typing.

My Man: *My last name is Carter. Might as well get used to it. Don't forget to save my number, we will talk soon.*

I laughed; he was cocky, and I liked it. So sure, of himself, beautiful mothafucker. I wanted to block him or tell him to get lost. However, I was intrigued, especially since my body reacted to the sight and thought of him. Not liking that he already had the upper hand, I changed his name to *Unknown* immediately. He'd have to earn the title if he lasted that long.

I could play this game for a bit, just to see if I liked it, right? What else did I have to do? What was the worst thing that could happen?

I closed my phone as Keysha opened my door. When I saw Lionel, my summation was that I answered my questions instantly. Lionel rushed pass Keysha into my office. He obviously couldn't wait and had some things on his mind.

"Dr. S, these hoes trippin' let me tell you what Winnie said to me…" Lionel said as he rushed to a seat on the sofa and reclined immediately.

This right here is why you can't talk to him, Sasha. He could be Lionel's fucked up Uncle. The one who gave him bad advice all that damn time. The one he suggested you meet, like that shit would ever happen! He could have no morals whatsoever under that beautiful panty-dripping exterior. He could also have herpes and eight kids. The thought of good dick ain't enough to fuck up your celibacy/re-virgin-nation, Sasha. Wake up. Get it together. Abort mission.

Keysha laughed quietly, then closed the door.

"Man, it's gonna be one of those sessions, is the tea kettle on?" Lionel said, sighing as if he had a long day.

It's always one of those sessions.

I grabbed my phone and went to turn on the electric tea kettle. After turning it on, I texted Dolph.

MDSCarter (as it appears in his phone): *Umm…cute, very. But I don't know you. Thanks again for entertaining Lorna. Also, for the attempt at a marriage proposal? Sweet, but I'ma pass. You be blessed. Peace. Love. Blessings. Dr. Sasha PHILLIPS.*

I set the phone down as the water finished boiling, and I grabbed the kettle along with the assortment of teas and put it on the table next to Lionel. As he sorted through everything, then I heard my phone chime, so I went back to silence it.

Unknown (as it now appears in her phone): *Nice try. Too late. Lunch tomorrow. Heard 12:00 pm is a good time. I'll be out front. You are a blessing. You are about to be really peaceful. And about to be full of love. Have a good day, Dr. Carter.*

I looked at the message again.

Was he serious?

I was so in my thoughts, I forgot about Lionel for a second, but he couldn't stay unseen for long.

"Aye, Doc, we got some lemon wedges and cookies today?" Lionel said, slurping his tea with his pinky up and adjusted his position in the recliner.

I silenced my phone, grabbed the wedges and cookies to place next to Lionel. Then I sat down and took a breath, then leaned back in my chair.

"Ok, Lionel, what did Winnie say now?"

"Oh, you're not gonna believe this shit, Doc!"

Lionel said as he dipped his cookie in the tea. After unpacking his spat with Winnie, we discussed Kenya and Breesha, his other two baby mamas. After his second cup of tea and two packs of madeleine cookies, Lionel was calmer and levelheaded. We agreed to meet next week in the afternoon.

"Thanks, Doc, you always get a ni---- I mean a brotha back on track."

"You're welcome, Lionel. Glad I could help. Now, please leave and be sure to check out some of those employment prospects we discussed, please."

Lionel nodded his head; he really was trying, but he got in his own way sometimes. Once he realized his true worth, he would be fine. Prayerfully, it wouldn't take another baby mama or baby to realize it.

After an eventful meeting with Lionel, I was more than ready for lunch despite sitting down to work on session notes. When the words started running together and dancing on the screen, I shut my laptop and closed my eyes. Keysha claimed she was tired and couldn't wait to eat, so she left without me. The truth was, when I mentioned walking, she was already planning her exit.

"Doc, my blood sugar is low. I gotta eat now."

This heifer didn't have diabetes; her ass was just hungry and lazy. But I got it. I told her to go ahead. Truth, I needed a break, a moment alone. Sensory overload was kicking my ass.

Get out of the office, Sasha. Sitting here is not going to make you feel better.

I nodded in response to my thoughts and grabbed my purse to head out of the office. As I opened my office door, a delivery guy was headed through the front door.

"Excuse me, ma'am. Can you sign for these?" He said, holding a large bouquet of random flowers. They were beautiful, different colors, shapes, but still neatly tied together with a jade green ribbon. As I looked closer, I realized they were silk flowers. That didn't change their beauty or my love for them. The bouquet consisted of blue (Forget-Me-Nots, Iris), yellow (Daffodils), and white (Azaleas, Gardenias) flowers. It was an odd bunch, but still amazing. I signed for the flowers. Then observed the card.

> *Azaleas for the femininity of you and the passion I feel every time I think of you.*
> *Daffodils for what I hope will be our new beginning and our success as a power couple.*
> *Gardenias for the secrets we will only share between us.*
> *Iris' because I'm in it for the long haul.*
> *Forget-Me-Nots because I pray you will never forget me.*
> *I love you, Key, hope you don't mind that they are silk. I just wanted to ensure you had a reason to smile at the thought of me, forever.*
> *Love You Always,*
> *Kyle*

"Aww!" I said, admiring the flowers again and putting the card back in the holder.

Kyle and Keysha had been together for two years. They were engaged last year and scheduled to get married this year. Kyle called her his "forever girlfriend" and treated her as such. Always sending flowers, gifts, and even meals to the office. It was some real storybook shit, but I loved every minute of it. Our women deserved to be treated with overwhelming love, passion, and desire. If one got it, there was hope for the rest of us.

Last month, Kyle treated us to a private Taco Tuesday, after hours, of course. Which included food, margaritas, and a small live band. We had so much food; we invited people from the suites near us to join us. It was a great time. That was where we met our new friends, Sarye (Rye) and Monet (Mo). Sarye was a whole vibe I couldn't get enough of. She worked as a Nurse Practitioner by trade, but she aspired to own a fashion boutique. She said she only entered medicine because she thought she loved it. However, her desire to design clothes was her true calling. But her family didn't play about being established and didn't support her dream, at least not full-time. But baby, she had talent.

The day I went over to invite her and her colleagues to "Taco Tuesday Happy Hour," she had just changed from her scrubs and wore a t-shirt she designed along with a jean skirt altered with various distressed accents. When I laid eyes on her, I was in awe.

"I don't know where you got that, but it's amazing," I said, sizing her up respectfully.

Sarye laughed, "Girl, this is a custom piece. If you ever need something or want to wow, ya man, here's my number." When Sarye took a closer look at my attire, she smiled, then added. "Better yet just call me period." She handed me her card as we both laughed and slapped hands at her statement. I'm sure the last part was in response to my "uniform" (suits or wrap dresses), as Keysha called them. I'd seen Sarye plenty of times, and I was usually wearing one or the other.

Too bad I didn't have a man, but maybe I'd get one with her designs.

Anyway, Sarye was 39, tall, medium brown, with thick, bone straight hair that went slightly passed her shoulders. At first glance, you would admire her eyes, which were medium brown. However, when she smiled, it made you smile. Then her laugh, goodness, who knew such a loud noise could come out of this slender person. Sarye was definitely an alpha female who was never short on conversation, but I was here for it. She told us she came from a big and loud family, so she was trained to command attention. By the end of the night, I felt like I knew her from the sandbox.

Monet was a ball of fun as well. She was 37, short but voluptuous, which included ass and breasts for days. Her bright red pixie cut perfectly complemented her medium brown skin. She wore personality glasses and was loud on purpose. However, you could tell she had a heart of gold and was confident in every way. She was the one friend every friend group needed: the life of the party and always aware of the latest happenings.

"Now, Sasha girl, you and Keysha are our new BFFs. Don't try to ditch us now, we is friends, boo!" Sarye said, giving me a hug at the end of our evening.

"I could never, love. Besides, you're going to help me revamp my snooze life. As you called it. And Monet has already promised to get me in them streets." I laughed jokingly; I appreciated their "consideration," but I was gonna pass on all that.

Thanks to Keysha's meddling and oversharing ass, Sarye and Monet now knew I was single and had been for a while. It was all in fun so I took it in stride. Thanks to these ladies, I hadn't stopped laughing all night. It felt good to be out and not go home or stay at work to do paperwork.

"You damn skippy. Sorry, boo, you're too cute to be vitamin D deficient." Monet was excited about the possibilities. Everyone laughed, and I shook my head.

"Well, ladies. I appreciate it, I do. But in due season." I smiled. I was only joking about my agreement, and they needed to know that sooner rather than later.

"Which season, Doc? Cause I've seen them come and go. Bout time you change your weather, cause you've been stuck, winter came and went. Time to bloom that flower, get some sunrays on it, let that shit loose before it closes up." Keysha added while she glanced in my direction.

Sarye and Monet clapped at her little speech.

Why was my shit always a topic of discussion? Urgh!

"Ok, great, we will go through your closet this weekend. Send me your address. I'm coming over," Sarye said, waiting for me to text her my information.

"Cool, I'm bringing wine," Monet said, putting a reminder on her calendar.

"What time? I got a cake tasting, but I can come right after. I'll bring us some nosh because this is going to take a while." Keysha said, shaking her head. I glared at her, and she added, "What Doc? It's gonna take a while to go through them old, ass, too-big clothes you got. Bout time you show off that cute figure you work so hard for."

Keysha had a point. After I lost weight, I looked amazing but still hid in my old clothes. Let's face it, I was a turtle afraid to come out of her shell. The spotlight was not something I liked or wanted, except for the man I dated. It was only then that I was on full display.

A while back, Keysha told me, "Doc, you can tell when you're not in a relationship." I wasn't sure what she meant, so she added. "When you got a man, honey, you're showing hips, lips, boobies, and legs. But, when you don't, you're stuck behind them glasses and ponytail. Hell, if your ass could come to work in yoga pants and a sweatshirt, you would."
I rolled my eyes. This was not the first time I'd heard this conversation or something similar. Between her and Lorna, this was all I heard.

"Keysha, you should be thankful I'm not on my glamazon. It means you get more in your bonuses and free meals." I said, smiling.

Keysha smirked and nodded, "Yeah, it is a perk, Doc. It really is. However, I'd rather see you smile with your heart. Not hide your head in your shell."

Keysha walked away, and I was glad. Her truth was a spotlight I suppressed. She didn't know it, but my shell was comfortable for a reason. I needed it at one point in life. It was safe, away from the reality that had a disastrous ending.

Fucking Blue!

I shook off the idea and went back to work, but he was the reason why my shell became a permanent home.

Chapter 3

"Doc, tell me about Blue." Dr. Kirkland (Dr. Kirk) said. She'd been my therapist for about a year when I finally decided to tell her about Blue. I had to admit, I wasn't ready to face reality or the shitshow that was our relationship. So, I talked around it and him, hoping for a different outcome. But the truth was the truth.

"Nothing to really tell Dr. Kirk. He wasted three years of my life with his lies and bullshit. I shouldn't have ignored the signs like a dumbass. That's what I get for being so damn stupid. Now I'm left with the bullshit. No need to rehash it." I said, looking away, waiting for her to move on.

"Ok, I see. Not ready yet. Still gut-punching yourself for a reality you couldn't see then. Ok, fine, hope your stomach is ironclad. How's the hair situation? Still falling out? The acid reflux still an issue? Too bad you won't do the work to resolve all this. But I digress." She cleared her throat, which meant there was more to follow. "You know you're still holding on to him, right? Giving him life and manifesting his return, you realize that, right?"

Was she serious? I didn't talk to him. Won't answer his calls or texts. Hell, I even threw them funky ass flowers he sent in the trash. She couldn't be serious. However, she was right. As soon as someone mentioned him, he'd pop back up. Same shit, different day. Then he'd disappear as if I fed the beast enough. Only when he was empty again, he'd be back…he always came back. I could guarantee that. This would happen before everything exploded.

Dr. Kirk sipped her tea and waited for my rebuttal. When I rolled my eyes and snapped my neck, she blinked multiple times. Which was her signal for, you know, I'm right. Truth is, she was right. I was in denial. Which was why he flooded my dreams. All the signs, warnings, his bullshit apologies and explanations. He consumed my mental.

Sometimes at night, I swore he got in bed with me to taunt me.
"I love you. Let's have a baby. I'm gonna make you happy."
But he didn't. I didn't realize it then; it wasn't till three years in that I realized…his wife wouldn't allow it. After the big reveal, I confronted him with his wedding announcement, which I found online. His conversation shifted to a sympathetic tone for his "adulteress" actions.
"If I leave, you got me, right? I can't do this without you, Doc. I was going to say something…I just didn't know how. Let's meet up, we need to talk this out, baby."
The revelation crushed me. I was even more ashamed that I allowed him to explain. Not once, but multiple times. It wasn't until I started to take myself and healing seriously that I was finally able to walk away from Blue. Only I was left with a trail of damage, I wasn't ready for. It would take five years to bounce back, and I almost didn't make it.

The next morning, when I got up, Lorna had already called me at 7:00 am. However, after her little matchmaking antics, I needed 50 feet on her. So, I was glad I missed her call. I went through my morning routine, which seemed to take forever because I was exhausted. Which also meant I was running late again. Against my better judgment, I went back to the gym and prayed Dolph would be nowhere in sight. After our last text, he hadn't said anything else, which meant he likely gave up. Part of me was ok but disappointed, somewhat. But I did attempt to end things so, I couldn't be but so upset.

When I got to the gym, I dreaded going in, which was the norm. The thought of working out was only intriguing once I got inside and actually started. If there was any other way to decompress, I would, but this was the only way I knew how…for now. Once inside, I scanned my QR code and started my routine. First, getting a few wet napkins. Some people were nasty and didn't wipe the machines before and after using them. The thought of getting a random rash from someone's germs was not appealing.

Today, I'll start on the angler. I need some more umph in my ass area.

After sanitizing, I was ready and stepped on the machine while I selected my workout music. Pretty much ass shaking/hustling/club music from the 90's and 2000s, because why not lean into an exercise while *T.I., Juvenile, Three 6 Mafia,* and others give you some motivation. With my headphones on, I was ready. When *"Like A Pimp"* by David Banner came on, I started moving. In my former life, I thought I could make it as a video girl. Shoot, I had ass and boobies. Might need some lessons on how to throw my ass in a circle or some shit, but I could learn. Hell, YouTube was a university for a reason.

Sasha, please, Lorna would have a prayer call immediately if she ever saw you in someone's video.

As I laughed at the thought, he entered my line of sight.

Fuck! There he goes, Lorna's new BFF.

He had a crisp white T-shirt, loose black pants, a du-rag on his head, and headphones; however, I doubt any music was on as he wasn't alone. He smiled and laughed with a woman I'd seen a few times at the gym. She was beautiful, built like a stallion. She looked more like she was going clubbin' than the gym. This heifer had on makeup, who the fuck wears eyeliner to the gym? Nonetheless, she was immaculate, perfect ass, breasts, a long ponytail, light-skinned, not a blemish in sight. The sky-blue jumpsuit she wore fit like a glove. Even her damn arms were chiseled. Why did she come to the gym anyway?

Probably to make us work in progress, women want to step up our game.

Fuck it, I was hating that Dolph was a man and single. If I were a dude or into women, I'd holla at her too. Putting the old, unhealed version of myself back in her place, I changed my attitude and leaned into my workout.

Well, I hope they are happy. Lorna will be disappointed when she hears this.

I kept moving and tried not to look in their direction. However, her fawning over him, touching his shoulder every time she laughed, was hard to miss. I didn't even know if he saw me as he kept talking, giving her his undivided attention.

Girl, stop! Whatever you're saying ain't that damn funny. You got his attention, relax, team too much!

As she walked away from him, he went back to his workout. However, she circled back and stepped closer to whisper something in his ear.

Bet she is offering him a personal spotting, so he can touch her beautiful mane. Damn, she got some nice hair or one hell of a sow-in. Urgh, let it go, Sasha…no need to give her or him another thought.

"Yep, that's true," I answered myself out loud. Feeling determined, I pushed harder and increased the resistance on the machine.

After 20 minutes, not only was my ass screaming, but so were my thighs. Sweat poured from everywhere, which felt great. I loved the tension in my body during and after working out. After a few more machines, I made my way to the exit. As I walked out, I passed by a group of men conversing in the weights section. Dolph was among them. He looked in my direction and slightly smiled. I nodded without so much as a smirk and kept moving. Dolph was no longer my concern. When we saw each other, a simple acknowledgment was all he would get.

When I got to the truck, I checked my messages once I turned it on. Typically, my phone stayed in DND (do not disturb) until I turned it off after sessions, possibly. There were four messages, all from him.

Unknown: *We not speaking this morning?*
Unknown: *Not what you think…*
Unknown: *Damn, just a nod. Ok, Dr. Carter. We don't ignore things; we address them. See you soon.*
Unknown: *Oh, and P.S., don't ignore My Mother In Love…she was just checking on you!*

Was he serious? Fuckin' Lorna told on me, damn, who did her loyalty belong to? She keeps it up; I'm putting her in a place like Shady Pines from the Golden Girls.

I was just being mean, I'd never unless I had exhausted all resources and the capacity to care for her. But if she kept this up, he'd be her next of kin instead of me. Pouting at the messages, I closed the phone and made my way to Dunkin' for some coffee. The more I thought about the messages, I became more pissed off.

You can keep all your yah, yah, yah, Sir! Ole' girl wasn't cackling to herself. No explanation needed. Good day.

I thought about responding to his messages, but what was the point? We had no ties with each other, and he was free to do as he pleased. Besides, I had other stuff to focus on. Which didn't include him anymore.

"So, Dexter and Maria, how are we today?" I said, smiling at my clients.

Dexter didn't say anything, just scowled at his wife from the corner of his eye. Maria tried to smile while addressing my question.

"Well, Dr. Sasha, we are not doing so well. Dexter is frustrated that I…"

Before she could finish, Dexter chimed in.

"I'm frustrated that my wife won't let me sleep. I work long hours, and my shifts are crazy sometimes since I work an overnight construction gig. So, when I'm asleep, I'm dead to the world. However, my darling wife feels the need to wake me up."

I looked at Maria, and she shrugged. Dexter was now fuming mad and awaiting her denial. But she didn't; she sat quietly while he continued.

"We live in a moderately sized house. But it feels like a one-bedroom apartment when she and the kids are up. Everyone feels the need to yell or stomp around, waking my ass up. Then, if I sleep on the sofa because my wife is snoring too loudly or if I'm too tired to make it to bed, she wakes me up. Come to bed, Dex. Then she waits for me to get up. When do I get a damn break, huh?"

Countdown before the meltdown. And here we go…5, 4, 3, 2, 1!

"I'm tired too, Dexter. We have twin toddlers who are full of energy. All day I work and then come home to them. So, yeah, I'm exhausted too."

Maria was on the verge of tears, so I handed her the tissue box. Dexter tried not to be fazed by his wife's emotions, but he couldn't help it. He put his hand on her knee, giving her a slight squeeze.

"Look, I hear you, babe. I do. I appreciate all you do, especially since my schedule is crazy." Maria dabbed her eyes and leaned her head on his shoulder.

"I know you do, babe. That's why I want to be as close to you as possible. Even if you are sleeping. I miss my husband." Dexter smiled at her words.

Why am I even here? They have obviously worked this one out, good job team! Now, if they both weren't living double lives, this might actually work.

When my timer went off, I was glad. The Elliots were an interesting couple. Dexter did work nights, but he also worked Michelle. She was a family friend whom Maria was well aware of. In turn, Maria spent some time with Myron, who happened to be Michelle's husband. Not sure if that part of the puzzle has been revealed yet.

I learned of Dexter's affair during a private session with Maria. She was a client before they started couple's therapy. Which was after she confronted Dexter. It was then that he demanded to come in and share his "side of the story." That was about six months ago, and here we were. They came in when they had a meltdown. Then they apologized to each other, and life was grand again.

At this point, they might as well be a poly family. No shame in it, everyone was happy with their part of the 'arrangement' anyway. They share everything else. Wonder when they will catch onto that idea? Ahh well. Grown folks' business.

"Well, our time here is up," I said, relieved. "I'll see you next week or whenever you're ready to huddle again. Good work!" I got up to open the door for them. The couple smiled at me, then each other. Dexter locked hands with Maria, and they smiled as they sauntered out of my office.

I went to my desk to check my email. Seeing an email from Carlton, I immediately rolled my eyes. Despite getting on my nerves, he held the key to my advancement, so I had to play nice. Carlton was an intelligent, handsome man, but he was arrogant as fuck. He wore his arrogance as a badge of honor. Don't get me wrong, he was good at his job. We met when I was in graduate school; we were a part of the same study group for our multicultural counseling class. On the first day our group meeting, he had already divided up the work and handed a schedule of duties to everyone. As he handed each of us a piece of paper. I asked him how he could make such an executive decision without our input.

His replied, "I see the effort, or lack of some of you put into this class. You all won't embarrass me. Now let's go over the paper. You can be my VP since you are close to being as smart as me."

I hated him immediately. However, I secretly respected his work ethic because we did have two lazy bums in our group. Not only was our presentation flawless, but Carlton and I took the same classes for the rest of our master's program. We studied together, quizzed each other, and successfully passed our board exams together. Although he moved to Houston a few years after we graduated, we remained in contact. Reading the email from Carlton, I took a breath and tried not to let my annoyance take over my mind.

VP Philips, Dr. Philips, if I must!

The Longhorns of Houston are awaiting you! The Community Health Board of Houston-Dallas just opened a position, and you would be perfect for it. Of course, I would apply, but I already have my dream job and have a seat on the board. Now all I need is my VP to join me. Aren't you tired of the DMV yet? Your ass still ain't married and likely aren't dating…so pack up your little practice and try something different. Read over the position and call me so I can help you with your resume. Better yet, come to Houston and stay at my ranch. I can help you and show you around your new city. Book your ticket and don't keep the board waiting. They are looking at other candidates from North Carolina and Florida. They don't stand a chance once they see my VP. Call me!

> *Your Forever President,*
> *Carlton*

"We take one class together and suddenly he's Barack and I'm Joe. Urgh, he's a pain in my ass even when he's not physically here," I mumbled. Carlton and I never dated, but we did hang out a lot. He was like a makeshift boyfriend, only we never kissed, slept together, or even entertained a romantic relationship. As far as I knew, he was straight, but that didn't matter anyway. If I ever considered anything with him, as soon as he opened his mouth, the thought evaporated. I knew I needed to respond, but he wouldn't get my attention until after lunch. It was after 12:00 pm, and my stomach was growling loudly.

"Guess I should eat something before it gets any louder." I grabbed my purse and headed to the waiting area, where Keysha sat.

"Doc, are you ready? I'm starving. Where are we going today?" Keysha said, putting on her purse and locking her laptop. "Can we take a long lunch? We don't have another appointment until 3:00 pm today." Sighing, I nodded ok to Keysha. It cracked me up that she said 'we' as if she saw the clients too. However, I guess she had to deal with them before I did, so she had a point. "Good, because I want to go to Sapphire. It's Wednesday, and they got smoked turkey today." She added as we headed out the door.

"Cool, but you're driving. I need a moment to close my eyes," I said as I locked the door, as Keysha headed towards the parking lot. As I locked the door, I heard Keysha stop walking but she didn't say a word. As I went to ask her why she stopped, she spoke.

"Ummm…Doc," Keysha said as my back was towards her.
"What Key…"

When I turned, Keysha was smiling and admiring the view in front of her.

Fuuuucccck! This can't be happening, not now.

Dolph stood before us wearing a gray short-sleeved T-shirt which exposed his tatted arms, a thin sliver rope chain, medium blue jeans, gray tennis shoes, and a gray hat to match. His silver watch caught the sun perfectly as it reflected the light in our direction. He was holding two plastic bags filled with Styrofoam containers. If he was smiling before, he wasn't now and didn't say anything but stared at the keys in my hand, then looked at my face.

I honestly had forgotten about his message yesterday about lunch and his gentle reminder from earlier. However, I honestly didn't care, but I was glad I was still cute in my various shades of purple wrap dress, which had hints of gray with purple peeped toe platform heels.

I stood silently, rolling my eyes, displaying my tiredness and hangry reaction. While Keysha sized him up, excitedly waiting to see what happened next.

"Going somewhere, Doc?" He said plainly while adjusting his grip on the bags.

"Yes, I'm going to lunch with Keysha," I said as if he was interrupting my progress, despite not moving.

"Interesting. I could have sworn you already had plans." He said, slightly lifting the bags.

"Well, I don't remember agreeing to those plans. Besides, I'm not hungry. I'm only going to lunch with Keysha as a supportive figure."

"Huh? I don't…" Keysha said, confused. When I glared in her direction, she shut up and returned her big smile towards Dolph.

Before he could respond to my comment, my stomach gargled extremely loudly. This caused him to smile, calling bullshit on my comment.

"Sounds like you are now…" He turned his attention to Keysha, who was blushing.

"Hi Keysha, I'm Dolph. It's nice to meet you."

He shifted the bags to one hand so he could shake her hand.

"It's nice to meet you, Dolph. I've heard so much about you." She said, still cheesing.

Was she serious? I had not said a word about him. If anything, I had completely forgotten about this dude.

"Miss Lorna speaks highly of you," Keysha said, still smiling.

Lorna strikes again. Calling her ass today!

Dolph kept his attention on Keysha, "I like her too. We've had some great conversations since I met her yesterday."

Are they besties now? Maybe he should fuck her and leave me alone. Can see where his loyalty lies.

Still addressing Keysha, Dolph glanced at me, then back at her.

"Look, Keysha, I've brought lunch from Sapphire as I've heard you all like their smoked turkey. So, if you wa…"

Before he could finish, she replied, "Hell yeah, I'll have some…we were on our way there anyway."

I could have smacked her for being so anxious. She didn't know him. Who was loyal to me? Anybody? Both she and Lorna had sided with Dolph like he was their day one.

"Umm, look…" Before I could finish, Dolph handed one bag to Keysha, and she took it. "Dang all this for me?" she said excitedly.

He nodded yep, "Yeah, figured you could surprise Kyle with lunch."

Keysha beamed and pumped her fist like she was on Arsenio Hall.

"That is so sweet, he's gonna be so happy. You good people's Dolph."

I just shook my head in disbelief as she headed to her car.

"Doc, I'll be back at 2:30 or 2:45 since you said we could take a late lunch. Love you, bye!"

Note to self…fire Keysha for talking too damn much! And going against the home team, trader!

I wasn't going to fire her, but I was going to lecture her about talking to strangers.

Hadn't she heard of stranger danger? I should call her damn momma.

"Nice, we've got time to get to know each other. Come on before the food gets cold. I don't like room temperature food." Dolph said as he walked past me to the front door.

I took a breath as Keysha sped out of the parking lot, waving. He stood off to the side so I could open the door. When I unlocked the door, I side-eyed him, and he just looked at me, smiling. His gaze was burning a hole in me, and I resisted the heat I felt from below since he was so close in proximity. I let us into the waiting area. Then I walked to my office door with the intention of unlocking it. My plan was for us to eat in the waiting area. However, when I opened the door, he headed in and took a seat at the meeting table. I frowned as he made himself at home in my space.

This is my office; he can't come in without being invited!

I folded my arms and looked at him, then at the door. However, he paid me no attention.

"You have some plates? Also, some utensils?" Dolph said as he unpacked the containers.

"Can I get you a hot towel and an after-dinner mint?" I asked unmoved, still processing that he was in my office uninvited.

"Naw, I asked for what I needed. But thanks anyway." He said unbothered and then sat down at the table.

I went to the cabinet with the paper goods to grab plates and utensils. After I retrieved them, I put them on the table. He had fixed his plate, and as I stood next to him annoyed but in awe of his comfort.

"Can you heat this for me, please?" Dolph said, handing me his plate.

Did I look like the help? This dude is getting on my nerves; he can get the hell out like now.

I snatched the plate from him and went to the microwave.

"You want me to make your plate?" He asked while I waited for his food to warm up.

"No, I'm good. I'm ok with room temperature food." I snapped

He chuckled, "Well, it's not good for you, babe. I'd feel better if you heat it a little, especially since the turkey looks a little pink. Don't want you to get sick."

No, he didn't try to act all concerned. And who the fuck was Babe? I ain't no little pig and he don't know me like that.

"I'm good. Thank you for your concern." I said while grabbing his food from the microwave. When I got back to the table, I set the plate in front of him.

He smiled, "Thank you, babe. I appreciate it. Come on, sit down so we can eat, please."

I plopped down in the chair next to him and began to make my plate while making annoyed faces.

"So, we gonna talk about this morning now or later?"

Was he serious? There was nothing to discuss. If that's what he came here for, he can leave now.

"There's nothing to discuss. So, WE are not going to talk about it, period." I snapped back as I made my plate.

He nodded, "I hear you, but like I said earlier…we don't ignore things, we discuss them. So, let's talk about it now. Besides, your attitude is saying we need to talk, so let's hear it. Better yet, I'll start first since you obviously need more time." Looking at my plate while I avoided his face, he spoke again. "You sure you don't want to heat your food, Sasha?"

I sucked my teeth, annoyed, and moved away from him, and he shook his head. Then he reached for my hand.

"Fine. Let's pray over this food."

I clasped my hands together and closed my eyes. Dolph did the same, but he purposely put his elbow next to mine so we touched.

Really dude? You can't talk to Jesus by yourself. I don't even know if he likes you enough for you to be praying on my behalf.

"Dear Lord, thank you for the food we are about to receive. May your provisions and intercession always keep us close to you. For anything that you provide will ensure we walk closer to you, together. Also, please bless Doc's stubborn stomach since she's likely about to get worms from this pink ass turkey. Amen."

Although Dolph was done praying. I kept my eyes closed longer, so I could finish talking to Jesus myself, privately.

Dear Jesus, what the hell is this? Why does he keep popping up? Please don't let him be drugging me or something with this food. If he does anything remotely dangerous to me, please kill him instantly, then remove his body without a trace, like in the movies, so I can meet with my clients in peace. Amen.

When I opened my eyes, I sat silently. Dolph shook his head as I forked over my turkey. It did look pink and a little undercooked, but it wasn't so bad.

"So, back to this morning…" He said after he chewed his first bite.

"What about it? Again, there's nothing to talk about."

"Nothing to talk about but yet you have an attitude. So, who's bullshittin' me or you, Doc?"His attitude was a bit more serious. He wasn't going to back down, and neither was I. "Look, Sasha, that woman was just some woman. I don't know her. Seen her a couple of times. She has been trying to get my attention for weeks. Today, she happened to be bold enough to speak. That was it. We didn't exchange numbers; I don't even know her name. Don't care too either. The woman I'm interested in is acting like she caught me cheating or something. Better yet, like a spoiled brat!"

Did he just call me a brat?

Having had enough of his rant, I replied. "Look, whatever you do is your business. It's none of my concern."

He laughed as if he knew I was bluffing.

"Ok! So, tell me why you're trying to act like it doesn't bother you?"

I had no response. Truth, I didn't know why it bothered me. Maybe it was because just yesterday, he showed me the same type of attention. Or maybe it was him, bum-rushing my world by talking to Lorna and now Keysha. Or him showing up at my job; having easy access to me, and I had nothing in return. I didn't even know him beyond his name. What the hell kind of game was this?

Here I was exposed, and he wasn't—it's not fair. The experience made me feel alone and anxious for the "other shoe" to drop so he could crawl back into whatever hole he came from. Something had to give; it had to, it always did. I wanted him to hurry up and finish so he could go. This was too much already.

Don't let him see you sweat, Sasha. Channel your inner Tasha Mack, "Emotional walls, emotional walls"

When there was no response, Dolph continued eating while we sat quietly.

"I'm going to say this last thing and then we're done with this subject."

We? Well, good, then maybe you can finish eating and go, since this is already done.

"Sasha, you don't know this now…but you will. My time is precious. So, I am intentional about where and whom I spend it. I don't entertain for fun or without a purpose. Let that shit sink in. While you work on that, can you grab us something to drink, please?"

I went to my mini fridge to survey my beverage options.

I hope he enjoys water cause that's all I'm offering. I'm not giving him my Clear Canadian nor my Lipton Teas. Enjoy the Deer Park.

"Let me get one of them Lipton's in there. If you have a Sweet one that will work. Thank you." Dolph said with his back to me. Shocked, I looked up and frowned. Dolph had his back to me. Also, my fridge was off to the side and opened from the opposite side, which would block his view inside.

Fucking Lorna! What did they spend all of yesterday and today gossiping about me and my life?

I grunted and grabbed the tea and a Cherry Clear Canadian for myself. When I got back to the table, I slapped them both down while looking at him. He continued to eat while I hadn't even touched my plate.

"Dang, I ain't seen a Clear Canadian in a minute. Where you find this at?" Dolph said, opening the glass bottle.

"Costco. They sell them in bulk." I said, still trying to decipher if the turkey was safe.

When the top was off the bottle, he took a swig of the drink.

Did he just drink my shit! What the entire hell! Why is he so damn comfortable?

"Umm, my guy! Did you just drink out of my LAST Clear Canadian? Really, dude!" I said, annoyed.

Dolph dropped his fork and faced me. While I gave him a piece of my annoyed face he looked in my eyes and spoke.

"Look, Doc, you're gonna have to learn how to share. We don't hoard our stuff. If you want, you can have some of my tea." He opened the tea and slid it towards me. However, not before he took a sip out of the bottle. My face further displayed my annoyance with his actions, but yet again, he didn't care. "Just drink it, man. I don't have cooties or some shit."

Are you serious? I don't know you. Nor where your mouth has been. Cooties or not, I'm not interested in backwashing someone else twat!

"Besides, you've been single long enough and you're faithful with them checkups. Which is good, proud of you for that. I haven't done nothin' either. Been holding off until I find my wife. So, high-five to us having good health." Dolph raised his hand, and I just stared at it.

You can't be serious! How in the hell did he have my hygiene history, damn it, Lorna? What else had she told him? Did he know my last pap was clear and I didn't have my wisdom teeth, too?

When I didn't move, he returned to his plate and smiled. I returned to my pink turkey, still trying to decipher if I should eat it or not.

"Babe! Can you please heat that. It's making me uncomfortable." He said as I again questioned the sight of the turkey. I almost gave in but didn't.

You're not the boss of me, Sir. All these directives are getting on my nerves. It would be nice if you were my man, but you're not. Please hurry up and eat so you can leave. Sincerely, management.

"It's fine. I don't need to." I said about to shove a forkful of pink meat into my mouth. However, Dolph lowered my hand and then removed the fork from my hand. "Stop being stubborn, babe, please. You ain't about to get salmonella on my watch because you want to be right. We don't have time to be in the ER all night while they pump you full of liquids. I mean, I would, but that's not the move. We got other shit to do."

WE wouldn't be doing anything after today.

He grabbed the plate to put it into the microwave.

You won't keep telling me what to do either. I'll show you!

While Dolph heated the plate, I opened the container with the turkey, took a piece off, and ate it. Then another piece and another. The turkey was fine; it wasn't unusual for smoked turkey to have a little pink sometimes. It looked like it was cooked with a slight pink hue. When Dolph came back, he instantly noticed the container was partially opened.

"Sasha! I know you ain't open that container and eat from it." He was frustrated as he was almost mumbling.

"I did, and I'm fine. Thank you, Sir." I said, purposely taking another piece from the container and chewing it in front of him. He set down the plate he had warmed for me and returned to his seat.

He groaned, "See, you like doing stuff the hard way. Cool, this really will be an interesting journey together. We're gonna see how right you feel in about five minutes."

I laughed, "Oh yeah, what makes you think you will last that long. Or if at all? I haven't even…" My stomach immediately grumbled. "I haven't even decided if I like you or will even entertain you again. Oh, and further to your point, in five minutes I'll be just fine, thank you!"

"Whatever you say."

Moments later, my stomach grumbled again, only this time my mouth watered as well. Dolph dropped his fork and looked in my direction. He leaned back and intently surveyed me.

"Guess that semi-raw ass turkey didn't need five minutes. Come on, let me help you to the bathroom."

I tried to play it off and kept eating, but something was terribly wrong. My mouth was watery, sweat was beading on my forehead, and my stomach ached. When I heaved the first time, I tried to push it down, but the second time I wasn't so lucky.

"Sasha! Let me help…."

Before Dolph could finish his statement, I got up and ran to the bathroom. However, I couldn't hold it and threw up on my way. The line of throw-up on the carpet led a trail to the bathroom. Everything came up, including some unprocessed dinner from last night. When I made it to the toilet, I let more of it out. As I hovered over the toilet, Dolph stood in the bathroom door with his arms crossed, shaking his head. Too embarrassed, I tried to hold my puke while I waved him away. However, he came over and pulled my hair back with a scrunchie from the sink.

Smart move taking your hair down before lunch, SMDH!

Tired of seeing me terribly attempt to hold it in, Dolph got closer to my ear and spoke up. "Look, I'm not leaving. Let that shit out so we can get you cleaned up."

No sooner than he completed his statement, I blew the rest of my chunks into the toilet. Dolph got up and went under the vanity to find the cleaning supplies to clean up the floor and carpet. After three more conversations with the toilet, I sat on the floor and leaned my head against the shower glass after I flushed the toilet and closed the lid. There couldn't possibly be any more fluids or food left in me.

How embarrassing was that, Doc? Good job trying to be right. That went totally and completely great. Mental eye roll and shade face for you.

When he finished cleaning and deodorizing the office, Dolph came back to the bathroom door. My eyes were closed and I was breathing deeply. I shook my head at my stupidity.

"Hey, you good, babe? Let me help you up."

When I opened my eyes, he was reaching out his hand to help me.

This guy.

I was about to take it but lowered my hand and let my foolish pride set in again. "I'm good. You can go. Lunch is obviously over. Thanks for everything." I said, feeling defeated and humiliated.

Dolph didn't respond verbally. He just moved his hand back, squatted, and put us closer to eye level. His face was serious, which matched his voice and energy.

"Look, Sasha, I don't know what type of 'men' you were used to, but I'm a man. A real one. So, all that dismissive, *I'm every woman* shit you've been on…cut it out. I don't do drama, and I don't do whatever it is you're attempting to do. Keep it up, and you're gonna get what you asked for. And I don't back track, for NO ONE." When he emphasized the last part, I knew he was serious.

But still, who did he think he was talking to me like that? I'm a grown ass woman. I hadn't agreed to be in a relationship with him or be his woman.

He stood up and reached his hand out again. This time, I took it, and he helped ease me off the floor. I immediately went to the mirror to survey the damage. There was puke on my dress. There was no hiding it, even if I tried. I stared at my dress as Dolph now stood behind me.

"Don't worry about that, it will come out. I'm sure you have another outfit here somewhere. Why don't you get cleaned up, and I'll get rid of the rest of this food?"

He was right, I had a mini wardrobe at the office. I kept several spare outfits in case I needed to be ready for a meeting, the gym, happy hour, or just chill. I went to my closet where my clothes were. I thumbed through a few outfits before I put my hand on my black wrap dress.

"That's a nice choice." He said, leaning back against the makeshift wall, which I used as my changing area. I eyed him and went past the outfit to select a green dress that had a scoop neck. "Nah, the first one is better. Might want to pin the front up, though." He said, returning to clean up the food. I selected the black dress and hung it on the makeshift wall.

I hope he knows he's gonna get out while I shower. This ain't no peepshow, brah.

After putting everything in the trash, he turned his attention back towards me.

"I'm going to step out and let you get cleaned up."

Maybe he was a gentleman, and I was doing too much. My attitude was a bit much, so I decided to shift my mood.

"You don't have to stay. I'm ok now. Thank you, I appreciate it." I said, smiling, attempting to let him know I sincerely meant it.

He didn't respond, just grabbed the trash and headed out. When he closed the door, I went to the bathroom to get showered and changed.

When I came back out, I felt more refreshed. I put my hair in a ponytail, changed my shoes, put on my other dress, and put the other items in a laundry bag to take home. It was almost 1:30 pm, so I opened my office door to let more sunlight in. When I opened the door, Dolph was sitting in the waiting room reading a magazine.

Did he really sit here the whole time? Doesn't he have a job? Don't get fired on my behalf; I won't be taking care of you.

"You look nice. You smell even better." He let out a slight chuckle, and I did the same. "The only thing I would adjust," Dolph said, getting up and coming towards me. "I'd pull this back a bit, so some dude won't be admiring the view. They are already spoken for." He said, adjusting the shoulder portion of my dress. As he smiled, I looked at his hand, then back at him, shaking my head.

"You are a whole trip, Dolph," I said, finally giving in to his antics.

"You finally acknowledged me. About time you see me, Sasha, because I see you beyond that tough exterior you put up, and I like you." He said, moving his hand to my face.

"Well, you have a whole damn cheat sheet thanks to Lorna," I said, laughing. Even Dolph had to laugh.

"Can't be mad she sees something in me that's made for you," Dolph said, rubbing my cheek. I wanted to move but did the exact opposite and leaned into the palm of his hand. His hands felt like they were bigger than my entire face. I felt like I leaned into a warm body pillow, gentle and soft. "Sasha…can't wait for you to actually see me." I looked at him, admiring his face which made me clinch my knees. His breathing into my air almost made me high.

What is he doing to me? What is this feeling, and why am I resisting it, fuck!

He leaned closer to me as if to kiss my cheek. However, we were interrupted by Keysha, who came in on her phone.

"Oops. Did I interrupt something…" Keysha was still holding her phone to her ear. She admired my dress and gave me the eye.

"Nah, you good Keysha. I was just heading out." Dolph backed away but kept his attention on me. While Keysha gyrated behind him as if she caught us doing the nasty. "I'll be home late tonight. I hope to hear from you. Hopefully, you will listen this time and we won't have a repeat of lunch." Dolph raised his eyebrow and tightened his lips after saying the last part.

Did he really have to throw that in there? Now he's Mr. Funny Man. Too soon.

"Well, I'll see if I'm available. I might be busy later tonight." I didn't have any plans, but he didn't need to know that.

Dolph smiled, "Ok, Sasha, we gonna do things your way for once. I'll leave the next move up to you. If you call me, then we will go from there." I nodded, feeling like I had the upper hand. However, he stepped closer to add to his statement. "If I don't hear from you, I'll be calling reinforcements." I knew he meant Lorna or now even Keysha.

"Snitching ass," I muttered.

He smiled at my comment, not before kissing my cheek. "Don't be mad, babe, just get on board and let me lead."

Urgh, negro, please! The only board I'm considering is the one in Houston. Note to self, talk to Keysha.

Chapter 4

"Come on, babe. We're almost ready." My husband yelled. I straightened my dress, which flowed over my protruding belly. Why did I agree to this photoshoot? Here I was, eight months pregnant, back hurting, hungry, and wishing he were rubbing my feet. But I agreed to this and hounded him for weeks about making sure we were ready. We stood in the foyer of our home. The sunlight illuminated the room perfectly as the light bounced off the white walls.

"Mommy, I ready!" Our son yelled as he rode his tricycle in the house. He was three and full of energy. We had to buy him a special tricycle for in the house since he insisted on riding it everywhere when he wasn't shooting his basketball into his Fisher Price hoop, which stood against the wall.

"Umm. Son, can you slow down?" I urged. We were in his "space" technically, since this was where he played, but still. Him all in white, and the thought of a boo boo or blood made me nervous.

We wore all white, father and son, in matching polo shirts and pants. I wore a floor-length, lightweight dress. The V-shaped front gave space to my swollen boobs. The way they felt, I was sure this baby would be here any moment. I smiled as I admired my hair, which waved down either side. With a natural crown on my head, I almost looked like Mother Earth.

"You look beautiful, Doc." He said as he stood behind me, putting his hands on our baby and his head on my shoulder. His hands on me were soothing, but also caused our baby to jump with excitement, kicking the hell out of me. "Thank you, love. I feel it, but also tired and hungry." I pouted through my smile as he stood taller behind me.

"Don't worry, we will be done soon. Mommy will be picking our son up soon. Then Daddy will feed you and rub your feet and back. If it wasn't so late, I'd…"

I smiled at the thought of making love to my husband. But I was eight months pregnant. There was no way we were doing that. I'd go into labor right here and now. It had been too long, I hope I could make it to the six weeks doctors urged.

"Picture, mommy! Picture!" Our son yelled as he rode his tricycle closer to us. His smile and excitement were everything and caused both of us to smile.

"You know this is your fault!" I said as I looked at his father, who beamed with joy.

"What?" He said as if he were oblivious to my next comments.

"You had to teach him to ride that tricycle!" I eyed him as I sat on the steps to give my back a break.

"You damn right. The agreement was that once he learned to ride the tricycle, we'd have another baby. Missions accomplished."

It was true, and he caught on quickly. But I made that agreement at a time of weakness. A session in the kitchen bent over the counter. However, he never let me forget it. Neither did the baby, which kicked me every time his/her Daddy was around. I rubbed my belly and closed my eyes.

My husband came to the stairs and squatted down, putting him closer to my stomach as he touched it.

"Hey, in there. It's Daddy." He smiled with joy as he looked at my stomach. "I know you're ready to come out. And we are ready to meet you. But, not too soon, ok? So, you gotta take it easy on Mommy, ok? Daddy loves you. I'm going to make sure you're well taken care of, I promise." Whenever he said the last sentence, he always looked up at me and winked. Which made my heart smile. Somehow, his words always soothed our child, as if they already had a special bond. When he stood up, he smiled and helped me to my feet.

"Thank you, babe." I smiled and kissed my cheek as we got ready to finally take our picture. Mommy, Daddy, Baby, and our son cheesing on his tricycle. It was perfect.

I finally got my family. The one I'd been waiting for, prayed for, and manifested.

But this dream was like all the others. When I dreamed of my husband, I only felt his presence; his face was that of a Rorschach. An inkblot in black and white that's only left to one's interpretation. Maybe that was God's way of preparing me without seeing the whole picture. However, he did give a sneak peek, and I saw our son clear as day.

After describing my dream to Dr. Kirk, she nodded and smiled then replied. "So, what does that tell you, Sasha?"

I sat in her office for our monthly session. Depending on the season, I saw more or less of her. This season was a quiet one, so once a month was perfect.

"It tells me that God has a sense of humor. Why would he show me my son and not my husband? You know God is rude for that one."

Dr. Kirk laughed at my antics; she always did, which I appreciated. If I couldn't say it how I felt it, then this therapy relationship wouldn't work. I wasn't as bad as Lionel, but sometimes I had to drop a few F, D, MF, GD, IKTFYD (*I Know the Fuck you Didn't*), GTFOH (*Get the Fuck Outta Here*), and other cussing bombs.

"God is not rude; you have all the information you need. Let's be real, if you knew what your husband looked like, you would AI the hell outta his picture and be on a search and rescue mission immediately. You're so wrapped up in not seeing the image, you're missing the big picture, Dr. Sasha."

Dr. Kirk was rude as hell for calling me Dr. She only did that when she needed to get through to me. But I understood her motives and nodded in agreement.

"He's showing me that he hears my prayers, and my time is coming," I mumbled, not looking at her face.

"That's good. What else? Cause you know there's more, right?" Dr. Kirk sat back in her chair while I finally looked in her direction. She motioned for me to finally say it.

"And that despite what I feel and keep struggling with. I'll be more than ready when it happens." I mumbled again and let out a breath of air while I pursed my lips.

"That's my girl! See, the only one kicking your ass mentally is you. That ain't God being rude, it's you not acknowledging what's in front of you." We were silent for a brief moment before Dr. Kirk continued. "You know, Sasha, I bet and I could be wrong…you have let several chances at love pass through your fingers. I mean, there was that one time you took a chance…but there's no need to rehash that we've worked passed it."

Really, Dr. Kirk! Rude!

"But, moving on…you've let that experience lock you into one vision of love. If love doesn't look exactly how you want it, then you're not interested. How sad is that? You are a multifaceted being with millions of qualities, talents, and beliefs that any man would love. But, because of one experience, you won't open yourself up to anything but one thing. How is that serving and feeding the being that is you?" She was right. I couldn't say anything, just allowed the silence between us to linger. "Do me a favor, here's a takeaway…if love finds you today, tomorrow, or the next day, welcome it in for a cup of coffee."

"Are you serious, Dr. Kirk?" She gave me the *do I look like I'm joking* face, and we both laughed, then she continued.

"I'm serious, you've been getting out more and trying new things, so it's time to be more open. So…if love finds you today, tomorrow, or the next day, welcome it in for a cup of coffee. Then, if you enjoy your coffee, invite it back for a scone or cookies. And…if you enjoy your scone or cookies…"

"Invite him to spend the night, then kick him out before dawn. No slumber parties in my good space." I laughed after my statement, and Dr. Kirk shook her head.

"Yep, session is over. Get out, Dr. Sasha. You need to get back on bi-weekly or weekly because you don't know how to act without supervision. Now be gone! See you next month." We both laughed, and I assured her I received her advice and would follow, minus my last statement.

On the way home, I thought about my session with Dr. Kirk. She was right about everything she said. My thoughts went back to Dolph and all that happened between us. I gave him a hard time because I didn't want to believe him. In truth, he was paying for burdens that didn't belong to him, and I knew better than that. At that moment, I thought about calling him. However, I had a better idea and called my girls for a late happy hour.

After the lunch fiasco, a cocktail and some all-flat chicken wings were just what I needed. When I called the girls, only Sarye was available for a quick meet-up up which was cool. We ordered our food and drinks while I told her about lunch. We both laughed until we cried.

"Girl, if he stayed around after that shit. You might as well marry him. Cause to clean up someone's puke is a love language itself."

Sarye sipped her drink while waiting for my response.

"Please, I can't even fathom the thought of looking at him ever again."

My antics went too far. Every time he was around, I turned into a silent, shit talking mess. Something was wrong with Dolph, too, because his ass kept coming back for more—insanity.

"Well, look, you grown boo. But give him a chance. At least let him knock the dust off that box, shit."

"There's no dust on my box, thank you, Sarye."

We both laughed again and nodded to the music.

"Yeah, them electric waves from…what you call it 'Black Vybes' is pounding them corners raw."

Did she really have to bring him into it? He only did the job I charged him for, literally.

Sarye moved her hair as if I would protest. However, I sipped my drink and kept movin' to the music.

"Let's be real, Sasha, you can only vibrate or pound so much until your body craves the weight of a man. His warmth, touch, smell, hell, the shit talking alone. Fuck! Girl, you're about to make me call Curtis and bust it wide for him tonight." Sarye stuck out her tongue and bounced in her seat. We both laughed again and tipped our glasses.

But she was right. I hadn't had a man since Blue and all his foolishness. After everything, I needed a break…a long one. I'd been on a few dates even entertained the possibility of getting a fuck buddy. However, deep in my heart, I knew I wanted and sought more.

There was a hole in my heart and the pit of my stomach, which sometimes caused me to burst into tears. I cried for the emptiness I felt. The part of me which felt unlovable or unhealed…better yet, incomplete. My family was who they were. Everyone had their cliques, and I grew tired of trying to fit in. At the end of the day, it was just me and Lorna. Oh, and Robbie, but he also had his people. So, I vowed that I'd get the family unit I wanted when I had my family—whenever that happens. I just knew that having my husband and our family would help make me feel complete.

"Rye, you're right. I very well could, and he'd probably do it gladly. But…" I hesitated then continued, "I want something more. There's something inside that won't allow me to just live that life anymore. I've been there, had a lot of fun. That's how I met my ex, Blue. He wasn't supposed to…we weren't supposed to fall in love. However, he pushed, and I drank the Kool-Aid, only I didn't throw up until it was too late. The End." I hated talking or thinking about him. But he was a part of my story. I didn't deny it, but I wouldn't dwell on it either. Not anymore, at least. "My point is, I want and deserve more. No more room for temporary people in my permanent space."

Sarye nodded and grabbed my hand to hold it. "Well, stop acting like your space is occupied when it's only filled with emptiness for someone to fill."

Damn, she just fucked me up with that one! She just therapied the hell outta me. Fuck.

A tear formed in my eye. As I thought about letting go and opening up, I got scared. But I was ready, truly ready. I'd come this far and worked hard to heal. Just needed a body of water to fall back and catch me while never letting me go—no matter what.

"Ok, Sarye. I hear you."

She smiled, then hit me with our classic line from *White Men Can't Jump*.

"You can hear Jimmy, but are you listening?"

We both laughed, and I nodded, "I'm listening. I'm listening!"

We discovered our love for movies during our first meeting at Taco Tuesday. Ever since we've been quoting up a storm, various urban classics.

After happy hour, I got into my Range Rover and let the windows down. I shuffled my favorite Old School R&B Playlist and turned up the volume in preparation for whatever came on. When Teena Marie's *Dear Lover* came on, my eyes immediately lowered. The words, the sound of her voice, ripped right through me. I wished I could write a letter to my future husband telling him all about me. Not wanting him to be surprised or unprepared for all that came with me. However, I was sure God had done some of that. Preparation and patience for us both were a part of my nightly prayer. I also asked him to heal us in those dark places. While I thanked him for our lives as individuals and our lives together.

You're ready, Sasha. Don't sit down now. Get up and get out there.

When Luther Vandross' *Wait for Love* came on. I let out a holla like the old folks when their song came on. It was almost as if to testify, the song told their story. The words resonated with me every time I heard them. Love was and has always been my goal. People criticized or reprimanded me for being a hopeless romantic. Often telling me "Move on", "your obsessed", "your (fill in the blank)" I heard it all. So, I kept my ambitions for love to myself or shared with those whom I felt were safe.

Fucking hate labels!

Maybe it was the music, warm air, the illumination of the moon, but I felt good. Bold. As I drove, I found the number and hit the call button. As the phone rang, I let the windows up, prepared to hang up after the 3rd ring. But he answered after the 2nd.

"Greetings, Sasha, you've reached your favorite person. How are you?"

I sighed as Robbie Bobbie, my favorite cousin, answered his phone. His company was always welcome on any day. We've been close since birth, although I was five years older than him. However, given our bond, who could tell? Robbie Bobbie was 37, slim with a low haircut that changed colors depending on his mood. He was 5'11", but you couldn't tell him he wasn't 7'11". He was bold, confident, and quick to read anyone who tried him. People thought he was mean, but he was a sweetheart and a giver. He used to tell me that's why he made a great lover.

Anyway, when he came out to me, I wasn't surprised but happy he decided to live his truth. My auntie (Lorna's sister) wasn't understanding, so their relationship was strained. But he had Lorna and me, so he said she'd come around or not. Either way, he was good. I thought after he relocated to Dallas to become an actor, we'd drift apart. However, it only brought us closer. We talked often, but there was nothing like having him home. Part of me hoped he would come back soon.

"Hello Roberto love, how are you? I miss you something terrible!"

As Robbie sighed, I could hear him smile. "Bitch, no, you don't. You've been listening to them sad ass songs. Now you're thinking about your boring ass life. Now you need your Robbie Bobbie to make you feel better."

We both laughed at his sarcasm and that he was yelling into the phone. He could always read me like a book, and I loved it. Robbie didn't identify as gay, bi, or anything…he said he was just Robbie and that was it. I loved it. He could be everything, and I wouldn't give a damn. I'd lose my religion if anyone fucked with him, and he'd do the same for me. After we settled down, he spoke again.

"Ok, love. Now tell your Robbie Bobbie what's wrong? Sit on my mental sofa, but don't get dirt on it with them baby shoes you wearin'."

Can never have a normal response to anything.

"Now speak chile, but make it quick, chop chop."

I couldn't help but laugh again. He always said this when we had a heart-to-heart.

"Whatever, just cause I ain't slinging yachts on my feet like you."

"Boo please, a yacht ain't only docked on my feet…Okkkurrr! Now hurry up, Kalvin is on his way and I need to relax my vocal cords so I can cheer for him during his big and I do mean BIG performance."

After hearing he was about to have company, there was no way I could even think about my feelings and thoughts. So, I got all in his business because why not? His life was way more interesting than mine. Robbie barely talked about his love life, so I needed to know who Kalvin was.

"Umm hmm. So, this Kalvin…when he performing are you…"

"Aht aht aht…stay out of grown folks' business. Kalvin will come when I tell him…tonight. But we're not talkin' about him or his gorgeous dool. My damn…it's just so. And Chile, the way he be having me…" Robbie got quiet. When I chuckled, he snapped back into our conversation. "Bitch stop deflecting!" I laughed then sighed, giving him the real reason I called.

"I just called to hear your voice, cousin. I do miss you, and my heart needs to see you soon."

Robbie sniffled and spoke as he faked crying. "You know…I knew you missed me. It's good to be loved." Then, just like that, he spoke normally and gave me my marching orders. The moment was over before it even began. "I'll be home soon. Have my room ready and all the shit I like. Cause you know I'm staying with you…them other people ain't got the good shit. Oh, and be sure to get that body wash you had last time. I like the expensive shit, not that grocery store shit. Oh, and I'm vegan."

He a damn lie!

"Bitch, since when? Last time I saw you, your face was knee deep in ribs. Get the fuck outta here." We both laughed; it was true. As a matter of fact, at a family reunion, Robbie won first place in a rib-eating contest. He took out our uncle and family friend despite being skin and bones.

"Well, Kalvin and I are exclusive, and he's vegan, so I joined the vegetable garden so I could keep riding in his pick-up truck, if you know what I mean." We both laughed again. He was a whole trip. Robbie said he would be home in a few months just to regroup and catch up. He was about to be in between movies, plus he had some other business to handle. He wouldn't say what or if he was bringing the infamous Kalvin, but I hoped he would. "Well, love, Kalvin has arrived. So, I have to go and give him this standing ovation. Love you."

"Love you too. Can't wait to see you, Robbie Bobbie. Oh, and we need to talk about something when you're free. I have a new opportunity brewing that might put us in the same state. Can't decide if I should take it or not."

"Really now! Yes, we must converse soon then. Can't wait to see you soon, too, boo. Oh, and Sasha…dial the number you really meant to dial. Don't think I don't know this was a 'stall-call.' Stop running from your own standing ovation. Aunt Lorna already ratted you out. Get it together, boo. Love you." Robbie blew kisses into the phone, then hung up while I laughed out loud. Damn, he knew me so well. Fucking Lorna, what is she parading my shit to everyone?

I looked at his number, which still said *Unknown*. Everyone else tattooed his name in their phonebook but me. But Dolph took up space in my mind which was now practically his home.

It was almost midnight; I couldn't call him this late. But why couldn't I? What was gonna happen? His momma was going to answer and say he can't have phone calls this late? Or better yet, his bitch? Urgh, this is too much.

I was almost home so I decided to bite the bullet. With my 3rd ring rule, I hit the number but kept my finger near the hang-up button. He answered after the 2nd ring.

"It's almost midnight…but at least you listened. How are you, babe?" His voice was so smooth, but he sounded a bit tired. However, I instantly smiled when his words hit the air.

He was waiting for me; he couldn't be this sprung already. But if he was, who could blame him?

"Why does it sound like you in the car? It's almost midnight. I don't like you being out this late, Sasha." Dolph sounded annoyed and waited for a response.

Smiling, I sarcastically answered his question. "First of all, RAN-DOLPH, hello. Second, I'm good, and you? Third, I'm grown. I can be outside after the streetlights come on. Thank you. Fourth…."

Dolph cut me off, tired of my sequential list of responses.

"Sasha, I know you're grown. From what I've seen, I like it. But the point is, you don't need to be out this late. If you do, you need to call me so I can make sure you're safe. I'll even pick you up from wherever. The point is, I need to know your safe, deal?"

He couldn't be serious. What am I five? Please, I'm not doing that shit.

Before I could reply, he added, "Before you snap back with more of your 'I'm a single, Independent woman Sasha-isms' don't. We ain't on that move no more."

We…who the hell is WE?

His words caused me to laugh but also turned me on. I loved a man who could take control. I loved a man who could be a leader I could actually follow. Little did he know, if he proved himself worthy, I'd be his right hand and gladly wear his ring on my left. Fuck that independent shit, them angry man-hating bitches can have that shit.

"Sasha?" Dolph waited for my response, but I just laughed and replied with a fake attitude.

"Look, I didn't call for all this Randolph. So…"

"But you did call, so you were thinking about me. That's good. I was thinking about you, too."

My face hurt from his sweet words, something else hurt too, but it was too soon for that information.

"I was. Now that I've heard your voice. I can get off the phone now."

"Oh, nah, we not doing that. Since you out in them streets, we talking until you pull them covers back. So, remove your hand from the end button and tell me how was the rest of your day?

Matter of fact, hold up…where you coming from? Let's start there."

Urgh, why did I call him again? He's giving Daddy vibes and not in the sexy way.

Although I was almost home, I ran into traffic, so the ten-minute drive took twenty. However, Dolph was alert and ready to talk. So, we talked. We discussed the remainder of our days and got to know more about each other. He owned a few barbershops in two different counties and had construction and contracting businesses.

How sexy was a man who worked with his hands? Talk about a pearl-sweller.

Dolph's family was from North and South Carolina; they migrated to Maryland when he was seven. His grandmother and great-grandmother still lived in the Carolinas along with his uncle and cousins. He had a large family, and he was the oldest of his siblings on both his mother's and father's side. His parents weren't married but still loved each other. In his heart of hearts, he still hoped love would help them find their way back to each other. As he told me about himself, I was intrigued and happy I'd given him the opportunity. Dolph was smart, cultured, handy, had a vast knowledge of many subjects, and was apparently quite a chef. He bragged he could put me on my ass in the kitchen. Part of me wondered if he meant cooking or literally on his countertops. But it was too soon to ask. However, I made a note to ask him later if we ever got to that point.

When I made it home, we continued to talk as I got into my night routine. After I changed into my oversized night shirt, brushed my teeth, I began to prepare to wash my face. Splashing water on my face, I added the cleanser and rubbed it in. Dolph still talked as I listened. He was quite a conversationalist, but I enjoyed it. As he kept talking, I rinsed my face as he made a big announcement.

"I also have a son, he's two," Dolph said, then paused.

Wait? Did he? There goes the other shoe, fuck! I knew it was something.

It wasn't a problem; I loved kids and enjoyed working with them, but it immediately made me nervous. Unsure if I heard him, I wiped my face instantly then cleared my throat and spoke.

"Come again?"

Speaking louder but still calm, he said, "I have a son, he is two. His name is Randolph Jr. (DJ), but we call him 'Little Man'. Wait, don't tell me that's going to be a problem for you?"

I didn't respond. Truth, I didn't know how to respond, but I just knew I didn't do baby mama drama.

"Wait, so you work with kids but won't date a man who has one? How does that make sense, Sasha?"

Mary wouldn't be knocking on my door looking for her little lamb or his Shepherd. Nip this shit in the bud, Sash! And quick!

Dolph's voice was slightly elevated. Which was understandable, but still, he needed to relax. I didn't have a problem with the kid. I liked and respected kids, hell, more than most adults. But again, I didn't do Baby Mama drama. Plus, this kid was two years old, fresh out the cooch and still young, the world turned once, who says it wouldn't turn again.

"Dolph, I don't have a problem with you having a child. That doesn't bother me at all."

Dolph let out a sigh of relief, "Good, so let's…"

"HOWEVER! I don't do Baby Mama drama." Dolph sighed loudly again, then grunted but allowed me to continue. "Plus, he's still young and…"

"And what, Sasha? I am his father. Me! I have custody, FULL custody. So, whatever you think is going to happen, it's not. So can we…"

"Dolph, you're being unfair! I'm trying to express my concerns, and you're being dismissive and a bit aggressive, may I say."

Dolph immediately relaxed his tone and took another breath before he spoke again. "My bad, Sasha. That wasn't my intention, and I apologize. I jumped the gun, thinking you were about to shut me down…"

"Oh, you are right, I was. But not for being an active father. I think that's amazing, and I love that. But he's young, and although his mother is not there now, she might change her mind. And he deserves…"

"He deserves to be with someone who loves him, cares about him, and will guide him to be a great man one day. And that's me, his father. Not with someone who has no interest in being a parent. She handed him over at birth and never looked back, the end." Dolph was upset. I hit a nerve unintentionally. We were both silent, but I had something else to say.

"Look, Dolph, I've seen this a thousand times…"

Before I could finish, he grunted again and then spoke before he ended our call. "You not even listening…you know what, never mind! Good night, Sasha. You have a good one."

When the line went dead, I instantly felt bad. I had no idea about his dealings with his child's mother, and my assumption led me to put my foot in my mouth in addition to kicking me square in the ass. The therapist in me knew better than to push. At that moment, I should have let it be and asked more questions at another time. The relationship between Dolph and the mother of his child was a sore subject and none of my business at this juncture. It was also personal, likely riddled with heartache and unresolved trauma. It was true, I needed to know what that looked like, but it could have waited. I should have waited instead; I pushed and then pushed him out the door in the process. While in bed, I pondered all the things I could have said or done differently. But it didn't matter, I fucked up.

At 2:00 am, I was still up. Not only thinking about Dolph, but the damn full moon didn't help. It always made me stay awake later or woke me up at 2:00 or 3:00 am as if to call me to it. So, I got up, drew my blinds, and pulled my ottoman to the window. I needed to have a heart-to-heart with myself and God as the mediator.

Sasha, you have to apologize to that man. Even if he doesn't respond. You should have held space for him to express his feelings and then respected them; you know better. Yes, your concerns were valid and should be addressed. But, honey, they could have waited. Don't let your defenses from the past keep you from enjoying your future. Even if he's not your man, you are going to need to do that for your future husband. Today, make time to call or text him. It's the least you could do.

When I resolved that I'd do that, I went to bed. Not falling asleep immediately, I stared outside into the trees that lined up the back of my home. The fireflies blinked off and on, almost creating a mythical scene. Although I wanted to call him then, I decided against it. The more I thought about him, my heart and stomach ached. I also thought about Dr. Kirk's words. Not only did I not invite love over for coffee, but I also didn't even bother to give it a chance.

Fuck My Life

With that thought, I drifted off to sleep. When I woke up, the sunshine was on full blast, and I struggled to get up. There was no time for the gym; I was running late again. A busy day, full of clients and an apology I still needed to send.

Chapter 5

"Hi, Dolph, it's Sasha…"

"Dolph, Sasha here…"

"Hey, this Sasha or whateva…"

"Fool this…"

"Dolph, baby…"

Really, Sasha…baby? Girl, bye!

My attempt to mimic Issa Raye's mirror conversation from *Insecure* was an epic fail. I practiced what to say to Dolph but felt foolish. He didn't text, and neither did I. Truthfully, I didn't blame him; I was the one who fucked up. He didn't owe me anything. So, if I never heard from him again, I'd understand.

After leaving the bathroom mirror, I went back to my computer to check my calendar. It was Thursday, so when Charity's name appeared on my calendar, I smiled. She was a young lady in her late twenties who came to therapy but didn't talk. We usually sat quietly, and she read a book or played on her phone. When she came in, she'd say, "Hey, Dr. Phillips," when she left, she'd say, "See you next week, Dr. Phillips." That was it. Nothing more or less. However, she was court-ordered to come, so she did just that.

At first, I'd try to make conversation with her. Ask her questions, talk about why she was in therapy, but she wasn't interested, and I was over it. So, while she entertained herself, I typed notes and waited for her to be ready to speak. Maybe today I could finalize my apology to Dolph so I could move on.

"Doc, Charity is here."

"Thanks, Keysha, let her in, please."

I stood up to greet Charity. As I smiled, she gave a half-smirk and sat down, then opened her phone.

Well, hello to you, too, Charity. Thank you for the warm regards and silence, much appreciated.

At the end of the hour, I stood again.

"See you next week, Charity." She chucked me the deuces and walked out without saying a word. I stuck my head outside my office to address Keysha.

"Damn, did she say anything this week?" Keysha asked

"Nope, silence is golden with that one. Look, did you order the supplies we needed? If not, can you do so? You know I hate to run out."

"Sure, Doc." Keysha turned to her computer and continued her work.

"Hey Keysha, do I have any messages?"

Keysha searched for her notepad, then replied. "No new messages since you asked an hour ago. What's up, lady? Who are we waiting for?"

She was so damn nosy, but I set myself up for that one. Not wanting to rehash my mess, I ended the conversation.

"No one, just making sure I didn't miss Steve Harvey telling me I won the Publishers' Clearinghouse."

Keysha gave me the eye, "Yeah, ok, Doc. I'ma let you have that one. But we both know you're bullshitting, boo."

"Language, Keysha, you know we're working."

"Yeah, yeah. I know my apologies."

The rest of the afternoon was quiet. I was able to finish my paperwork, edit my next book, clean my desk off, and start preparations for my next project. At 5:45 pm, Keysha entered my office and sat in one of the available chairs.

"Umm…unless we're getting paid OT, what's wrong?" Keysha was right, usually by now she was gone, and so was I unless I had late appointments or I went home to work. "And before you say nothing…just know I call bullshit! So, fess up!"

"Keysha!?!?"

"Nope, Sasha! We're off the clock, so all professionalism out the door. What is bothering you?"

Fuck it, what did I have to lose?

"Ok, Key, I fucked up with Dolph, and I need to apologize. I just don't know how, yet."

Hearing his name, Keysha's antennas went up. "Oh, we need to fix that shit immediately."

"We? Key? And why it gotta be me?"

"You the one working up the apology, Sasha, so…."

Duh Sasha! She got a point.

"On a scale of 1 to 10, how bad did you fuck up? Does he like flowers? Is it too early for a BJ? I mean, you still know how, right?" I could not with her foolishness and laughed while my face reflected my confusion at her suggestions. However, Keysha didn't care, just kept talking.

"Ok, too soon for the BJ. But, how about a nice text or call Sasha? You got the gift of gab and have helped me smooth things over with my boo plenty of times. So, come on, let me help you get out the doghouse. Wait first, tell me what happened…what have you done?" Not wanting to tell Keysha what happened, I fessed up and told her the truth. The look of judgment from Keysha further let me know I had to fix this and quick. "Really, Sasha! I can't believe you pushed like that. You know better."

"Urgh, I know, which is why I need to at least apologize. My spirit won't settle until I do." Keysha shook her head, and we sat silently. She nodded and sipped her tea, full of judgment. Then she sat up in the chair, folding her arms on my desk.

"Yeah, you know better. Put on your big girl thong and call him. Don't bitch out and text him; he deserves that much. We're not letting him get away. He's cool, plus I like free lunch. So, do we need to do a roll-up? An ass kiss. I can call Kyle now and tell him I'm gonna be late."

I hate it when she's right! A text is a cop-out out and he did deserve more.

I reached for my cellphone and set it on the desk. As I looked at it, Keysha looked at me. "Come on, Sasha, it can't gonna dial itself. Plus, Kyle gonna be looking for me soon, and I can't leave until I know this is done. So, hurry it on up."

"What if he doesn't answer Key?" I whined, hoping she would show me some sympathy. But Keysha didn't.

"Leave him a 90's R&B voice message, you want me to play some *Shai* or *Hi-Five* in the background. Trey Songz, my cousin, and my sister know C Breezy backup singers, sister, baby cousin. We can have them sing on your behalf, you know, they know all about fucking up."

Black people swear they know somebody famous, I cannot!

Her comment made us both laugh. That was the type of message I needed to leave. But I didn't have that kind of time. All the music and celebrities in the world wouldn't make up for what was really needed. After a breath, I went to my call history to find his number.

"Damn, Sasha, you ain't even saved his number with his name…raggedy! Give him that much respect. That is, if he ever talks to you again." I hit the call button and put the phone on speaker. After the third ring, I attempted to hang up, but Keysha popped my hand. "Don't you dare!" she mumbled as he finally picked up. There was silence on the line. My throat went dry, and the words escaped me when Dolph didn't say anything.

"Dolph…it's…"

"I know. Sup!" His voice was plain and indicated his disinterest in hearing from me.

Damn funny how the tables turned!

"Ok, cool. I won't keep you. I wanted to apologize for last night/this morning. I was wrong for pushing the subject. Also, for not respecting your boundary. It was clear you set it, and I pushed anyway. I didn't mean to disrespect or question how you parent your son. I don't know much, but I can tell you love hard and protect even harder. My mentioning your son's mother was completely out of pocket, and I was wrong. I just wanted to say, I apologize. I truly apologize, Randolph."

He was quiet, we both were. I looked at Keysha, and she smiled half as if to say, at least I tried.

"Thanks. Appreciate it."

Yikes, he's still pissed. Damn, ok. I'll take this L. Apology is done and obviously so is his interest in me.

His voice held no inkling of hope, remorse, or anything. My apology was as dead as this conversation. I nodded and then hung up the phone. There was nothing else to say.

Ouch. Well, you tried, Sasha.

"Maybe he needs a little time," Keysha said uncertainly.

"Nah, Key, it's done. Gone, gone, and done." Keysha gave me a side hug and went home, while I went back to work. If I never heard from Dolph again, at least I attempted to make things right.

The next day, I went to the gym at my normal time. Part of me wanted to go to the gym a couple of miles down the road. However, I wanted to run into him. Maybe I'd have a better outcome if he could see my face and I could see his. I'd even tried to spice up my look a bit in hopes a nice view would help my case. So, I wore the athleisure wear I usually wear in the house or on a quick run to the store. In my grayish blue form-fitting, matching two-piece casual long sleeve tracksuit set, I walked into the gym with my head held high. Since I abandoned my hat and glasses for a high-tuck ponytail, sweatband, and contacts, I walked a bit taller.

Before I left the car, I gave myself a nod of confidence and put on extra gloss on my lips. For the life of me, I couldn't remember what I was supposed to be working on today, but it didn't matter; my mission wasn't myself but finding him. I did a quick scan and found him immediately. Seeing him sent a mixture of emotions through my mental.

Ok, he's here…don't fuck this up, Sasha.

I went through my normal routine, only I hit the treadmill this time and then moved over to work my arms and back. I tried to focus on my workout, but I couldn't. Dolph was in his usual place at the front, lifting weights in the mirror. As he moved around the gym, I followed him with my eyes. Although he never looked in my direction.

I said I was sorry. I know he heard me, even though he didn't respond, at least not like I wanted or hoped.

It felt like he purposely avoided anywhere I was or even looking in my direction. It hurt, but I got it or attempted to. Before I finished my workout, Dolph headed towards the exit. I immediately got off the machine and headed toward the exit. By the time I made it out of the gym, he had already reached the parking lot, so I picked up the pace to follow him, but I needed to get his attention. Although part of me knew he realized I was behind him.

"Dolph, wait!"

He turned around and stopped. The look of admiration he usually displayed was gone. When he admired my attire with his eyes, I flashed a partial smile, but his face didn't change. Dolph just stared at me and waited for me to speak. So, I took a breath and said what came to my mind.

"Look, I'm sor…"

"Yeah, I already know that…what else you got? I need to go pick up my son since I AM his only parent." He was more than annoyed and pissed was an understatement.

I immediately regretted this decision; I should have left him alone. So, I hesitated and hoped he would just walk away after I was done. Saving us both from whatever this was about to be.

"Ok, well, I won't keep you."

Dolph immediately turned away from me. However, my conscience wouldn't let me just let him walk away.

"But Dolph, I…" I couldn't find the words. I'd said I'm sorry, he didn't want to hear it. Whatever planned words had next escaped me, but I had to try. "Maybe, we could…"

He laughed sarcastically, and for the first time, I saw the smile that used to be mine.

"We could what, Sasha? Come on, let's hear it!"

Fuck, he's mean. I was wrong, but damn, this is torment.

After a pause, he spoke again.

"You made up this whole story about my baby momma coming back and us living happily ever after. Although that shit is never gonna happen, but whatever. You used that as a reason, better yet, as a reason to say you're done, so what you want, man? And hurry that shit along."

What I want is to leave your evil ass alone now. But my stupid ass won't give up. Always a sucker for self-inflicted punishment, Sasha.

"I want you to stop and put yourself in my shoes."

My words were soft, hesitant, but I hoped they showed my sincerity. If I knew this was going to be his reaction, although warranted, I would've kept my thoughts to myself. Although what good would that do? This would have happened sooner or later. I couldn't allow my feelings to fester too long; it's something I learned in my healing journey. So, I had to say what I had to say now, we'd either move past it or not.

"Your shoes? What about me? You question my ability to take care of my son. I tried to show you I cared about you. You shut me down continuously with some past bullshit you can't get over. Now you coming around for what? What's your point, Sasha? Like I said, I got other stuff to do."

He was cold and stern, but he wasn't wrong. But I was about everything. What was my point? What did I want from him? Part of me wanted to tell him, I wanted another chance. I wanted a redo, for him to go against his word and circle back this one time for me.

I want you to stop being an ass and give me a chance to make it right.

Dolph went to walk away, but I grabbed his hand. He looked at my hand, then pulled away. "Too late, Sasha. Remember, I don't double back for no one."

Fuck! And there it is.

That was it, he was done. Dolph got into his large black SUV with super dark tints. I stood off to the side, hoping he might roll down his window, but he didn't. He pulled forward, and I watched him speed out of the parking lot.

Dang Doc, it really is a wrap…he ain't have to do us like that though, sheesh!

After that, I conceded with the plan to go to the gym down the street. Dolph could have this one, considering it a parting gift. It would add 30 more minutes to my morning routine. However, I had to keep moving forward, and that was a start.

Later that week, Sarye, Monet, and Keysha (who eventually arrived) came over to rummage through my closet.

"Umm, Doc, what the hell is this?" Sarye asked as she held up my college hooded sweatshirt.

It was gray and displayed the school's name on it. In it, I was comfortable and felt ready for any task, and it showed. The front pocket of the hoodie was slightly ripped from being snagged too many times. The front was cut slightly because I didn't like tight things on my neck. Plus, it had a few stains on it from whatever never came out. But in my eyes, it was still wearable.

"That's my favorite sweatshirt. I wear it all the time. What's wrong with it?"

Sarye looked at me like the *Nick Young meme*, like I had three heads, as she frowned.

This is not going to end well for us.

"It's raggedy, dingy, and needs to be thrown away. Please tell me you don't wear this outside."

With sarcasm, I replied as if I didn't see a problem.

"Yeah, I…"

Before I could finish, Sarye replied.

"Nope, trash it."

Monet took the sweatshirt from Sarye and put it in the trash bag.

"Wha…"

"No ma'am. If you love that school so much, buy a new one. You out here looking like you don't care about life in that rag."

"Dang Rye, you cold! How you gonna make Linus throw away his blanket, you rude AF!"

Monet had a point, and I tried to give a sad face, then frowned. However, Sarye was a tough cookie and was unmoved.

"Fine Rye. Bye-bye sweatshirt. Although it's seen me through some difficult times. I wrote some of my best work in that sweatshirt, just so you know."

"Yeah, looks like it. Besides, it wasn't the sweatshirt…that was all you."

Sarye gave a disgusted look then winked and smiled. Then she continued swiping through my clothes and threw more stuff in the bag as she made comments under her breath. We all laughed as she tossed my once-beloved clothes and shoes. By the time Keysha arrived, we were still in my closet. Which now only consisted of mostly hangers and some lingerie, which I only wore for myself.

"Damn, Doc, does this come with a whip and chain. Because baby, this is some sexy shit." Monet said, holding a hunter green lace bodysuit against her chest.

"It used to. But I didn't want to cross-contaminate, so I threw them out."

The ladies laughed as I winked.

"Good one, at least we know you will be ready when Mr. Right comes along."

Keysha said as she made herself comfortable on my bed. Usually, I didn't allow outside clothes on my bed, but I planned on changing my sheets later. The mention of a man for me to entertain soured my mood a bit. Now I wished that man was Dolph, but I royally fucked that up. Of course, Keysha picked up on it instantly.

"Don't worry, Doc, someone else will come around. At least you put yourself out there. It will happen again." I instantly regretted showing any emotion and Keysha's oversharing. I already knew what was about to happen, so I braced for impact.

Here we go! 5…4…3…2…1!

"Wait…what we miss?" Monet beat Sarye to the question, but now they all looked to me for an answer. Keysha conveniently looked away, then glanced at me from a distance.

Urgh, damn Keysha…

"Did something happen with 'Throw up Bae'?"

Lawd, did she just call Dolph Throw up Bae? Hilarious.

We all looked at Monet, with the *what the hell* face, before we busted into laughter.

"What?!?! Tell me the naming isn't fitting? I mean Sasha did blow chunks up and down her office in front of him."

We all couldn't help but laugh hysterically.

"Really, Mo. He does have a name." I was trying to get myself together, but that shit was funny.

Yeah, it's more like Don't Circle Back Bae! Fuck his rules; he could have made an exception. Fucker!

"Yeah, yeah, but who cares about all that. Anyway, what happened with throw-up bae?" Mo was right; it didn't matter. Besides, Dolph was gone, and he made it clear he wasn't going to return. It was time everyone knew the truth, so we could all move on with this new reality. I was about to answer the lingering question, but Keysha held her hand up and then spoke.

"Well, shit, if we gonna talk about it, can we get some wine and food. I had too much cake, and I need some food and wine to top it off."

Everyone agreed, and we headed to the kitchen to chew, sip, and gossip. We sat at my island as the spread of food and drink sat on the surrounding counters. Once everyone had their portions of everything and sat down on the barstools, I let it out.

"Well, y'all long story short. I fucked up. I pushed him away in more than one way and then insulted him, and now he's done. And he said I quote, *I don't circle back for no one!* So, it's a wrap."

"Dang, what, you insult his dog? Call his mama a hoe or something, cause them is some fighting words." Monet's comment caused us all to laugh again.

"Naw Mo, she told him his Mama look like his Dog! Unless she must have done something deeper. Something crazy like insulting his child, if he got one." Sarye and Monet smacked hands and laughed at her comment, but Keysha and I lowered our heads and shook them, ashamed. Monet slapped the counter with her hand before she spoke, while Sarye sipped her wine and shook her head.

"Oh Shit! Not the baby Doc! Did you call his baby ugly or something? Girl, you supposed to lie! Lie like a rug if you have to. Although some of them babies be fu-ugly! I was dating this one dude…" Mo was about to take a trip down memory lane. When Sarye swatted at her and she stopped. Then Sarye asked the question they wanted to hear. "So, girl, you really lost your boo…tell us what happened."

The ladies listened as I told them what happened. From the looks on their faces, they agreed with Dolph.

"Damn, Doc! Yeah, children are a touchy subject. But I kinda see your point." Sarye said as she leaned on my shoulder.

"Maybe give him some time. Who knows what can happen?"

Yeah, talking to him feels like doing 5-10 in prison for the whole conversation, I'm good. We don't ever have to talk again.

"Thanks, Rye. But it's done, really done, and I'm good with that, for real."

Now that things were out in the open, I was even more ready to move on. Another opportunity with Dolph was the furthest thing from my mind. It hurt how things ended, but it was what it was.

We were all quiet for a bit, then we engaged in small talk as we ate and drank. Keysha filled us in on wedding stuff. Then we continued to laugh and joke throughout the evening.

"Anyway, let's go get these clothes and donate them so Doc doesn't try to revive them." Sarye said, making us all laugh.

"Matter of fact, get rid of that…whatever you're wearing now, too!" Monet nodded at Sarye's comment.

"What? I haven't been outside today. I did take a shower, but this is my around-the-house dress."

We all have that one dress that done seen better days. Well, mine was an oversized spaghetti-strapped orange dress; I created knots are the top to make it fit better. It had some subtle grease stains on it and a few pin holes, but who would see it but me?

"Girl, you done fried your last chicken wing in that oversized mess. Now go upstairs and take it off." Sarye motioned for me to head upstairs. But not before Monet added her two cents.

"Yeah, besides that ain't sexy. No man wants to see random spots on a dress he knows he ain't put there…period! It's giving used condom vibes."

Where did she come up with this stuff! That's just nasty!

We all shook our heads, then laughed, and I headed upstairs to change.

When I changed, I leaned against my closet door and looked at the empty hangers. The space reflected the current state of my life. I'd spent so much time hanging on to what-ifs and the past that I'd missed out on a lot of the future. When I was with Blue, my life was different. Our love consumed me; with a phone call he could make or wreck my day. That was problem number one. I'd given him too much power and control. He became a priority, and I became second to last.

When we finally broke up, I was different was like it stopped everything. I didn't know how to exist on top of dealing with the pain of our breakup. Since I never exposed him or our discretion, he went on with his life and his wife, while I struggled to put myself back together.

One of my former friends at the time said I should have called his wife or shown up at his house. But what good would that have done? Funny thing is that we women know when our men are unfaithful. It's a part of our intuition; whether we choose to ignore it or accept it is on us. The wise say, we don't leave until we are ready, and it's true. We don't, and not a second before we are finally ready. So, all the advice in the world can't save a soul that's tied to another, remember that.

After Blue, I had a series of physically intimate relationships, but nothing panned out. I'd even lost some friendships, including one I thought would last forever. The "revolving door," as it was once described in a joke that was funny until it wasn't, represented my dysfunction. Initially, I laughed until I realized what it meant and represented, then it hurt silently. Funny how people see one thing and run with it and stand on it. It's their punchline every time until it's their gut punch, but I digress.

However, the funny thing about that joke was that it inspired me to bolt my door shut and really deal with myself. Now, like my closet filled with hangers, I'd had space for new things in my life. Now it was time to figure things out. Dr. Kirk always asked me, *What does that look like?* Or *what does that mean for you?* Sometimes I'd have the answer, but other times I didn't. However, I'd rather take the time to figure it out than settle for the first thing in front of me.

When I took too long to come back downstairs, Keysha came up to look for me.

"Hey Sasha, you good?"

I smiled at her to let her know I was good, seeing the emptiness was what I needed to move forward. My saddest days used to consist of crying spells, gorging on junk food, staying in bed, and drowning in whatever movie or song that could make me feel lower. But I traded that all in for reflection, peace, ease, grace, acknowledgment, and plans to move forward. My feelings for Dolph wouldn't disappear in a day; it would take time. Now that I'd done the work, I could manage myself better and reroute when needed until I could find peace with everything that happened.

Keysha stood inside my closet opposite me. I smiled at her and took a breath, then responded.

"I'm good, Key, looking forward to a fresh start."

She smiled slightly, then grabbed my hand to squeeze gently. I appreciated Keysha; she was more than my assistant; we were like sisters. I knew she had my back no matter what, and I appreciated it. It's rare you find treasures like her in life.

Keysha was studying to become a licensed clinical mental health counselor. In less than a year, she'd do it successfully; my girl was a hustler. During her interview, she said she wanted her own practice. I slightly frowned at her statement; it was bold and would make most owners nervous. However, when she said she wanted to get into the field and learn the ropes, I was sold. She was willing to start at the bottom and work her way up.

Keysha was hungry, showed initiative, stayed late, never passed up an opportunity to learn, and always represented the business in a positive professional way. She was the Pippen to my Jordan; one day, if she wanted, I'd give her the keys and retire happy. Hopefully, married with at least one child, but either way, the business would be in good hands. I still needed to talk to her about Houston, but that conversation could wait.

"Look, I know you don't want to talk about him. But I gotta say something."

I raised my eyebrow while looking at Keysha skeptically, then waited for her to speak.

"I heard what you said, Sasha, but sometimes people say things they don't mean like…"

"Like me!"

Keysha didn't want to nod, but she did slowly. I appreciated her words, but I really was ok with how things were. I was ready to move on and wished everyone would as well.

"Sasha, it might not be today…tomorrow or even soon. But I feel like you two will work it out at some point."

I pulled Keysha in for a hug and let her go without responding. She could dream and hold hope for both of us, but as for me, I wished him the best. We headed back downstairs, where Sarye and Monet were chatting as they cleaned up.

Time to focus on the next exciting task at hand!

The next day, Sarye and I were going shopping for my new clothes.

"Time to get you some action, Doc. Or at least a wink." Sarye bumped me with her hip. I wasn't bolting my door shut, but I wasn't in the mood to entertain just yet either.

"Ohhhh…maybe you can hook her up with…" Monet said too excited.

Oh hell, let's nip this in the bud asap! These heifers are getting ideas, abort mission!

"Nope, nope, nope! I don't do hook-ups or blind dates."

Monet frowned. "Well, Doc, maybe you should, cause you ain't doing shit right now. And that other shit is done, so you say." Everyone nodded at Monet's comment. I was over it and was about to change the subject when she started again. "Let's make a deal, Doc." We all waited for her to finish. "If you don't get a date after a month with these new threads. You have to let each one of us hook you up."

That sounds like some desperado crap or a recipe for a bad reality TV show. HELL, THE FUCK NO!

Everyone agreed out loud, but I frowned at the idea.

"What Doc? It's a good idea. Besides, Curtis got some cute cousins. They might be a little rough around the edges…but at least you could dust off ya box a little."

Why does everyone think my pussy is dry and dusty, urgh! It might be moister than theirs, but that's going too far…focus, Sasha!

"I'm not agreeing to that mess. No deal."

I walked into the living room and sat on my sofa, folding my arms to further reflect my disinterest in the topic. If they couldn't see it in my appearance, they'd hear it in my dismissive tone.

"What do you have to lose, huh?" Keysha's joining felt like the ultimate betrayal.

Did Keysha just join in? Urgh, she's fired! You're no longer Pippen, I'm trading you, damn it! Mo would make a good Rodman.

Keysha's agreement was the co-sign Monet needed. If she agreed, the group knew I'd at least consider it. After a few minutes of bouncing my leg, I considered the idea.

It's not like you're on the internet, not meeting anyone when you're out. Hell, the nigga ain't gonna break into your house, and if he does, that's a problem. Cause who is waiting 5-10 for him to get out? Urgh, what do we have to lose, huh?

"Fine. Fine. I'll agree if everyone will leave me alone."

"We will," everyone said in unison.

This is complete bullshit, and they know it. But it is true, what did I have to lose?

Chapter 6

ONE MONTH LATER…

It had been a month since everything happened with Dolph, and I hadn't seen him since our last interaction. As a matter of fact, I made sure I didn't see him. My gym routine now consists of a night workout at my usual gym. Which helped my schedule; I was no longer late and could crash after my shower. Problem solved.

Anyway, not seeing him physically didn't change what went on in my mind. I thought about him a lot, but my remedy was to send him light and positivity, then let the thought go. Sometimes it worked while other times it didn't. When I talked to Lorna eventually, after gently scolding her about telling my business, I asked her not to mention him to me. Part of me wanted to know if they were still talking. Who would blame him if he stopped dealing with her, too. But I never asked, I set a boundary with her and she kept it. No Dolph meant no Dolph!

However, there was no action in another department, which forced me to do something I thought I'd never do…go on a blind date. As much as I tried to renege on the idea, the ladies were not giving up. So, I had to suck it up.

No date in sight! So, a Deal is a Deal! Why the hell didn't I get pneumonia or a hangnail that required surgery? Fucked up shit never happened when I needed it to! But let it be a sunny day, then here comes the bullshit!

Date Number One ~ *Monet's Pick*

I can't believe I'm doing this shit…this ain't even me! Further, I don't even look like myself. Fuck!

I squirmed in my seat as Sarye finished pulling my weave into a high bun with two spiral curls coming down the front. Although they were pulled back as Monet put on my make-up, which they wouldn't let me see. I felt like it was all too much, including the royal blue off-the-shoulder sleeve bodycon midi dress. I'd stick out like a sore thumb in the color, although it did complement my medium brown skin. And the diamond studs and necklace did make everything pop; from the one glance I did get before Monet started on my makeup. I did look beautiful despite my attempt to act differently. The only thing I was not looking forward to were the black strappy sandals, which tied around my ankle. They were at least 6 inches and too tall in my opinion, but no one seemed to care. I could walk in them, so to them it was problem solved, according to them.

"A promise is a promise, Doc." Keysha reminded me as all the ladies sat in my bedroom as I tried on a dress for my date.

Damn her memory. Why couldn't she be this thorough at work? I'm being messy, she was, that's what I loved about her.

"I know and I intend on going on this date, hell or high water." As I mumbled through my teeth while Monet applied a medium brown lipstick to my lips. I had every intention of getting this over with as quickly as possible. As if reading my thoughts, Keysha replied sarcastically.

"It doesn't count if you ruin it. So, stop planning to fuck it up, Sasha. You've done enough of that already."

Well Damn, she have to put me out there like that? Urgh.

Keysha was getting on my damn nerves, and I wanted to tell her verbally. However, I shut up before my words got me into an even further mess. After taking a deep breath and closing my eyes, I replied in my most professionally annoyed voice.

"You're right. I'm a woman of my word. So, I'll give it my best shot."

"That's right, Sasha! Now come on and let's finish up so you can go meet Reid."

Monet was overly excited about her pick. How the hell they let her go first is still beyond me. Apparently, they drew straws or some shit, and she was second. Sarye initially had the first pick, but her date had a cancellation or something. And Keysha wanted to go last, so here we were. So, Monet anxiously stepped in to get the first shot.

Monet was my girl, and I had all the confidence in her when it came to clothes, accessories, and beauty shit. However, her taste in men and mine were like night and day. She liked her men really rough around the edges and unhealed. However, I had a different standard. A little rough was one thing, I mean, having a man who can hold his own in any room was sexy. But a man who made you hold or hide your head in the same room because he didn't have table manners or said ignorant shit was another thing. I hoped and prayed her pick was more towards my end of the spectrum and not hers.

When I agreed to this, I didn't realize was the "us" I agreed to included all the ladies having their separate matches. Apparently, that was spelled out clearly to me, no matter how I tried to plead it wasn't. Every woman would get their turn to hook me up. Fucking fine print and selective hearing, now here I was, since they wore me down, about to embark on date number one. How bad could it be, right? He sounded nice, but something made me nervous. Like something was missing from the puzzle.

Reid was 45, an entrepreneur, and had no kids. Which was a breath of relief. At least I knew I couldn't fuck it up in that regard. We talked on the phone a few times, and he seemed nice. Reid called at a respectable hour; his vocabulary was great, and he had manners. From the picture he sent me, he was handsome. The picture was a professional shot from when he sold real estate. He recently transitioned into owning his own business, so the picture was about two years old. However, he was dressed in a navy-blue suit and, tie. Although I couldn't see his whole frame, he looked nice from the mid chest up. Medium brown skin, clean-shaven brown head, brown eyes, salt and pepper goatee. He was tall, about 6'1", with strong arms that displayed some muscles.

When Sarye and Monet finished, they looked to Keysha for approval since she supervised everything. Once Keysha gave her a nodding approval, they prepared to turn me around.

"Ok, Doc, you ready!" Keysha said excitedly.

When they turned me around, I was astonished. I looked like a completely different person. Everything was in place perfectly. I wanted to cry but didn't want to mess up my makeup. My girls had done amazingly!

"Say cheese, Doc," Sarye said as we all took a selfie. The picture was perfect. Me and my girls. As we all headed out, we agreed to get on a group call after my date. As I headed to the restaurant, my nerves and thoughts settled a bit. When I arrived at the restaurant. I took a deep breath.

Tonight, will be great. I will enjoy just being beautiful. Just let your hair down, Sasha, you deserve it.

I walked into the restaurant with a smile as if I owned the place. The waitress showed me to the table where Reid waited. Reid stood as I approached the table. He was dressed in a khaki brown suit, with a light blue button-down and brown wingtip shoes. He had a bouquet of flowers in his hand. He was off to a good start, although I hated carnations; in my opinion, they weren't real flowers unless you were in middle school on Valentine's Day. However, the gesture was nice, so it was no big deal.

"Sasha, you look amazing."

Reid pulled me in for a hug; he smelled good, but the cologne was a bit overpowering, which made me cough a bit.

Goodness, if he lasts, we gonna have to teach him not to bathe in this shit. Fuck! He ain't gonna be stinking up my whole house for days with this shit, urgh.

Shaking the thought from my head, I tried to reset.

"Sit down, love, let me get your chair so we can finally get this date going."

I sat down, and Reid took his place. I smiled and turned my face slightly up, trying to catch any piece of fresh air that passed.

Optimistic Sasha, be optimistic! Smile and be present.

Four Hours Later...

I was back in my car and headed home. After I calmed down and cursed myself, agreeing to shit I didn't want to do in the first place. I placed a call to my overly anxious girls, who were blowing up my phone individually. I should have known they would; they had my location and saw it moved from the restaurant an hour ago, going from Bowie into the heart of Northwest, DC. The neighborhood wasn't the best, so I really called them in case I got carjacked or robbed. Part of me tried to remain calm as I spoke. But the other half was like fuck it, let your feelings go…so I did.

Before everyone could get on the call, when I saw Monet, I immediately started talking. Practically yelling into the phone, I needed to know her thought process with this one. Why did she even remotely think Reid was even my type, let alone even in my league?

"Really!??! Monet! How in the hell did you think he was a good match for me?" Everyone laughed (including Monet) as I waited for a response while I drove home. Moving quickly through the streets of DC, I wanted to get out as fast as I could.

"What Doc? He was nice!" Monet yelled back while laughing a bit. Reid being nice wasn't the problem, and she knew it based on her reaction.

"Monet, he said he was an entrepreneur!" I mumbled through my teeth.

"What he is?"

"Yeah, an aspiring one! This negro does Uber Eats at night and practically sleeps all day." Everyone fell out laughing. I shook my head as I sat in traffic.

"What Sasha?!? The sheet and comforter business is slow sometimes. He just hit a rough season. Plus, he also sells supplements."

Was she fucking kidding me? Urgh! This is why I didn't want to do this; everything is a big FUCKING JOKE!

"Monet, the website he showed me is for the Dick Gregory juice from the 90s. I don't even know where he would find that shit now. Ain't no one mentioned that juice since Robin Harris in *House Party One,* God rest his soul." The ladies fell out laughing, but I hadn't said the worst part. "Plus, the other supplements he sold, said Dr. Sebi, but the dude on the bottle looked like Uncle Ben's. Oh, and let's be clear, he never had a real estate license; his license that shit was a whole damn lie. Make it make sense!" I roared loudly, and the ladies laughed, but I wasn't finished yet. "Oh, and icing on the cake, not only does he have three kids. Although he claims they are not his biologically, he just took them on. His baby momma/ex-girlfriend lives in his apartment, so he stays in his momma's basement. Since she doesn't have a place to go. This man is in no position to do anything for anyone. Again, make it make sense! I feel like Theo when he thought he was getting a Gordon Gartrelle"

Being funny, Sarye hit the *Denise Huxtable* response, "So you don't like him?"

And I shot back, "Ask me again!" They all roared in laughter again. After Monet composed herself a bit, she finally spoke up with a hint of sincerity.

"Damn, Doc, I didn't know all that. My bad, boo. I tried; I really did; these niggas be lying."

It wasn't her fault, not totally. Reid obviously had us both fooled with his "half-truths-truths" and mythological lies. After dinner, Reid confessed to not really being a real estate agent. Turns out, he was an "aspiring" real estate agent. He used a picture he took at a church job fair event that offered professional photos. He said he "couldn't" take the class or test for the license because they only offered it once a year. I didn't even bother to address his lying ass. I was more pissed that he actually thought I'd fall for that bullshit. My ass should have put him out right then and there for insulting my intelligence, fucking asshole.

"Then to make it worse, y'all, he needed a ride home." The ladies roared again with laughter. One would think I was lying, but I couldn't make this shit up if I tried, because why would I? "That's why I am stuck in this damn traffic at 10:30 pm clutching my necklace, hoping no one snatches it while I drive through the city." As they laughed, I couldn't help but join them. It was funny, but at the same time it wasn't.

"You better than I am, Doc. I would have left his ass at the restaurant." Sarye commented as she tried to contain herself.

"Oh, I would have, but he only had enough for dinner and not enough to go home. I had to leave the damn tip." They all laughed again.

"Girl, you're a Saint. God is going to bless you. Keep the faith, boo." Keysha laughed as she tried to make me feel better.

You damn right! And I'm about to bless y'all with this reality gut punch!

"Good thing this is a one-and-done. No more blind dates for me." Everyone stopped laughing, then groaned and complained as I had two more dates left.

"What? Y'all set these dates up and don't vet them enough, and I'm stuck with bullshit like this? Nope! I'm good, move on." I was so serious about my words, but of course, the girls were not letting up.

"Sasha! Come on, this was a fluke, my bad. Look, he fooled me like he fooled you." Monet whined, trying to change my mind.

"Right, and my pick is going to be better, I promise. I will vet him like he's going overseas, I promise! Please don't give up now!" Sarye never begged, but now she was. I couldn't overlook this, so I took a moment and a breath before I responded.

"Fine. Fine. I won't let one bad date ruin things. But I hate this, I want everyone to note it. Oh, and these last two better be who they say they are, damn it. If not, I'm leaving immediately."

They all mumbled in unison, "Fine, Sasha!"

The ladies talked to me all the way home and until I got into bed. As I lay in bed with no trace of the night I just experienced. I truly wondered if I could do it again. This process didn't make me feel good; I wanted to be chosen (again). My thoughts ran back to Dolph. If I had done things differently, I wouldn't need to do this.

Guess it's true you don't miss your well until it runs dry. Oh well, lesson learned.

I pulled on my eyeshades and rolled over to get some sleep.

Two Weeks Later...
Date Number Two ~ Keysha

It took me two weeks to work up the courage to do it again. But here I was going on date number two. Apparently, Sarye and Keysha switched places. Keysha had the perfect match and didn't want to wait until it was her turn. The ladies tried to repeat the same glam cycle; however, I wasn't having it. Plus, I decided to leave from the office, which further meant no glam team. The only person allowed to even see my version of glam in person was Keysha, and that was because her nosy ass refused to leave the office. However, she called Monet and Sarye on FaceTime, so technically we were all together again anyway. Keysha set her phone on the soap dish in my office bathroom so everyone could see me. When she tried to touch my hair, I moved out of reach.

"Nope, I'm doing this one solo."

I put on a simple black pencil dress with cap sleeves. The website I bought it from said it could serve as an office and date dress, so it was perfect. The V-neck allowed me to adorn my favorite silver necklace, which had Doc in cursive italic letters. I pulled my hair into a neat bun on the top of my head, added some eyeliner, and a light eyeshadow. The End. Of course, Monet and Sarye tried to make suggestions while Keysha tried to add more makeup, but I wasn't having it.

"Come on, Doc, at least let us…" Having had enough of the commentary and dodging Keysha, I put my hand up to her and then pointed it towards the camera.

"Aht, aht, aht…no thank you. I'm going on the date as myself. Be satisfied with that and move on." No one said a word. Keysha took her phone and left the bathroom. If I was going to do this, it was my terms only, I'd let them control enough.

Keysha's pick, Connor, was meeting me at the local watering hole for happy hour. Connor and I hadn't spoken, so this was a true blind date. Against my better judgment, I agreed to this because Keysha said, "It's better to get to know him in person." It sounded like a recipe for disaster, but I went with it.

However, when I considered the possibilities, I forced Keysha to show me a picture. He was cute at least. Connor knew he was fine; his seductive, bright white smile said it all. She verified his credentials and even showed me his company website as proof. It was updated a few days ago, so that gave me a bit of relief; after everything that happened with Reid. Funny thing, Reid called me the next day after our date as if we had a grand ole' time. I gently told him I wasn't interested, hung up, blocked him, and prayed he found what he needed elsewhere.

As I stood in the bathroom putting on lip gloss, Keysha came back in.

"Dang Doc, you look good. Guess you didn't need our help after all."

Dang, she right, I do look good! See, I don't need a glam squad, I'm fire as is.

"Well, I've been a whole woman for about 42 years, and I did have a man at some point. So, I think I know a little something." Keysha laughed and nodded.

"Well, hopefully you will wow Connor tonight, so at least you can say you had one in your 40s." We both laughed; she was a whole trip.

Sad but true…that other mess didn't count. Although he did claim you instantly, but I digress.

It was time to get this over with, so I ushered Keysha out of my bathroom and the office.

"Whatever, Keysha. Go home so I can get going." She went to grab her purse while I shut down my computer and grabbed mine.

"Ok, cool, remember to call us on the way home." I locked the office front door, and we headed to the parking lot.

"I will. I will."

Getting into my truck, I started it and sat for a second. My nerves were getting the best of me again. However, I didn't want Keysha to think I was backing out, so I pulled off.

When I arrived at the bar, I was a ball of nerves and tiredness. I'd never been on a true blind date, only seen the horrible aftermaths on TV.

Their stories ain't your story, Sasha. This will be fine.

When I walked into the bar, I surveyed the area and found a smiling face immediately. He was very handsome. He had short dark brown wavy hair, gentle brown eyes, light skin, almost looked Cuban with Afrocentric features. He wore a tailor-made hunter green suit and spotless/creaseless brown leather shoes. When he smiled, it lit up the room and other private spaces.

Damn, maybe Keysha was on to something with this one.

When I approached him, he stood up to greet me. Once closer, he took my hand and held it as he spoke.

"Dr. Sasha, how are you this evening?"

"Connor, I'm doing great, and you?"

His presence made me smile, and suddenly I felt comfortable.

He smells amazing, I could sniff him till my nose hair shriveled up.

"Please sit, let me get you a drink so we can finally catch up."

The date was perfect, and we talked about our college experiences, work life, and aspirations. It was all perfect. Connor wasn't married, didn't have any legitimate or illegitimate children. He owned a house, a car, and was going to visit St. Barts this summer. I always wanted to go there. We discussed places we'd traveled to and others we've yet to explore. By the end of the night, we agreed to see each other again. Our date ended at about 10:30 pm, and Connor walked me to my car.

"Sasha tonight couldn't have gone any better. If I may say so myself." Connor gently grabbed my hands while staring into my eyes.

"I agree, Connor, I had a great time." Hearing Connor say those words soothed me even more. Man, if he believed it to maybe there was something more to him or us. We'd already exchanged numbers inside, so I knew he'd likely call me tomorrow or soon.

Finally, a great first date! What a relief.

"So, how are we gonna do this?"

Wait what?

Confused by what he meant, I slightly smiled.

"Come again?" Connor licked his lips and smiled slightly as he moved our hands, which he still held.

"Do I follow you home? We could get a room. I mean, I didn't think you'd be comfortable coming to my house. But babe, I'm ready for whatever you want it."

Please tell me he is fucking kidding me? When did I give him the impression we were gonna have that type of DATE (Dick At The End)?

I eased my hands out of his and tried not to hurl off and cuss his ass out. My tone was calm, but I was on the verge of going full-blown *IKFYD(I Know the Fuck You Didn't).*

"Umm, what are you talking about? WE not going anywhere. I'm going home. Alone!"

I tried to do a mental rewind as to why he would think we were going to sleep together. However, Connor interrupted my thoughts with his response. He was now a bit uncomfortable and appeared confused, although he said that dumb shit.

"Oh, I thought…" I folded my arms as I leaned against my truck door. I spoke a little louder but still contained myself. I needed to know at what point I gave him any impression of us sleeping together.

"You thought what?"

Connor looked away, then he answered hesitantly.

"Well, I know Kyle said you hadn't been dating for a while. So, I figure you just needed some entertainment. If that's the case, no need to hide it, I'll gladly…"

I nodded and sucked my teeth. I turned to open my truck door, and he stood back. When I slammed the door shut, I started the truck and let down the window.

Note to self: Cuss Kyle the fuck out for sharing that bullshit.

"I don't know what you think you know. But you don't know shit. And yeah, I've been single for a bit, but it doesn't mean I'm interested in fucking you! And by the way, if I was, you just fucked yourself outta that. Good night, Connor."

Yet again, another man had me all wrong. I didn't even bother to call the ladies on the way home. I just sent them a text in our group thread.

TacoTuesdayLadies: *Another one bites the dust. He wanted some puss, but I didn't want his dick. Going home. We will talk tomorrow. BTW, Sarye, cancel your date…I'm over this. Oh, and Keysha, talk to Kyle about sharing my apparent sexual history…aka teach him to keep your pillow talk on the damn pillow. Or better yet, stop telling him my damn business, how about that! Please and thank you. Good Night.*

On the drive home, I rode in silence. The ladies tried to call me collectively and individually. However, I wasn't in the mood. I couldn't hold space for anyone, and I didn't. Beyond business, I didn't talk to Keysha for a week despite her constantly saying she was sorry. Plus, telling me she scolded Kyle's oversharing ass. Kyle even sent me flowers to say he was sorry. But it was a nice gesture, and I appreciated them both apologizing. However, this was yet another moment ruined, which I needed time to process so I could get over it.

Two Weeks Later…

After spending weeks reeling from yet another unsuccessful date, I decided to enjoy a late happy hour with the ladies. Keysha couldn't make it as she and Kyle were spending some time alone before his business trip. So, it was Sarye and Monet, but still good times, although we missed Keysha's presence. Funny thing, we ended up at the same bar Connor and I went to. But I didn't care; the food, drinks, and music were awesome.

The ladies placed their orders of chicken wings, firecracker shrimp, and their drinks. I ordered my wings all flats, of course, covered in moon dust seasoning. When it was time to order my drink, I was about to order a glass of wine. However, I decided to be a little bold. I usually didn't drink brown liquor, but after a long day and the past few weeks, I ordered a double shot of whiskey but vowed to sip slowly. After that first sip sent a shock to my system, I knew I'd nurse that bad boy all night.

The ladies were finally off the hook Sasha up train, so now we focused on planning Keysha's bachelorette party. From all the plans tossed around, it sounded like it was going to be a lot of adult fun. Keysha's sister, cousins, and other friends, in addition to us, were planning the event. Keysha was lucky we loved her because this was going to be the event of the year, next to her wedding and after wedding brunch. Thank goodness the Bride and Groom's parents were paying for that. As invested as I was in this wedding and bachelorette party, I should have adopted Keysha. But I was glad to help. My girl deserved the best because she showed up for everyone else anytime and all the time.

Some of the ideas Sarye shared with us via Keysha's sister had me questioning if this was getting a little too grown. When someone mentioned auditioning entertainment, I took a heavy sip of my drink. I was not prudish, but the word "entertainment" caused my eyebrow to raise a bit. Strippers were cool, but what the hell was entertainment? Some of these ladies were known to let loose, from what I was told. Someone had already requested private rooms and tents. I shuddered to think what would possibly happen in any of those spaces. But I had my marching orders and would stay in my lane.

"Ohhh, I know I meant to tell y'all something. Keysha's sister said it's gonna be a joint bachelor-bachelorette pool party." Monet was excited about Sarye's announcement. I took another large sip of my drink and swallowed hard.

Just keeps getting better. I love it.

"Yes, I'm about to go find a next-to-nothing bathing suit now." We laughed at Monet's comment. She was already anticipating the action since the males would be in abundance as guests, servers, and entertainment. My girl knew her train would be pulling out of the station at some point during the festivities. I loved that for her. Hell, who was I to judge? At least she lived in her truth and proudly.

"Well, let's cheers to Monet getting a ride or two during the festivities!"

"Yess! Sasha, claim it bitch! I'm over the saddle I got now. Mama needs a reclining seat, sitting on some cash in addition to a good stash of that green. I can handle the rest."

We all laughed and raised our glasses to Monet. Sarye had a man, Curtis, they'd been together since grade school. He'd cut a fool about her, and she did the same despite breaking up with him every other week. We always joked with her that they'd break up every week until one of them was in the dirt. Sarye agreed and indicated one of them would have likely put the other in the dirt. Then the other one would come back from the afterlife to get the other, since they couldn't live without each other.

The thought alone made us crack up laughing. At least two of us were in love, hopefully, us remaining two would catch up or at least get close enough to our "ideal mates." Whatever that looked like.

Driving home after happy hour with the ladies, I felt good. Really Good! The feeling you feel when the world is alright and you have zero fucks to give. I opened the moonroof in my truck and turned up my music. When Summer Walker's *Pull Up* played, I smiled. Her crooned voice gave me the essence of Erykah Badu but with Summer's amazing twist. The words took me back to a mental space I avoided for weeks. I imagined the words becoming my reality. Only I'd pull up on him and let my seat back so I could say and show him how sorry I was.

When my phone rang, I wondered if I had missed that part in the song. I'd already replayed the song a few times, but when I saw a number pop up on my dash, I answered instantly. I purposely didn't say anything, just waited for the caller to speak.

"Sasha, we need to talk. I know what I said, but we need to clear the air…" The deep voice was soft but hadn't lost its tempting authority. I hadn't heard it in what seemed like forever. There was nothing to say. I thought he'd forgotten about me. Maybe there was still some hope. When I had yet to respond, he continued. "Look, last time we met I shouldn't have said what I said…"

Without thinking, I replied. "I'll send you my address. Let's do this in person."

Everything in me needed to see him. It had been too much time and space between us. We needed this if there was any hope of fixing us. I didn't usually text and drive, but I quickly balanced the wheel and the phone to send him my address and some other information. Besides, I was in my development and there was not a car in sight.

"Really…Sasha, it's almost midnight." He was unsure if I was serious, however, when he got my text there was no need to question any longer. "Ok, you meant it, I'll read the rest before I arrive. Got your address. I'll be there in 20 min."

I hung up and prepared to head into my house.

This is finally happening. Whew! I'm ready, though, really ready!

I didn't know what I was doing and why. But I was over all feelings, fuck 'em. This wasn't a problem before he came along. Now I can't stop thinking about the feeling of a man touching me and holding even if it was just for a moment. I wasn't new to this or this feeling, but I tried to avoid its lingering, which could lead to recklessness. Given the drink I had and my boredom with electronic things, I was giving in to it all tonight, lucky him.

Before Blue, I had a life. I won't say I was reckless, but I did have some fun. A lot of fun. It was nothing to have some fun and not fall in love. My mistake was I let Blue convince me otherwise. He sold me on a dream that would never come true, and he knew it, sorry bastard.

While I sat on my bed and prepared for our conversation. My mind was void of emotional thoughts. It was perfect. Just like old times. When the doorbell rang, I was ready. This was like riding a bike, and I could handle a 10-speed, Mountain Bike, Mongoose, whatever. But I knew he wouldn't disappoint; something told me his shit was top of the line, which excited me.

When I reached the bottom of the steps to the front door, I swung it open as I stood behind it.

"Sasha…"

The sound of his voice was everything. I couldn't wait for him to get on the other side of the door. Although I didn't reveal myself, I stuck my hand on the other side of the door and motioned for him to come in. When he stepped inside, I closed the door and let my sheer robe fall open. No need for foreplay, I was naked, he just needed to join me.

This is to get the edge off, no feelings, no thoughts. Just plain ole hump and dump, no slumber parties, no conversation. We wrote the book on this, Sasha; we do this, definitely not new to this.

"Damn, babe, umm…you look…"

His surprise and hesitancy enticed me; I had to restrain myself from attacking him.

"Shh…no words. Unless you're talking to Candy, she likes it. I, on the other hand, don't need them." He nodded in agreement and stepped closer to me.

"No words. Got it. I've been thinking about you…about this." His warm arms around my waist only intensified my energy.

Looking into his eyes, I saw the signs of the man I knew cared for me. I could tell he missed me, too. I'd fuck him into submission if I had to; we belonged together, and I wasn't giving him up. He opened his mouth to say something else, but I put my finger to his lips.

"You're still talking, no more talking, Dolph. Please, just…"

He raised his eyebrows, then nodded in agreement as if he caught my drift.

"I got you, Sasha."

My baby is hard of hearing; we will fix that! He will learn to follow orders before the end of the night.

"Dr. Carter…" He nodded again and smiled.

"Got it. Let me take it from here, Dr. Carter." Dolph picked me up and pressed his lips against mine. He carried me up the two flights of stairs without missing a beat or losing his breath. My baby was strong! While walking, he continued kissing all over me as if he really did miss me. Inhaled his scent, and my body reacted to his hands gripping my ass and my thighs, not letting there be any space between us. When he laid me on the bed, he admired my body. His mouth didn't move, but it was like we had telekinesis; we said everything, if only with our minds.

Dolph: *Sasha, I missed you.*

Dr. Carter: *I missed you, too, Dolph.*

Dolph: *Show me, Babe.*

Dr. Carter: *Gladly…all night if you let me. Forgive me, let me make it up to you…please! I promi…*

Dolph: *I forgive you, babe, no need to circle back…let's start over!*

Dr. Carter: *Yes, babe, let's start over. Come here, let me please you.*

When he finally got undressed, he was handsome and as tasty as I imagined. Immediately sat up and grabbed his hips.

"Wait, Sas…"

Before he could finish, I was on him, having a private conversation between his dick and my mouth, and he allowed me. His gentle groans only made the experience more enjoyable. From the first time I saw him, I imagined us just like this, which is why I couldn't respond to his questions.

"Shit, I know we not supposed to be talking, but damn…" The sounds of him sliding in and out of my mouth drove him crazy. The bigger the swell, the wetter my mouth became. I eased off of him momentarily so I could clarify my statement. He looked down at me, semi-confused and disappointed. However, I smiled and leaned up a bit to address him.

"It's different when you're telling me how good it feels. Let that shit out." Dolph glared at me, glad for the permission to release what he tried to hold in.

"Fuck, Sasha, I can't hold out much longer, babe." I pulled Dolph closer and leaned my head back, allowing him to slide to the back of my throat. The motion drove him crazy, so he gripped the back of my head while I looked at him.

"Dr. Carter, it's yours now. Finish your meal." I slid back off again, then smiled. As I eyed his dick, which stood at attention, I turned my attention to him.

"I'll gladly finish my meal. The rest is for another day." Dolph smiled, and I went back to work. The sound of Dolph's enjoyment only caused me to speed up. Truth was, I really enjoyed this; it was like he was made to fit perfectly in my mouth. His growl only pushed me to suck my personal lollipop harder.

"Sas…Doc…I'm about to, shit, babe." Dolph couldn't find his words, but he didn't need to. I wanted the ending; he just needed to give it to me. When I didn't ease up, he welcomed my invitation and held my head as he released right where I wanted him to. When he was done, he let out a sigh of relief, and I leaned back on the bed. Happy. Content. Relieved.

Dolph climbed on the bed and hovered over me. We didn't speak; he just surveyed my face like he was trying to figure out who I was. What just happened. Why did we wait so long? He went to speak, but I put my finger to his lips.

"Don't. Stay in the moment. Let's just explore each other. Please."

Dolph nodded and lowered his body onto mine.

Then he whispered, "Whatever you say, Dr. Carter. Just tell me what you want and how you like it."

Pleased he listened well, I responded, "Make Candy weep." Dolph eased up and looked at me as if he didn't understand. So, I explained, "Candy is sweet, she likes to…release when she's happy. So don't just make her sniffle or drop a few tears, make her weep, Dolph. Give her the release she desperately needs. Tonight, she's all yours." He smiled and licked his lips at the requests.

I knew he was up for the challenge. This is going to be fun.

Dolph didn't say another word, except "I got you." Then he lowered himself into me in many ways. It was nothing but pleasure and ecstasy the rest of the night. He filled every need and touched every space more than once. When he needed a break, I returned the favor; he deserved it. Everything I had stored up, I gave him. The sound of his pleasure only intensified my want to push him to the brink of no return. When he tapped out, I was satisfied and smiled while I looked into his eyes.

"Sasha."

"Dolph."

"Damn. What the entire fuck, babe…"

He is worn out. Mission accomplished. This was definitely fun. I wished he could stay, but rules were rules.

"Look…" I cleared my throat, then tried to smile through my carefully crafted exit statement. "Thank you for an amazing time. I enjoyed it really. But it's check-out time. Remember, no sleepovers, no discussions, nothing else. We can discuss the other stuff later."

These were the rules I texted him when I sent him my address. So, he wasn't surprised—at least he shouldn't have been. When he went to speak, I lifted my finger, and he just nodded. I got up and grabbed my robe, then headed into my bathroom. He got dressed and smiled in my direction. I stared into my bathroom mirror, I could see him sitting on the bench in front of my bed.

Finally got what you want…needed Sasha. Good job! Kudos to you for sticking to your rules, cause he could definitely spend the night or more. Maybe another time, definitely another time.

I smiled at my thoughts and waited for him to finish getting dressed. He came and kissed my cheek; I turned and looked at him. Dolph rubbed his hand along my face and kissed my cheek again. But his touch felt different and his beard was gone. But was it ever there? It was one of the things I couldn't wait to rub and touch when I met him. His hands weren't as rough as I remembered. They were soft like butter, as if he didn't use them. Suddenly, it felt like everything shifted; now, nothing seemed to make sense. I couldn't put my finger on it, but it was different. Dolph grabbed my hand, and I followed him out of my room downstairs to the front door. While I was still trying to place the difference in him. When we reached the door, he slipped on his shoes and stood in front of me.

Suddenly, I felt like I was coming down from my euphoric state back to reality. When he finally turned around with his hand on the doorknob, it hit me like a ton of bricks as reality stood before me.

What the entire fuck, Sasha! Damn it!

He smiled at me again, then kissed my cheeks softly as he held me close.

"Glad you enjoyed yourself," I said with a slight smile, feeling disappointed, I tried to mask it as being tired with a fake ass yawn.

End this now. We need a whole moment, A FUCKING SAP SASHA!

"Hell, yeah, I did, I enjoy that role-playing shit. I like the name Dolph. Is it short for something, maybe you wanted me to be your Rudolph so I could shine my nose in your…"

Are you fucking kidding me with this lame ass joke! Urgh, get the fuck out and now!

"… and then calling you Dr. Carter. That's something different. You really into that freaky shit, Sasha? I can get used to that."

I'd imagined he was here the whole time. Goodness, how you gonna explain this one in therapy, doc?

My worst reality was now true. This wasn't Dolph, it was Conner.

Wow. This really didn't happen. None of it. Dolph wasn't even here.

With each moment I was becoming even more turned off and pissed. The whole experience was now a waste. My "re-virgin-nation" was trashed, five years down the drain.

Damn, did I imagine the dick was good as well? The whole experience was based on fantasy. Why the fuck is he still standing here…go home, damn it!

Seeing my face, Connor wasn't smiling; if anything, he was wondering what had happened. However, he still proceeded to palm my face in his hands.

"Dr. Sasha Phillips, I mean Carter. You surprised me, and I don't surprise easily. But you…are amazing woman…are everything I've been looking for. Shit, since we both ain't looking for nothing serious, this will be a lot of fun."

Connor rubbed his hands along my shoulders and leaned in to breathe into my neck.

"Now that I've met Candy, I am her sucker. Call me whenever she's ready again."

Little do you know, you'd never get a suck, lick, or even sniff her ever again. There was no need for us to talk again.

When he stood back up, I nodded, then I reached to unlock the door, then grabbed the knob.

"Good night/morning, Connor."

My lackluster response didn't faze him in the least bit. He was still riding the high from our interaction. Connor winked his eye at me, then left. When I closed the door, I cursed myself for my part in whatever the hell this was. I was turned off, disappointed, unhinged, now that he had been revealed. He wasn't what I wanted. Not even close. Connor wasn't the one; no need to settle or fake it.

Fuck Sasha! Fuck! This shit makes no sense…what the hell was wrong with you? Better yet, what was in that damn drink that your ass out here with an imaginary playmate? Cancel the day, try again tomorrow! Can't do shit for no one else when your ass ain't right.

I immediately called out "sick" from work. Which meant I sent a message to Keysha that I wasn't going to be in. She could handle all the dealings for the day and everything else. I didn't have any appointments on Fridays, thank goodness. But any work I had to do would wait till Monday. I turned off my phone and treated myself to a spa day and naps for the rest of the weekend. It was time to decompress and detox.

Chapter 7

Three Months Later...

"Doc, you slept with him?" Keysha grilled me while I tried to ignore her during our weekly staff meetings. Eventually, I had to come clean to Keysha. For multiple reasons, first, keeping it in was driving me crazy. However, I swore to her that if she even thought about telling anyone, I'd never tell her anything else. Then I'd fire her for breach of confidentiality. Not really, but it sounded good with my speech. The second reason was one I didn't want to reveal yet, but I would have to soon.

"Key, we are on the clock. Please, let's move on."

I handed her an email I printed and pointed out what she needed to reply to. She acted like she was focused, but her next statement said otherwise.

"Sasha, look!" I cut my eyes at her, and she sighed, then spoke again. "This right here. These actions, your mood lately. This is unlike you, I'm concerned. Maybe..."

"Maybe what Keysha?" I snapped. Keysha didn't back down and met my frustration right where it was.

"Maybe you need to take a break. A real one." Truth be told, she earned the right to let loose on me a bit. I'd been a bit of a raging bitch lately. Although I tried to control my emotions, they kept getting the best of me, specifically with her. Keysha took a breath and spoke more calmly. "The schedule is light, so you can take a week. Even if you did virtual for a few sessions." I tried to ignore her and waved her off, but she wouldn't let up. "You can't give your best for the client when inside you're falling apart." It was obvious our meeting was over. Her words were too much to bear. So, I gathered my papers and went into my office.

When I left, Keysha followed me. I needed a moment, so I looked out the window and didn't say a word. However, Keysha had a few more words to share with me.

"Doc, look. I know you're the one with the counseling degree, and I'm not, at least not yet. But you've allowed me to sit on your mental sofa plenty of times. So, now I'm offering you a seat on mine." We used the term "mental sofa" when we needed to have difficult conversations. This kept us aligned and reminded us that the other was speaking from a place of love. "Look, I've looked up a quick trip for you. And before you groan or moan or even respond, I'm only trying to help. Whatever you're feeling or thinking about is weighing on you. My guess is it has to do with Connor. So, what, you had some fun, shoot, we've all been there. But going there didn't set you back. Or delay what's waiting for you. He's still on schedule and will be here before you know it. You just need time to regroup. And now…is that time before it's too late."

My back was still towards her, but I felt every word as tears ran down my face. Keysha knew I was in pain; I made a decision that I strongly regretted and went totally against my nature. That decision landed me on the cold table alone, letting go of the future I wanted. I wished it were different, and it would have been if he were actually there. I knew better and should have been more careful. Then Connor's reaction didn't help the decision either. He didn't even attempt to care.

When I found out a month and a half ago about Connor and mine's indiscretion, I decided to call him immediately. Not sure what to expect but giving him the courtesy of informing him what happened. We hadn't talked since, and I had to really search my phone list for his number, as I had deleted it along with any trace of him. Although I could have asked Keysha to get it from Kyle, I was too embarrassed and ashamed about even being in this mess. He sounded excited when he answered the phone.
"Dr. Carter…is Ca?" Getting right to the point, I cut him off and blurted it out.
"Connor, we fucked up…" He was quiet and cleared his throat, unsure what to say.
"Umm…Sasha, are you saying…"
"Yep." There was no need to hide it or beat around the bush. It was already growing anyway.
"We used…"

"Not the first time, second time yes." Connor cleared his throat again, as if something was lodged in it.

"So…"

"So, I'm giving you a courtesy call."

"Well, I'm kinda seeing someone now. So, I'm not available to nor do I…"

"That's fine. At least you know."

"Are you sure…" I hung up the phone; he would not get the satisfaction of insulting me or insinuating I was trying to trap him. Connor never called back, and he didn't need to. He said enough, and I made my decision.

The next day, I made an appointment. They tried to get me to wait a few days to think about it and all that other shit, but my mind was made up. They insisted I bring someone with me to drive me home. However, I didn't have anyone, at least that I wanted to tell. But I had to tell someone as my appointment was in three days. Worst comes to worst, I'd beg Robbie to come home and go with me. He'd give me a load of shit, but I could take it from him and no one else. On the day of my appointment, I was still without a next of kin or a ride. Turns out Robbie was on vacation with the Kalvin person, so he was out. The crazy, ridiculous part of me thought about calling an Uber and hiring my driver for the next couple of hours to be my next of kin. Or paying a staff member off to let me go. They both sounded good for 2.5 seconds, but it was the dumbest shit I'd ever thought of. It was stupid, dangerous, and could get us all into a lot of trouble. But desperate times made you think of stupid shit. It was almost time for my appointment, so I had to get going and figure out the rest.

I was on my way out the door when Keysha grabbed her coat and purse. I hoped I could brush her off quickly and keep my appointment.

"Umm…where are you going? I have an…appointment. I'll be back tomorrow." Keeping my head down, I hesitated to reply as I kept moving towards the door.

"I know, and I'm driving, Sasha. So, let's go."

Keysha was firm in her response. I stared at Keysha, and she continued. "The nurse called to confirm. When she said where she called from, I put it together. I've been there, and you don't want to go alone. I promise you. Plus, they won't let you leave if you don't have a ride. No matter how much you pay them, which is an ethics violation for both parties." Keysha raised her eyebrow; damn, she was good. Before I could say another word, she added more words. "Sasha, I won't say a word to anyone. Just let me take you and get you home. Kyle is out of town for work, and I can tell him I'm with you, working on whatever. Then we can get you revamped, and you can start fresh again in a few days. Ok?"

I wanted nothing more than for someone to take control and relieve me of the pressure of thinking, feeling, or facing the one thing I promised myself I'd never do. If Keysha wanted to take care of me, I'd let her. No more hiding or questions asked.

"Ok, Keysha, let's go."

We didn't speak anymore that day. Just some nods and assuring hugs once she got me home. Keysha spent the night with me for two days. She transferred the phones to the separate line we had for the office, and she set up a home office in my house. After Keysha left, I stayed home for a week. I was back in the office the following week, but with virtual appointments. That was a month ago.

After I returned to the office, everything was going well, but I still couldn't shake the emptiness in my spirit. The feeling ate at me often, and I tried my best to remove it, but I was wounded. It was time to stop trying to put a Band-Aid on my wound and just let it flow so I could begin to heal for real.

I asked Keysha to give me a moment alone. When she closed the door, I held myself as tears flowed down my face and pain engulfed my chest. I let it all out. Next, I went to the phone and found the Bat Signal for Dr. Kirk for an emergency appointment. Before I could consider Keysha's request, I needed permission to pause. It might sound weird or even crazy to some, but if you think about it, we all need that sometimes. We need our people to give us a hug, kick in the butt, or nudge to do the unthinkable or what we know we need to do. So, after my discussion with Dr. Kirk, she offered to pack my bags herself. I stuck my head outside of my office and responded to Keysha. When I opened my door, she looked in my direction. I took an exhausted breath and then replied.

"When do I leave?"

"Tomorrow."

"Fine." I closed my door and that was that.

After leaving the office early the next day, I went home and prepared for my flight at 9:00 pm. It didn't matter what I wore; I planned on sleeping most of the day and then heading to the beach to stare into the abyss of the water before me. My nights would be early; no need to be out late anyway, as there was room service, so I didn't need to leave my room if ever. Five days to regroup, that's all I needed.

I called for an Uber to drive me to the airport. I didn't want anyone I knew to take me, nor know where I was going. Although I did have to tell Lorna, I was going out of town for some R&R. I assured her Keysha knew where to find me, so she didn't push. Lorna simply replied she understood, as I seemed "out of sorts" these last few months. I was glad she didn't push; I couldn't take not one more thing.

When I got to the airport, through security, and waited for my flight, I felt relief. Per my usual travel routine, I went to the nearest stand and grabbed some magazines to read and a few snacks. When I finally sat down, I did a body scan by closing my eyes and mentally checking in on each section of my body. Everything felt somewhat normal. For the first time in a month, I could breathe. Although I didn't inhale too much, in fear of breaking down at any moment. But I was ok...I really was.

Everything is ok, Sasha; we are on the road to healing! For real this time.

When they called my boarding section, I got up proud and even smiled. Keysha knew I was bougie and made sure to get me a round-trip first-class ticket. As the lady scanned my phone, it chimed twice. Once because of her, and the other time for a message that came in. When I got to my seat, strapped in, I leaned my head back and smiled.

Grateful for Keysha's pushy ass! When I get back, I'm going to give her a bonus, especially with her wedding less than a month away.

Once I pulled out my eye shades, I adjusted my blanket so I was comfortable. My meditation music was ready and was the full length of the flight and ready to go. My EarPods were the last missing piece. I checked my phone to put it on Airplane mode.

"Damn, I forgot about this message. Let me check it before I disappear." I chuckled at my thoughts and smiled while I opened the message. However, when I read the name, my heart stopped as well as my world. I wasn't expecting this; it couldn't have come at a worse time. But, then again, maybe it was perfect timing. I stared at it and re-read it before I put the phone in airplane mode.

Not now, Sasha, we need you!

I nodded to myself and put on my eyeshades, then turned on the meditation tape. That was what I needed and wanted. Everything else could wait. However, the words from the message permeated my mind as if the sender had read it aloud.

da Negro: *Have a safe trip. We have some unfinished business to discuss when you come back. Let's talk soon.*

What business would that be? He made a decision and stuck by it. It hurt, but I couldn't do anything but respect it. The rest was history.

I'd worry about the world when I return to it. Right now, I was only concerned with myself and my peace of mind.

When I arrived back in the office after my time away, I was excited. I was grateful for Keysha's pushy ass and even brought her favorite breakfast burrito and coffee as a thank you.

It was time to get back to my clients, whom I missed. My first appointment was with Sheldon. I was excited to hear about his latest adventure. Tomorrow was Lionel's appointment; I missed his butt, too. Couldn't wait to hear about the latest with Winnie, Beesha, and the others in the *Baby Mama Crew*. But most of all, how he was only doing his job by spreading his seed. Hopefully, he would have an update on the job front as well.

As I sat at my desk, it felt good to be in the "Captain's Chair," as I called it. I surveyed the office, which was cleaned and polished.

You've done good, Doc. Welcome back! Let's get it.

Typing on my computer, I made notes of things I needed to follow up specifically regarding the board opportunity in Houston, TX. Carlton and I worked together via Zoom to prepare and submit my application. However, Carlton left me several messages and was still pushing for me to come to visit soon. But I wanted to wait until Robbie was available so I could visit him and the Kalvin person, too.

The good thing is that if I got the job in Texas, I wouldn't have to move suddenly or at all. Most of the work was virtual, so I could keep my practice in the DMV. The opportunity would mean more exposure and reach for my practice. I already held licensure in multiple states, including Texas. Plus, I heard big things came from Texas. If I decided to stay in the DMV area, I'd have to travel to Houston, Dallas, or Atlanta each quarter for a few days, but that worked. I was looking forward to a big plate of southern food and whatever other things the South had to offer.

"Note to self, call Carlton to discuss next steps."

Carlton annoyed the hell out of me, and I hated to call him. However, he was doing me a huge favor by even mentioning me for this position. If he weren't such a pest, he might have a chance.

Really, Sasha, we are settling for Carlton, yuck!

The thought made me shake my head, and I moved on to my next task. When I finished writing my words, my phone chimed. It was time for me to silence it and go through my ritual of praying, being silent, and reaffirming myself before Sheldon arrived. However, that would have to wait a few more minutes since Keysha came through the front door of the office.

"Hey Doc, welcome back!" Keysha yelled as she came through the front door and stopped at her desk. I couldn't wait to wrap my arms around my pushy assistant. She tapped on my office door, then came in. I rushed towards Keysha and squeezed her tightly. While we embraced, I held her tight to extend my gratitude for all her support.

"I missed you, Keysha. You're the best. I'd fire you for being in my business…but I needed it, and for you to just take over. I love you for it. Thank you, Keysha."

Tears were in both our eyes, we broke our embrace and wiped our eyes.

"Oh, you're welcome. You know I got your back. When you good, we good! Oh, and thank you for breakfast, Doc! Welcome back, I missed you so much! So come on, let's see these clients, we need some money, honey." Keysha was a whole trip. But she was right, time to get back to the clients. She got up and headed back to her desk. I went to mine and checked my schedule.

First up, was my favorite young bull, Sheldon. Keysha returned to my office to close the door so I could prepare for my session. Before I started my routine, I checked my phone as I had an unread message.

da Negro: *Good Morning. Let me know when you got a minute.*

I shook my head and let out a sigh. This was the second message I received from him since I'd been back. I got the first one when I arrived home, almost instantly when I turned my phone off airplane mode.

da Negro: *Welcome Back. Hope you enjoyed yourself. Get settled, and let's talk. We've waited long enough.*

He was determined to talk by any means possible. Only I wasn't sure if I was or if I'd ever be. My time away gave me clarity, peace, and refocus. Everything that happened was behind me, and that's where I wanted it to stay. Every day I was intentional about forgiving myself for all my doings. Nothing and no one would set me back, especially not like before. I set my timer and prepared myself for my sessions, which always began in prayer.

> *Thank you, God, for this gift. The opportunity to hold a safe space for people who need support in this world, including myself. Let me use my gift to be an inspiration and not a hindrance to others. Let me be alert, open, receptive, and put healing, not hurt, into the world. All that I am is because of you. Thank you for the provisions and support to carry out this vision and plan. Give me strength and support where I am weak. Give me discernment where I have limited visibility. Give me provisions where I am running out. But most of all, allow me to use them to put more greatness into this chaotic world. Thank you, God, that there is more. Grow this vessel and this space into what you've called them to be. Cover all those who walk through those doors, and when they leave. I ask all these things in your son's name. Amen.*

After meditating for five minutes, I opened my door and I smiled.

"Dr. Sasha!"

"Sheldon!"

"Where have you been? Did you have a nervous breakdown or something?

Damn, what did he hear, or better yet, what did he sense?

Sheldon looked at me skeptically as he rubbed his chin. I slightly laughed and moved aside so he could enter my office. I looked at Keysha, and she snickered and shrugged.

"Huh, no. Why do you ask?"

Sheldon whispered, "I can hold space for you, too, Doc. We all got our shit."

No, he didn't…too hilarious.

"Sheldon. Language."

"What? You always tell me to say what I feel." He was right, and I couldn't help but laugh as I took my seat.

"You are correct. So, I apologize. But thank you, I appreciate you holding space for me. You're a real one for that. But I'm fine. I just needed some time to regroup. Now I'm ready to take on the world again. I appreciate you checking in on me, I really do."

Sheldon nodded. "Yeah, it's real in them mental streets."

I laughed again.

This kid is a whole trip, but boy, he was right. He's gonna be just fine if he realizes this much already.

"So, Sheldon, what's keeping you up at night lately?"

Sheldon paused and then responded.

"Why do the nice guys finish last?"

Damn, welcome back, Doc. He's in the puppy love phase. This will be interesting.

Sheldon had a crush on a girl in his class. He'd spoken of her a few times during our sessions. He had a bad case of puppy love. Knowing it was going to be one of those sessions. I grabbed his favorite snacks for both of us, a chocolate Yoohoo and a bag of Pop-Chips. Once I handed him the snacks, he nodded.

"Right on time, Doc."

We toasted, and he got comfortable and discussed his crush. By the end of the session, I understood his original comment. The young lady liked him, but she was "dating" another boy named Andrew in his class. At least this was the word around the playground, allegedly. Andrew was Sheldon's former best friend; she was crossing their school yard politics and Bro Code boundaries. Sheldon appeared to feel better after our session as we devised a plan to help him at least speak to his crush.

"If this doesn't work, Dr. Sasha, I might have to break out the moves."

Oh shit, what the hell does that mean? Lawd, he can't get expelled from school.

Curious yet concerned, I hesitantly asked Sheldon what he meant.

"Umm, clarify that statement for me, Sheldon."

He smiled and stood up, then busted out in some old school dance moves.

"You know, kick it old school. Bust out some J5, the Temps might even have to hit her with the Elements." Sheldon busted out in his dance moves. He'd obviously seen the *Jackson's American Dream* and *the Temptations* movies one too many times. He had the moves down packed, though, if they ever needed a stand-in, he was ready.

I cracked up laughing.

"Sheldon, what do you know about that music?"

"I know enough to know girls can't resist a good ole split, toss the mic, spin, and catch it." When Sheldon completed the move, I stood up to clap for him.

"Very good, Sheldon, you got that down packed. But you got more than moves, Sir…you got respectful words and most of all a good heart. If she doesn't see it, don't worry about it; someone else will."

Sheldon nodded in confidence and brushed off his shoulders.

"Yeah, like Lisa, her best friend. Ole girl loves the kid." I rolled my eyes and ushered Sheldon out of my office to the waiting room, where his mom was waiting. He was growing up right before my eyes.

Maybe he should talk to Lionel, help him get on his wavelength.

I laughed at the thought and closed my door to finish answering some emails and returning calls, which included calling Carlton before I finished the rest of the day.

Chapter 8

Since coming back from my vacation, my sleeping pattern had been off. I was up later than normal, which meant when I woke up, my routine felt like pulling teeth. I'd gotten home well after 9:30 pm and was too wound up to fall asleep. So, I changed my clothes to a peach body suit, oversized gray crop top, gray shoes, and a hat, then headed to the gym. Since it was nighttime, I decided to go to the local gym. I would be closer to home, and I could get in and get out. With my playlist ready, I fell into my usual routine.

"The treadmill will not kick my ass tonight."

The treadmill won, but I was determined not to give up. So, I pushed harder, forty-five minutes into my workout, and I was dominating it. I only planned to stay thirty minutes, but I couldn't stop. When I was done, I wanted to do some arm work, but all the machines I was interested in were occupied. So, I ventured into uncharted territory. The weights section. I usually didn't go there, mainly because it was always packed. The people who used the weights likely already had their "desired" bodies and then some. Wouldn't say I was intimidated; it just wasn't my jam.

However, I decided I wouldn't be no punk bitch. So, I made a bold decision and went over to the section. I grabbed some wipes to clean off the dumbbells and the bench. However, when I sat down, I was dumbfounded about how to move forward.

"Good idea, Sasha, get here without a plan." I laughed as I looked at my phone to change the song that was playing. Also, to get some ideas on how to start.

As I searched on my phone, someone entered the area. But I didn't even bother to look up. The space was empty, so there was no need to care. Still not finding a workout routine I thought was reasonable, I got frustrated and grunted. I closed my phone and my eyes with my head still lowered.

"Don't worry about finding the perfect plan, just try something. Here, let me show you."

When I looked up, there he was. I hadn't seen him in months, but here he was in the flesh…for real this time. Dolph looked and smelled amazing. He had on a white t-shirt with the sleeves cut off, loose black workout pants, and black shoes. We made eye contact for a moment but didn't speak. His face was plain, and so was mine. No smiles, I miss you stares, just two people who encountered each other's presence. Even his voice was even-toned, void of emotion. We acted not like quite strangers but acquaintances at least.

For me, enough time had passed for us to move beyond our last conversation. However, I wasn't sure how he felt. Then again, it didn't matter. After my fiasco with Connor, I was at peace regardless. Dolph walked away and went to grab some different weights, then he came back.

"Here, take these."

Part of me hesitated, not because I felt anything, but I just did. I looked at his hands before I stood and took the weights. I turned towards the mirror so I could see myself. He adjusted the position of my arms.

"Hold them like this." I lifted my arms. "Wait, don't lock your arms, just lift and lower." I did as he said while he watched me in the mirror. He showed me a few more exercises and helped me with my form each time. His expression never changed, but he stayed focused on the task at hand, and I did the same. For a while, it was just the two of us in the section. However, another lady came by and smiled at him.

"Hey, Dolph, how are you?"

Initially, he nodded at her through the mirror and didn't speak. However, when she didn't leave, he finally spoke to her. He didn't leave my side, just looked at her through the mirror.

"Hey, Tiffany. I'm cool, and you?"

It was the same lady he spoke with previously. The one who laughed too hard and obviously wanted him for herself.

Came at the right time, he's all yours, boo. I'm good on him.

"I didn't know you gave private lessons. You should have told me; I could definitely use some."

Dolph never responded to Tiffany's shady comment. Not even a facial expression, including an eye roll. He kept his eyes on me as I kept working out. From her physique, it was clear baby girl didn't need help at all. She was a damn stallion who probably came to the gym to troll for dudes. If her body didn't intrigue you, her outfit choice did. She wore what I called "ass eaters," those leggings that disappeared in the crack of your butt. It not only made her butt look bigger, but it also gave way to the roundness and plumpness. I wasn't into chicks, but even I thought she had a phatty.

Not being one to stand in anyone's way, I was about to make my exit. Plus, I was good with the weights and exercises. As I was about to leave, he put his hand on my shoulder for me to wait. I looked at him for confirmation, and he looked down at me while I looked back at the mirror. Tiffany picked up the signal and tried to draw attention to herself by addressing him again.

"Well, I guess I'll catch up with you later. If you're free, give me a call later."

She gave me a shady smile as she walked away as if she'd won some invisible challenge. However, Dolph never looked back at the mirror or her. He simply kept his eyes on me. The last comment made me laugh silently; she didn't need to do all that. It didn't bother me that they had each other's numbers. He wasn't my man, and I was not competition for her or any other woman. Dolph was a free agent just like I was. I didn't step on toes; if she was his, then good for her. I'd gladly step aside.

"Let's try a new exercise, lift your arms." I looked at him and frowned; we'd done like three exercises before Tiffany came over. However, he didn't care and was ready to get to work again. "Come on, Doc, let's get it." It was the first time he called my name since he'd come over. Hearing it caused me to take a breath and roll my eyes. However, I did as I was told.

But of course, Tiffany, who was not too far away on the treadmill, was showing out trying to get his attention. It was hard not to miss. After I made a few glances in the mirror, he stood in front of me. I stopped my reps and looked up at him with a blank annoyed stare.

"Hey, hey! Don't focus on anyone but you. You're the only one that matters when you're working out. It's plenty of people here who wish they could look like you. If you want results, be the crock pot. Not the microwave like this IG generation. Let's get it."

For the first time, I slightly smiled. I appreciated his words and support. Dolph showed me a few more exercises. We only focused on the task and not the words unspoken. When he was done. He gathered his things and walked away. No pleasantries or anything, which was cool. I went to the locker room to gather my things.

Moments later, I came out with my things to leave. As I was about to make my exit through the front door, he caught up to me.

"Hey, let me walk you out." Dolph's voice was still even, but his face was a little more relaxed.

"I'm cool. You don't…" He took a breath and replied, still using his even tone.

"It's after 10:30 pm, too late for you to be out here by yourself." He really didn't need to walk me out. The parking lot was lit, and I felt safe. He didn't have his bag, which meant he stopped his workout. So, I didn't say another word. We walked out the door; he opened each one, and we headed towards my truck. When we got to my truck, I unlocked it and he opened the door.

"Thank you, Dolph. Appreciate it."

"You welcome, Doc."

He usually called me Sasha or Dr. Carter; this time, it was just Doc. Which was cool, it made things a little easier—I guess. When there were no more words, I got in, and he closed the door. I drove off, and that was that.

When I got home and showered, I felt better. Now tired. Ready to get some sleep. My phone was in DND mode, but I saw I had a message when I went to ensure my alarm was set.

da Negro: *Did you make it home safely?*
MDSCarter: *Yeah, I did. Thanks again for everything.*

da Negro: *No, problem. At some point, we still need to have that talk.*

MDSCarter: *We've said all we need to, Dolph. Let's follow your lead and not circle back.*

da Negro: *Maybe it's not about circling back.*

MDSCarter: *Then what is it about Dolph? Look, from the bottom of my heart, I apologize again for everything. I've had some time to re-group and do some soul searching…I can see things and myself even clearer now.*

da Negro: *What does that mean?*

MDS Carter: *It means I see and respect why circling back is a no-go for you. Hell, I might adopt that shit myself. But the point is, I'm sorry again for all that's happened. But I'm glad I got the lesson from knowing you, Dolph. You take care of yourself and that amazing little version of you.*

da Negro: *You do the same, Sasha. Sometimes circles are meant to be broken. Take care.*

I didn't know what he meant, but it didn't matter. I'd made my peace with the situation before my vacation and even more while on vacation. Which was why I changed his name in my phone. So, he didn't owe me anything, and I'd apologized, so we were even. I went to sleep and slept better than I'd ever had since everything happened. When I woke up, I was refreshed. My sleep pattern was back on schedule, and so was I.

The next day, I agreed to go with Keysha to the bridal shop after work. She'd made me Maid of Honor and Honorary Godmother to her invisible child. Said and I quote:

We are tied together forever, whether you want to be or not. So, suck it up!

With an invitation like that, who could turn it down? As if I even had a choice. Keysha decided on an interesting color choice for the wedding: crème and gold for the bridal party; however, red and black with gold accents for the Best Man and Maid of Honor. It was a terrible choice in my opinion, but this was her event, so I shut the hell up. When I inquired about her selection, she only said she wanted to incorporate her and Kyle's favorite colors. I nodded, keeping my comments to myself.

When I saw the dress, I gasped mentally. The two-piece dress was something else. The top was black, form-fitted with a red color block down the center with gold lace trim on each side. Along with a gold tie that laced the back and was tied. The skirt was all black and full. Nothing to it but a sheer overlay, thank God. When Keysha showed me a picture of the Best Man's tux, I almost shrieked.

This is horrible. OMG, what was she thinking? It's giving me a toy soldier from The Nutcracker. We're gonna look like we're attending a formal ball for some armed service overseas. All he would be missing is the tall furry hat, WTF!

Keysha was so excited, so I tried to smile and model the dress as if I loved it. She deserved to be happy; I'd make sure this day was as close to perfect as possible.

"Doc, you look great! Wait till you see the gold accessories. Plus, with your hair straight and parted down the middle, it will be perfect. Especially since we will be adding about 16 – 22 inches. Haven't decided yet." I snapped my head around as if Keysha had lost her mind. *What the entire hell!* When she pouted, I just rolled my eyes and gave in. Why I needed hair that would almost touch my ass was beyond me.

This is about her, Sasha, just nod and smile. Smile with your heart and not frustration.

"Ok, Key, let's do it. Drip me down, boo, and make sure my edges don't move, cause I will be backing my thang up on one of them groomsmen."

Keysha laughed and snapped, "Yes, Doc and I got one…" Before she could finish, I gave her the face that suggested she had gone overboard.

"Ok, ok, we're gonna exit stage left on that plan. But, yes to the hair and the edges laid baby. I'm so excited."

When the dress and the accessories finally came together, it didn't look so bad. Still not my first or ever choice, but whatever, my girl was happy, so I was too.

After leaving the dress shop, we headed to grab a quick bite. It was Taco Tuesday, and I was in the mood for some guac and chips plus a Cadillac Margarita. We placed our orders and enjoyed the music while we waited. When the waiter returned with our drinks, we raised them to toast.

"Here's to my girl about to get married in less than two weeks. Cheers to Kyle for recognizing a real one. And cheers to my future Godchild, who I am about to spoil for life."

Keysha beamed at the toast as we tapped glasses, then the table, and made eye contact on our first sip.

"Doc, what's the point of the eye-to-eye again?"

"Girl, so we don't have seven years of bad sex!"

Keysha laughed, "Oh yeah, don't need them type of issues. Let's run that back just to make sure it sticks."

We laughed and toasted again, then we continued to chat and catch up. When we were silent, I cleared my throat and addressed Keysha.

"I saw Dolph at the gym." Keysha eyed me as if she didn't believe me. So, I added, "He was actually there, this time."

She nodded, then replied. "Are you ok?"

I smiled and told her about our interaction.

"Well, it sounds like it went well. Do you think…"

"No, Keysha, it's done, and I'm cool with it. No harm, no foul."

She was quiet, then responded. "Well, did you tell him about…"

I laughed, "No, I didn't tell him about him being my imaginary playmate."

Keysha laughed as well, then smiled and grabbed my hand. "Yeah, probably a good idea. Well, good, if you're good, I'm good, Sasha."

As maid of honor, I was partially in charge of the bachelorette party. Per Keysha's request. She was worried about the quality and taste level of her sisters and cousins. From the ideas I heard them toss around, she was right. I was glad to ensure it was somewhat classy. Now that all the details were finalized, we were ready to party. We decided on a *Ladies Night* theme. It would be a replica paying homage to the 90's music video with *Lil Kim, Missy, Angie Martinez, Left Eye (RIP)*, and *Da Brat*. It also included cameos from other amazing females in the entertainment industry. If you don't know, you're missing out. It was a whole vibe—still is. We wouldn't be on a tropical island but in a nice mansion which had an amazing pool.

However, there was an interesting twist: they wanted it to be a masked pool party. The atmosphere would include male and female servers, waiters, bartenders, masseuses, and any other necessary attendees. The guys would dress in dark green shorts, no shirts, and a mask. Since Kyle and a few of his groomsmen needed some eye candy, we'd have female attendees for them. The ladies would wear dark green bikinis, a mask, and clear heels. Optical illusion was key; if you couldn't see full faces, there was no guilt. Some of the ladies wanted some additional spaces or rooms for private parties. I wasn't interested, but hey, if that was their jam, who was I to judge?

Anyway, at the end of the night, Keysha wanted to do a big "revealed" for everyone in the bridal party to get to know each other. That would be an interesting concept with an element of surprise. Since that was her "job," I left her to it. We had the remaining events in order. I secured the mansion and provided the food/drinks while Keysha's sisters and friends did the rest.

"So, Sasha, did you pick out your bathing suit and mask for the party?"

Urgh, here we go! Third degree coming in for a landing.

"Yes, I did, Keysha. Did you?"

Doc, you know you lying…but it's on the list of shit to do.

Keysha smiled and reached for her phone.

"Hell yeah, I'm wearing all white and no mask, but I will have on a veil."

As I thought about the party, I mentally clutched my pearls for all the interestingness about to go down. These chicks were about to let loose for real. I planned on parking my ass on a lounger and watching it all unfold, of course, with a drink in hand.

Snapping me out of my thoughts, Keysha turned her attention to me as she typed without looking at her message.

"So, what are you wearing?" She asked as she took another sip of her drink.

Fuck think fast, Doc, she's gonna smell bullshit.

"Oh, a one-piece and some shorts."

Keysha immediately frowned as if she smelled something foul.

"Hated It! Nope, I'm texting Sarye and Monet, we're gonna hook you up. So put that granny suit you likely brought during your time off back in the closet for later."

Before I could say another word, she texted our group chat.

TacoTuesdayLadies (Keysha): *Doc does not have a fit for the bachelorette/bachelor party. We need to spring into action ASAP party is in a few days.*

Sarye: *Already on it, figured she wasn't ready when I asked her last week. I'll send y'all a picture in our separate chat.*

Sasha: *How y'all got a separate chat? That's rude AF.*

Monet: *How we supposed to help you without you resisting every idea, urgh! Grow up, Sasha!*

It was radio silence in the chat. However, Keysha was still typing, which confirmed Sarye's comment. I pouted and continued to nurse my drink as I ordered another.

They can go to hell! It's not a granny suit, they some damn haters!

The night of the party, the ladies showed up at my office to get dressed. Which included Sarye bringing my outfit with her. When I saw it, I almost ripped it to shreds. Although there was nothing much to it in the first place. A rip would have had a nipple or my vag lips hanging out.

"Y'all was trippin' with this piece of thread, I'ma need three leaves to wear this. I'm not wearing this shit!" I folded my arms and stared at the red two-piece bikini that Sarye held up.

My boobs would be covered as well as my ass, despite a little side cheek showing. But I still made a big deal out of it.

These bitches done lost their entire mind with this, nope! Not wearing it!

"Doc, come on, it's my party…" Keysha whined and stomped like a child in the grocery store on the verge of an ass whoopin'.

She, like everyone else, was already dressed in their party attire. Shit, Keysha had on a one-piece with a long zipper down the front, which exposed her perky boobs. I'd worn that shit before this piece of mess before me. Sarye had a cute black halter top with extremely tight jean cut-off shorts. The most exposed thing about her was her thighs and her boobs, of course. I'd even consider that. Monet even had on a decent swimsuit, although it was most mesh and had patches that covered her nipples and vaginal area. But it was black, and she looked cute with a sarong around her waist. I don't know if I'd considered that, but she looked beautiful and ready for action.

"Whatever, Sasha, you about to put this shit on and we're gonna head out. Come on before you make us late. My undiscovered boo could be there by now." Monet said as she finalized her makeup.

"Monet, we going to a pool party with masks on. Do you really need makeup?" I was trying to change the subject. But no one was buying my diversion.

"At some point, the masks come off. Besides, who goes to a pool party and gets in the pool? I mean, putting your feet in is one thing. But the full body is giving thirst trap behavior."

Monet continued to apply her makeup. Then added, "Now hurry up, I need to do yours so we can go. Chop, chop! Dr. Bridesmaid." After a few more back-and-forth comments, I got dressed.

Sarye secured a lace front wig on my head. When I protested about the wig, she said it added a level of spice and mystery. When I looked at the straight deep burgundy wig with a few highlights that stopped mid-back, I had to agree it was perfect. Monet did my makeup, which tied the outfit and hair together. One thing I could applaud that Keysha did was provide a black sheer cover-up which went to my ankles but it had two huge slits up the side. Also, it was form-fitting and still left nothing to the imagination. I was giving Lil Kim *Crush on You* video vibe. Only she was bold enough to pull it off and I was a nervous wreck. But fuck it, I put on my wedges and grabbed my mask, then we left.

Sarye insisted I ride with her because everyone was worried, I'd ditch the party early or altogether. Which could have happened, but I also knew this meant the world to Keysha, so I would stay the entire event or until she left. Either way, I had a car coming to get me at 3:00 am.

"Showtime, Sasha, masks on and responsible behavior on chill." Sarye said as she closed her visor before we got out.

"Sarye, it's not about to be that type of party." She was a little too excited and had too many expectations. Sarye slid on her mask, then looked at me.

"So, you think…we're about to have some fun. Just enjoy the ride, boo."

I put on my mask, added some more lip gloss to my lips, and we exited the car. Once we got into the mansion, everything was laid out perfectly. A gentleman greeted us with options for the signature drinks. He looked amazing in his dark green shorts with a ripped, oiled, and exposed chest.

"Good evening, ladies, are you a Baby Girl or A Daddy's Girl?"

The waiter smiled and winked through his mask.

Baby Girl: "Rum Punch with An Extra Punch" | Daddy's Girl: "Old Fashion"

"Oh, I'm both." Sarye grabbed one of each and smiled brightly at the waiter.

"Sasha, what are you tonight?"

I smiled and grabbed the Daddy's Girl; at least I could nurse this one drink all night.

"Come on, let's head to the backyard." Sarye extended her elbow, and I locked my arm around her, and we headed towards the music, which was concealed by a black curtain. When we got outside, I stopped and surveyed the area.

"OMG!" Were the only words I could say. It was a mix of the Garden of Eden and the video we envisioned. The masks everyone adorned were like a chef's kiss. Sarye smiled and then sipped her drink. Leaning closer to me, she whispered.

"Told you this was about to be fun, boo." A gentleman approached us and I let her go then she took his arm. "Sasha, this is Curtis."

Curtis smiled and nodded. He was 5'11' and nothing but muscle and white teeth. The dark Gladiator that stood next to Sarye was proud to have her on his arm. He wasn't bare and didn't adorn a mask but adorned a fresh wife-beater and black trunks with slides, and of course, white socks.

"Nice to meet you, Sasha. My girl hasn't stopped talking about you since y'all met. Thanks for looking out for her." He kissed her cheek, and she giggled.

"It's nice to meet you, Curtis. And she talks about you as well." We shook hands, then he took the Daddy's Girl drink from Sarye's hand.

"Well, boo, go mingle, see the sights. When you meet your match and remember, take it off." I did a double-take, so she added. "…the mask that is." She winked and left me standing at the entrance.

When did taking anything off become a thing? Da Hell! Ok, Doc, let's go have some fun or at least some mental laughs.

After another large gulp of my strong ass drink, I did just that.

Chapter 9

I had to say, Keysha's sisters and friends went all out for the decorations. I walked around the entire event and marveled at various things. There were vines everywhere, along with tropical flowers, a decent-sized dance floor that lit up, warm lighting, a heated pool with lights, and plenty of seating around the pool, which included lounge chairs, tables, a few tents with curtains or covers, and everything was color coordinated as well. The food was inside, and it was a large spread for all types of palates.

I made sure there were two bars: one inside and one outside. They were both open and free until midnight. The pizza truck was coming at 11:00 pm to help sober people up by 2:00 am, then the cleaning crew would come. There were also a few designated drivers available for those who had too much fun, so everything was covered.

Keysha insisted on creating a BINGO game to help people mingle. As I walked by a table that held the cards, I stopped to pick one up and review it. The rules were clear: *find someone who had done something in each category.* No harm, no foul. The top of the card read "Find someone who…" The first box said, "had a threesome."

Really Keysha, that's what you decided, urgh!

"No way in hell I'm playing this shit," I mumbled and put the card down immediately.

I get wanting to embrace the mood, but what the entire hell. That's creating something else, I wanted no parts of it. The last thing I need is another man looking to get his rocks off while mine were on shore with "do not disturb shades on."

I took another sip of my drink and hurried from the table, hoping no one saw me looking at that foolishness. As I walked around, the vibe was lit! Some ladies whom I recognized were getting massages from hunky guys who were a part of the weight staff. Lady servers were providing drinks to some gentlemen engaged in a conversation. Other people were on the dance floor. While others were in the pool. It was then that I thought about

Monet's comment earlier, and she was 100% right. Getting in the pool did say thirst trap.

I surveyed a young lady who obviously wanted attention as she kept acting like she was drowning, so some gentleman near her would rescue her. He obviously was intrigued as he kept trying to calm her down while gripping her entire ass and pulling her a little too close for public display.

Girl, shut up that hollering! He gets it, and from the look on his face, you will too, later!

I also saw a few people going in and out of the tents.

Yeah, I want no parts of them tents. I shudder to think what's happening behind them walls.

After finding an open lounger, I decided to sit my grown ass down and enjoy the music while people watching. I was glad we pulled this off for the bride and groom. They deserved to be celebrated, and the small fortune it was costing everyone was worth it.

Their asses better only do this shit once, if not, I want a refund!

"Goddess, can I get you another drink?" One of the waiters who mingled throughout the party asked.

The light-skinned man was chiseled from top to bottom, his hair flowed down his back, and he had entirely too much gloss all over his body, including his lips. However, he was playing the part well. Too bad he was barely legal, I could still see the Similac escaping the corners of his mouth. He looked me up and down and tried to look past my cover-up to admire the little ass red bikini underneath. I immediately felt a bit shy and hesitated to speak.

"Umm…"

About to say no, I smiled.

Have some fun, Sasha, relax!

I smiled at the gentleman again.

"Yep, another Daddy's Girl, please. Extra cherries if you have them."

He nodded, smiled seductively, then leaned closer to me to whisper.

"So, you want be Daddy's extra good girl, huh? Don't worry, Goddess, I'll sweeten it up for you myself." Before I could respond, he blew a kiss with his pursed lips and went on his way.

Oh, my goodness! Either this drink has me feeling good, or that young man is about to catch this cougar.

I laughed at my comment, knowing I was not interested in entertaining that poor baby. Monet insisted on the waiters being extra flirty in their approach. I felt ashamed when she said that at the meeting with the owner. However, after one drink, I could see her vision—it did make things more interesting. Monet saw me sitting and came over to occupy the lounger next to me.

"Sasha, boo! I know you ain't about to park your ass in this chair all night. We worked too hard on this outfit for it not to be seen. Get moving sexy! Go walk past some men and at least get a whistle or an accidental ass grab." Monet had her hands on her hips and rolled her neck while she spoke.

"Mo, I'm waiting on my next drink. Then I'll get up and mingle again. I promise."

Hoping my speech would win her over, I smiled and waited for Monet to leave. But she didn't just reclined even more in the lounger next to me.

"Fine, let's wait on your drink, then you're coming with me."

Damn it! So close, yet so far from her leaving! Fuckity Fuck!

"Mo, what are you doing here with me. Why are you not going to get a whistle or an intentional ass grab?" Mo laughed and raised her glass to me.

"Don't you worry, Doc; I got my eyes on a few potential victims here. Trust and believe, I won't be leaving unapproached." We slapped hands, then turned our attention back to the party, grooving to the music.

"Sasha, can I ask you something?" Her voice was quiet, so I looked over at Monet, nodding for her to continue. "Do you think…I mean. How do I say this?" Feeling her uncertainty, I grabbed Mo's hands and spoke.

"You can ask me anything, Monet, let's hear it, love."

"Ok." Monet took a breath, then spoke again. "Do you think guys take me seriously? I mean, I tell them straight up, I like to have fun and but I'm also looking for more. Does that make me a hoe or hypocrite? You know what I mean?"

I sat and thought about Monet's question. It was something that us women, or even men, had pondered for ages. We debated about who was ready and who was not. Whether having sex on the first day ruins a relationship or not. At the end of the day, no one had the correct answer. It was different strokes for different folks. But truthfully, did it matter? Not sure what to say to Monet, I said what came to mind.

"Monet, do you take yourself seriously?" She frowned but thought about it, then replied.

"Hell yeah!" We both laughed, and I rubbed her leg.

"Then that's all that matters. Shit, it's somebody for everybody, and if you decide to ride the bull before committing to the saddle, do you. Hell, most people judge you because they can't be as free as you."

"You damn straight, Sasha." We laughed again, then I finished up.

"Hell, my alter ego is you, and baby, she is a beast."

"Ohhhh!! Tell me more, Dr. Sasha." I laughed as I thought about my antics when I channeled Candy. She allowed me to let loose and just be free unapologetically. It wasn't until her ass went back in the bat cave that I struggled with self-inflicted guilt. However, on vacation I decided that shit needed to stop. Why not just embrace all facets of me, shit all of them deserved to be loved and seen. After being quiet for a moment, Monet sat up in her lounger to face me.

"Ok, Sasha, I'm going to challenge you."

What did she mean challenge?

Monet was smiling too hard, so I frowned and braced for her response.

"I mean, we got these masks on. So, I challenge you to channel your inner Mo and have some fun tonight. But…do it unapologetically, just let whatever happens happen, and don't give it a second thought. Agreed?"

Huh? Maybe this drink has me tripping. Did she just….

"Mo…I don't…"

"Sasha! Come on! Look, no one is going to know it's you. You got the mask, hair, and you're practically naked. No one is gonna know the nun you really are around here."

I laughed at her calling me a nun; I wasn't that bad.

"Look, you ain't gotta go all out. But, just live a little." I wanted to say no, but part of me (the unsober half) was up for the challenge.

"Fine, Mo. I got one rule. What happens at this party stays at his party. Deal?" Monet slapped my hand so hard it stung.

"That's my bitch! Now, where should you start…hmmm. Ohhh!!!! Have you been in any of the tents yet?" Monet said as the waiter approached us with my drink.

He smiled at me again and licked his lips. "I made this extra sweet for you, Goddess. If you need anything else, I'll definitely make myself available." He grabbed my hand and kissed it wetly. I smiled back and giggled, then he left.

"Yess bitch you already letting it go. Now back to the tents." I took a swig of the drink. Not only was it sweet, riddled with cherries, but it had extra brown in it. I was going to be fucked up for sure. Good thing I had Pedialyte at home on ice. Tomorrow, I wasn't gonna be shit. Taking another sip, I answered Mo's question.

"No, I saw them, but I thought they were just empty tents for decoration." I stirred my drink, adjusted my mask, and then took another sip.

"No, Sash…you gotta go in and see each one. They each have a different vibe. Matter of fact, I'll wait here and you go. I'll save your space since I doubt after the scavenger hunt, I'll be sending you on, your ass will be moving anymore tonight."

Scavenger hunt, what the hell?

My face reflected my thoughts, so Monet replied instantly.

"How am I going to get you to loosen up if you don't move around. Don't worry, I got some plans in motion, now go so I can finish." We both laughed, but Monet stopped and scowled at me.

"Well, come with me, Mo…" Monet put her hand up and motioned for me to hurry along.

"Nope, it's a solo experience…go on now and take your time. Explore and enjoy."

I stood up and brushed off my cover-up. I was feeling the second drink more than I knew. My body felt warm, my legs felt loose, along with all my ambitions. However, I was relaxed and really ready to party. As I was about to walk away, Monet stopped me.

"Put on some more lip gloss."
Urgh, too many rules…let's get this over with.

Once I secured my lip gloss to my lips, I was off to explore the tents, which were less than 100 feet away, with my drink in hand. The music playing caused me to groove and move. As I made my way.

Ok, Dr. Sasha, don't hurt anybody!

I wasn't a part of the tent discussion. My only job was to make sure they were on the property, and the other bridal party members handled the rest. The owner didn't seem to mind the request. He provided three large tents that mimicked ones at concerts for the artist to change. They were white, had four sides, and a zipper down the front to close them. Seemed pretty standard to me. However, from Monet's excitement, I could tell there was more to them than the basic outside.

When I reached the tents, there was a sign outside each one.

Caution: *Each tent is an experience; take your time and soak it all up or let it all fall down.*
Either way, enjoy the ride.

I turned back to Monet and frowned. However, she waved me off and smiled as if to mimic the sign.

Tent number One:

It was like an igloo with light blue lights. It was chilly, and had makeshift snow on the floor and tables, which looked like igloo ice. A mist machine puffed peppermint into the air to cool your nostrils, while a smoke machine billowed white puffs into the air. Plush white chairs were adorned throughout the tent. There was a bed in the corner covered like all the seats in various animal skin throw covers. When I saw a polar bear, I went over to get a closer look.

Damn, they got a whole bear. He almost looks real. Roar!

There were several mirrors all around. It was nice yet semi-kinky at the same time. The music seemed to match the vibe as Tweet's *Oh My* played. On the long table near the back of the tent, there were blue and white edibles.

It included a note: *Taste if you please, enjoy the blue coolness. The items with the * are the real edibles. Take it at your own risk.*

"This place is something else."

I thought about trying one of the edibles but decided to pass. I didn't know who brought these and what their tolerance level was. Plus, I wasn't a partaker anyway; I heard it wasn't good to get high alone, at least not your first time.

Also, on the table were wraps that looked like blue fruit roll-ups, blue and white condoms, cooling oils, and lotions. There were even some blue and white gadgets. I almost picked one up but decided against it. Besides, who knew where those had been.

"Boy, I bet people done had some fun in this tent." As I said the words out loud, a person entered the room. I didn't turn around, only looked through the mirror.

It was a guy, or so I thought, since they didn't have boobs. He, too, had a mask which covered his face. However, he was completely covered, unlike the waiters. He had a form-fitting black top and bottom with shorts on top to match. His frame was beautiful, although I couldn't see his skin, including his hands which were covered. He didn't say anything, but he smelled amazing. A scent I'd never smelt but wanted to smell again. When I turned around to address him, he was gone as if it was an optical illusion.

"Imaginary playmates again, Sasha? Girl cut back on the drink." I laughed at my comment and took another sip. Having my fill of tent number one, I left to explore the next one.

If that was tent one, I can only imagine what the next few will be like.

<u>Tent number Two:</u>
Sign Outside: *Take your shoes off before entering.*

I took off my shoes and stepped inside.

"Wow, they did it again. This is awesome."

The tent was warm with the amber lighting to match. The temperature was just right. Sand covered the floor; it too was warm and felt comfortable to walk on. It smelled like warm amber, and if you closed your eyes, you swore you were on a beach thanks to the sound of rolling waves. The chairs provided looked like zero-gravity chairs. They could be adjusted or secured using the knobs on the side. When I thought about the possibilities, I smiled. A rotating and reclining chair, very interesting. You could do a lot with nothing but gravity holding you in place or out of place. There were a few loungers around and a bed in the corner. Everything had yellow accents. If anyone wanted to have fun, they could get dirty in the sand or lie back in one of the chairs or a bed. The sounds of Skip Marley & Popcann's *Vibe* bellowed through speakers; it was perfect. The sound gave the perfect summer vibe.

Perfect song for this warm feeling.

The walls also consisted of mirrors and hanging warm lights. It was awesome. The table of goodies consisted of all things yellow. This included bananas, candies, and other trinkets, also found in the previous tent.

It included a note: *Let this room warm you up for what's to come. Enjoy these treats, play in the sand…just don't do it alone.*

"These people are a whole trip. What in the after-hours spot is this?"

I sipped my drink more while I lingered a little longer, touching the inflatable objects which were also everywhere. When I left the tent, the masked gentleman was outside. He stood next to the foot washing station. I reached to grab my shoes from the mat outside, but he already had them in his hands.

"Thank you, I can...."

He put his hand to his lips as if to hush me. I wasn't sure if the drink gave me liquid courage, but I was intrigued and didn't protest. He took my hand and led me to the nearby chair. He rinsed off my feet, massaged them, and my calves using some nearby oil on them as he dried them. Part of me couldn't help but enjoy the sensation and the intentionality of his touch. Even with gloves on his hands, he did wonders to my legs. When he finished, he put my shoes on then helped me to my feet. I smiled at him. If he smiled back, I had no idea because his mouth was covered. I could barely make out his eyes through the slits in the mask. All I could do was relish his scent. It was driving me mad. Since both of us had on masks, I just enjoyed the moment.

I smiled and squinted to see any part of his eyes but there was nothing to see.

"Thank ..."

He put his finger up again as if to shush me.

Either this drink is strong, or this is the kinkiest non-sexual shit I've ever seen. I like this, and I don't even know what he looks like. What the entire fuck.

I nodded in agreement, and he touched the side of my face as if to say *Good girl.* He was about to walk away, but I grabbed his hand.

"Come with me," I whispered. He turned his head to the side as if he didn't understand the request. "Let's go to the next tent together, come on..." When he didn't move, I pouted then smiled. The masked gentleman took my hand, then gripped and motioned for me to lead the way.

Tent number Three:
Sign Outside: *Can you take the heat? Enter at your own risk.*

The tent was hot, but not in an uncomfortable type of way. It was comfortable but steamy. The red lights all over definitely set the vibe. Still holding on to my mystery man and my drink, we started at the beginning and made our way slowly through the tent. This was definitely a place for lovers or people with chemistry. There were some adult images on the wall, which included some ideas of toys and activities. We stood and marveled at each one. He didn't say anything, just looked at the images, then at me. The mirrors everywhere added to the vibe. Plus, there were multiple places to sit, which included a bed, a chaise, a recliner chair, and an ottoman. They were all black but with red accessories, which included furry blankets and pillows.

"Man, they went all out for this room. Can definitely see a running theme, right?"

He still didn't speak and just nodded slowly.

I took a sip of my drink. However, when I attempted to lower it, he tilted it higher, and I guzzled the last of it, including the alcohol-soaked cherries. It was the sexiest thing I'd ever experienced. TLC's *Redlight Special* played when we first entered. However, when Aaliyah's *Hot Like Fire* played, I started to groove. My mystery man drew me closer to him from behind, and I let him. I was now tipsy and wasn't sure about anything. All I knew was that between the wig, liquid courage, this outfit, and the room, I was feeling bold as fuck. He turned me around, and he held me close as we slowly rocked. He placed his hand on my lower back, and I pulled him closer. I stared at the mask but gave up trying to see what he looked like.

When the song was over, he let me go but still held my hand. Then he motioned for me to keep going so we could explore the rest of the room.

We walked to the goodie table, which consisted of everything red candy, edibles (adult kinds), and more of the objects from the other tents. I looked at the note, and he pointed at it.

"You want me to read it?" He nodded slowly. "Out loud?" He nodded again and lowered my lip with his finger. Then motioned towards the note. I picked up the note, then he turned my face toward him and pointed at the note again.

DAMN! What the entire hell, Batman? He is turning me on!

I nodded, read the note, and recited it back to him.

"These are meant to turn you on and turn things up. Taste and see, how HOT it can be." He quietly applauded and touched my face again.

I smiled and went to walk away, but he gently pulled me back. Still facing me, he lifted a red-hot from the candy dish in front of us and held it up. On cue, I opened my mouth and he dropped it in. I typically hated this candy, but today it was everything. He gave me another. Between my taste buds and the moment, this was intense, and I wanted more of it. This masked man had me about to channel my inner Mo/Candy and possibly risk it all…Possibly. However, I was still sane in some parts of my mind. So, I didn't. Seeing I'd had my fill; he turned towards the exit and moved us to head out.

Wait, we can't just leave like that! I need a little sneak peek…come on, Sasha. Fun, remember…just a little, not a whole lot.

He was about to exit, but I pulled his hand to stop him.

"Wait!" He turned around and waited for me to speak. "Look, Black Panther, Spiderman, Iron Man…whoever you are, you can't just leave without me knowing who you actually are." He turned his head to the side. "I mean, you done grinded on me and fed me candy, plus you washed my feet. And I don't even know who you are. You can't just leave me with nothing. I'll take off my mask if you take off yours." He didn't respond, just rubbed the chin piece of the mask. Seeing he wasn't giving in; I tapped back into my pouty face bag. "Give me a clue, please…" When I pushed my lips out, he thought about it as he sized me up. When he sighed, a sound came out of the mask which scared me a bit but made me perk up a bit.

"Ok, more than a sigh, Sir!" I laughed and smiled, then stopped, "Wait, you are a man, right?" He chuckled, and a robotic sound came from the mask, which surprised me even more.

"Ok, I'll give you a hint. But, let me blind fold you first."
This is getting freakier by the second.

I didn't respond, just nodded. He grabbed a red eye mask from the table and slid it over my mask. When he was sure I couldn't see, he spoke again.

"Ok, I'm going to sit you on the ottoman, just relax." He helped me sit down, and I rested with my legs crossed. If they were open, it could be a problem. Seeing me clinching my knees, he laughed.

"Relax, Maid of Honor."

Wait, he knows who I am. This was becoming even more interesting.

I felt him kneel in front of me, then he put my hands on his waist, and he put his hands on mine.

"I'm going to kiss you. But with one condition. Nod if you understand me." I nodded slowly and smiled. "You can't take your eye shades off." I grunted and folded my arms as if I couldn't speak. "Those are the rules, nod if you agree, Maid of Honor." I let out a breath and pouted, then he laughed. "Them sexy ass lips can't help you get your way this time." I smiled, then nodded yes. "Good, now no peeking, just relax." He was quiet again, then he spoke. "Before, we get started…what's your name, Maid of Honor?" I smiled and laughed; we'd been this close, but we didn't know each other's names. I really was risking it all or partially.

"What's your name first?" He growled at my question. I knew he wasn't going to answer. But it didn't matter; he wanted to be a mystery, and so could I. So, I laughed again, "Sa--Candy. My name is Candy." I whispered and smiled. He squeezed my thigh, and I laughed again.

For a few seconds, nothing happened. However, I could feel his presence hovering over me as if to build the anticipation. He breathed on my neck; at one point, I could have sworn I felt the tip of his tongue. He moved my hands to his neck, and then he slowly kissed me. It was explosive, slow, wet, and exploratory—just how I liked it. When I tried to touch his face, he moved my hands. When I tried again, he locked my hands in his. Then he let out a slight laugh. Which caused me to smile. Then he kissed me again. After a few minutes, I was weak and my knees hurt.

"Please…let me see you," I whispered between kisses. He didn't respond but released one of my hands to allow me to touch his lips while he licked my fingers slowly. Feeling his tongue playing in between my fingertips made me release onto the ottoman. The more he explored my fingers one by one, I relented and opened my legs to draw him closer. He moved closer but backed up but I felt him nearby. Then he put my hand on his shoulder and lowered his body closer to the floor. I leaned back as if to give him a personal view. I felt him get closer to Candy and hover purposely, blowing in her direction to see if she would respond.

"Do it again…" I whispered after he hovered, then he blew again, and I moaned in pleasure. He spoke, of course, with his mask back on.

"She smells amazing. I can't wait to see her myself. We definitely need a personal introduction soon." He took his hand, swiped it slowly from the bottom of my pussy up to my thighs and back while helping me sit up straight again. Then he slowly closed my legs and wetly kissed both my knees. It was then that I felt a slight brush of a mustache.

Another piece of the puzzle.

Then he did something that almost made me lose it completely. He whispered something in my ear, but I couldn't make it out. This time, the mask was not on. I relished the air that lingered from his mouth into my ears. The words, his breath, were enough to make me let loose right then and there. He gave me one last kiss as if to say goodbye before he disappeared. I could still smell him, but I knew he was gone. There was no need to attempt to see him. If anything, I was satisfied with the illusion. He knew which buttons to push, and I was turned on. When I finally took off the mask, after he was long gone, I needed a moment. There was a note next to the ottoman.

"I'll see you soon...next time everything comes off."

When I walked out of the tent, I couldn't help but smile and laugh. I felt like I was on a high. I didn't even care if my mask was off. Fuck it, I'd met my match even if I didn't know who he was. Monet was no longer on the lounger, so I headed inside to get some food and hopefully sober up.

All the ladies were inside, grabbing plates as well. Feeling good, I smiled so hard my face hurt.

"Where have you been, Sasha?" Sarye asked, still fixing her plate.

"Yeah, I sent you into those tents about 30 minutes ago. They ain't that interesting, or are they? And…didn't I send you in with a fresh coat of lip gloss on them lips! Hmm…" Monet said with a hint of intrigue. Keysha eyed me with a smile on her face.

"Y'all said have some fun, so I'm having fun. Relax. Let's eat and keep the party going. Our girl is getting married!"

We all cheered in celebration of Keysha. She smiled and danced as we hyped her up. Tonight was about Keysha and Kyle. What I shared with the mystery man was guaranteed to be revealed at some point, and I was ready for it and him. He left me with that promise, and I knew he'd make good on it and soon.

At the end of the night, as Keysha requested, the wedding party was introduced to each other. It was nice to put faces to all the people Keysha talked or complained about. Kyle had left early, so had a few of his groomsmen, so a few faces were missing. However, we still partied and enjoyed ourselves.

For the rest of the night, I danced and mingled with my girls alongside me. At 2:00 am, the house was empty, and the cleaners showed up to revamp the catastrophe we had left behind. From what I heard, everyone enjoyed themselves. Although one of Keysha's cousins was caught in a compromising position by her sister with the young boy waiter who served my drink. That ended very well.

Other than that, it was a great night to remember. On the ride home, I peeled off my wig and smiled at the good time had by us all. However, my mind was still on my masked gentleman. I tried to piece together what I knew about him. But I couldn't come up with anything. All that lingered was his whisper in my ears. The words might have escaped me, but the sound was etched in my mind. I couldn't wait for our next encounter.

Chapter 10

After the bachelorette party, everything was pretty quiet until the three weeks before the wedding. Everything was going well until I came down with a damn head cold. I felt like my head would explode due to my sinuses building up. I fought for two days to get them under control, but I kept losing the battle. I was miserable that I couldn't find relief. It was times like these that I wished I were married or had someone to take care of me. Trying to cook, keep track of a meds schedule, and trying to find an ounce of sleep when I couldn't breathe at all was making me miserable.

After the second day, I was a wreck, exhausted, and defeated. So, when my phone rang, it was Lorna. I tried to sound halfway alive; keyword tried.

"Hello, Mother."

I sniffled into the speaker while stuffing more tissue into my draining nostril.

"Sasha, why didn't you tell me you were sick. I could have come or sent you some meds."

Whenever either one of us was sick, the other would order supplies and have them delivered. Truth was, I was too lazy to go down the two flights of stairs to answer the door. So, it was no use sending anything.

"I'm fine, just a bit of a head cold. I have on my hat, under the covers, and got a box of tissues." I said as I sneezed, which hurt like hell.

"Whatever, Sasha, I'm sending you supplies. What don't you have?"

"Are you asking me to think right now?" I whined, I didn't know what I needed other than a big sucky thingy to get the clog out of my head. But no one sold that—at least I didn't think so.

"I'm putting in the order now, should be there in a few hours. I'll let you know once it's enroute."

"Lorna, that means I need to get outta the bed." I sneezed and sniffled, "Fuck, that hurts."

"Language, Sasha, language. Look, why don't you go get a shower and put some of those oils you have in something and see if that opens you up? Warm steam and peppermint or eucalyptus does wonders."

"Good idea, I'll do that."

"Do it now and brush your teeth. That helps too. Sounds like you've been living in sickness for a few days. Time to start feeling better."

Before she could finish, I added, "Remember, a clean car drives better than a dirty one."

Lorna laughed, "That's right, so go get cleaned up. Comb your hair too. I'm sure that's a mess too."

"Should I put on make-up and a pageant dress too, Lorna?" I sniffled and tried to mentally prepare myself for the tasks ahead.

"Don't get smart, but yes, if that will help. Call me later, let me know how you are doing."

I hung up with Lorna and did as she requested. This included changing my sheets and sanitizing my life. Funny how I was still sick but found the strength to do everything she asked. I put on a lounge suit which included a hood, then a knit hat with satin lining. I fixed myself some tea and lay on the sofa with a blanket over me while I waited for Lorna's supplies. Thanks to the Vicks under my nose, I could breathe enough to take a nap.

As soon as I was almost asleep, my doorbell rang. I wanted to ignore it, but part of me wanted snacks and whatever Lorna ordered. So, I got up and stumbled down the stairs to answer the door. When I swung open the door, I readjusted my eyes, unsure if what I saw in front of me was actually there. There was a car in my driveway, bags on the ground in front of my door, but the driver didn't leave. I bent down to grab a bag, but a voice stopped me.

"I just needed you to open the door, go lie back down. I got this." I frowned as I stood up, and there he was. At my door. *How did he? That damn Lorna!*

"How did you…" I wanted to respond more, but I started to sneeze and was too tired to formulate words. The medicine I took when Lorna told me the supplies were 30 minutes out started to kick in. I was not only drowsy but could barely stand up.

"Let me help you upstairs, then I'll come back for this stuff." Dolph ushered me upstairs and back onto the sofa. He pulled the covers back over me and adjusted my pillow. He didn't move, just looked at me as I still tried to process him being in my home.

"Thank…you. Umm, how…" I was trying to hold in a sneeze and talk but failed at both. Poor Dolph just handed me a tissue and continued staring at the mess of me in front of him.

"Get some rest, Sasha." Those were the last words I heard for the next three hours. I slept like I was on a vacation. It felt amazing not to have to think or move.

When I finally came to, I could breathe and my head cold was almost gone. My eyes fluttered open as I inhaled, grateful to be able to feel halfway normal. I saw the mist from a humidifier, which was pumped with peppermint mist. I felt a new layer of Vicks under my nose, and I was grateful my ears were unclogged for once.

Everything in me wanted to return to sleep, but I felt something against my feet. I inched up and rested on my elbows, and Dolph was at the end of the sofa. He was reclining in the last chair and was asleep. My feet were against his leg. It wasn't a dream; he was here. I laid back down and tried to inch my feet away from him, but he grabbed my foot.

"Don't worry, I'm used to having little feet kick me. My son is a wild sleeper. How are you feeling, Sasha?"

I didn't even bother to move anymore.

"I'm good, feeling better, but still tired. Guess the last couple of days catching up to me." I inched back and sat up to lean against the back cushion of the sofa. Dolph turned his head in my direction.

"Why didn't you tell anyone you were sick. Could have done this days ago. You could be feeling better or almost by now."

Urgh, I'm so not in the mood for a lecture.

"Because I'm used to doing this by myself. Plus, it wasn't that serious, and I didn't want to get Lorna or anyone else sick." I said as I turned my head to sneeze and sniffle.

Dolph handed me a box of tissues. I blew my nose, and finally everything came out. I must have blown it at least ten times, but it was finally coming out. I chucked the tissues in the nearby automatic trash can and then sanitized my hands.

"Sasha, you got a head cold. It's a big deal, and shit happens; let someone help you for once. Next time, say something."

Fine, next time I'll call someone else so I don't have to listen to this shit again.

I didn't have the strength to argue, so I just nodded, fighting the urge to sleep again.

"When was the last time you ate?" I tried to think, but I honestly didn't have an answer to his question.

"I don't know…I've been medicating and eating snacks. Had some Cheetos earlier. Oh, and a plum, it was good. Wanted apple sauce, couldn't open the jar, gave up." Thinking about how good the plum tasted had me in a daze for a minute. Dolph just looked at me as I stared into space.

"No wonder you're barely functional, you're full of sugar and bullshit." Dolph got up, and I was about to do the same. "Nah, lay down, I got this." However, nature was calling, and I had to get up; my bladder was full. "Sasha, what are you doing. You can barely walk straight. I know you're not going upstairs." Too tired to explain or argue, I got to the point as I struggled to keep my nose from running.

"I have to pee. The bathroom is in the corner. I can make it unless you want to clean up piss." He nodded and went to the refrigerator, then began rummaging through my pots.

When I finished, I looked in the mirror as I washed my hands. I was horrified. I had tissue stuck in my nose. My eyes had gunk in them, and my lips were dry. Luckily, I had a hat and a hood on. I tried to spruce up, but it was a terrible attempt. Beyond cleaning up my eyes and nose, I looked the same. So, I came out of the bathroom. Dolph looked me over as I reached for my lip balm on the table. I was about to sit at the island, but he stopped me.

"Nope, get back on the sofa. I'll bring everything to you."

"Dolph…"

"Sasha, please…we gonna do this every time I ask or suggest something to you?" He had a point; besides, I was over the back and forth. He won, so we would do things his way.

Feeling somewhat emotional, I whimpered, "Can I at least have something to drink?"

He reached into my refrigerator and grabbed a beverage like he knew his way around. Dolph handed me an Orange Gatorade.

Orange is my favorite, aww.

I opened the bottle and took a sip, then frowned. I almost wanted to spit it out. My mood went from whiney to annoyed.

"It's sugar-free. What the hell is this?"

"Think you had enough sugar for the week. Drink that or water. That's it."

He ain't my daddy!

I frowned, but Dolph didn't care. He went back to the stove while I stood there.

"Now go get back on the sofa. Miss Lorna's soup is almost done."

Damn, he went to her house to pick up soup, too. That was nice of him. Guess I can drink this terrible ass Gatorade. But I'm not gonna like it.

I returned to the sofa and downed the drink. It felt good to get some electrolytes in my system. I felt somewhat alive for now, at least. It was almost time for my next dose of meds, so I filled the medicine cup with liquid. I set the bottle down to close the top, but Dolph took the medicine cup.

"What are you doing? I'm about to take that." I sniffled

"Not before you eat this soup and crackers. Then you can take it, killing your damn stomach and liver."

"And who are you, Dr. Quinn, the Medicine Man?"

"Nah. But you don't have to go to medical school for that type of basic knowledge, Doc."

He didn't have to go there. That was a dig. Besides, I knew that…I think. I just want to go to sleep.

Annoyed, I sucked my teeth. "Just give me the damn soup and crackers, man."

Dolph set the soup, crackers, and another Gatorade, along with water, on the TV tray near me.

"You need me to feed you or do airplane like I have to do my son?"

Seriously! Urgh, you can get out and now!

"No, Ran-DOLPH, I think I can handle…" Before I could finish, my hand swiped the bowl and splashed hot soup on the table and my hand. "Damn it!" I yelped as I tried to wipe off my hand, which hurt. Dolph grunted, then he grabbed my hand to assess it.

"You are worse than the baby. Let me see it!" But I snatched my hand back and pouted as I covered it. He blew air through his nose and sat on the sofa, then moved my hand to his lap. He looked at my hand, which had no bruise or burn, just some slight redness. Then he went to the ice maker and got a cube of ice and wrapped it in a napkin. "Here, put this on it." When he tried to put the ice on my hand, I swatted at him.

"It's gonna burn more and I'm fine."

"Sasha, we're not going to keep going back and forth. You might have the PhD, but I'm the doctor today. So put this on there and hold it. Apparently, asking you to do anything else might result in us both getting 3rd degree burns." I snatched the ice and held it on my hand.

"Nobody told you to make the soup so damn hot anyway."

Dolph chuckled. "We saw what happened last time you ate lukewarm food. Don't need a repeat of that again, now do we?" I rolled my eyes; he didn't have to bring up the lunch fiasco.

I mumbled, "Whatever, throw up bae," I chuckled a bit thinking about Monet. Dolph was so busy blowing on the soup he didn't hear what I said.

"Ok, come on so you can eat and take these meds."

Dolph lifted the spoon and waited for me to eat from it.

Was he crazy? I'm not doing that shit! I never let any man feed me; that shit creeps me out. I barely like holding hands. I'm not doing that shit.

When I leaned back and folded my arms. Dolph put the spoon back in the bowl and stared at me.

"What's the problem now? Wait, let me guess…there's a clause in the *Destiny's Child* oath for independent women. *Thou shalt not be fed. Hold your spoon at all costs.*" Dolph laughed at his comment.

He really thinks he's funny. Ok, that shit was funny, a little.

I closed my eyes regarding Dolph's comment. He was getting on my nerves. However, when I opened them again, he was back with the damn spoon full of soup. I smiled. I was tired and my meds were wearing off, so I gave in. When the spoon was empty, he loaded it up again, and we continued that bullshit until the soup was almost gone.

"Aww, look at Daddy's Big Girl. Eating her soup with no smart-ass comments. Making me proud." He winked. I grunted, and he loaded the soup again.

"No, I'm done. I don't want any more."

"Fine but at least drink the broth. It's good for you, please." He put the spoon back in the bowl and added some broth to it.

"I'm not about to have you spoon-feed broth to me."

Dolph laughed, then returned the spoon to the bowl.

"Oh, so you think you're ready for the big time now. Do I need to get a bib or something, butterfingers?" I couldn't help but laugh at his smart comment. So, to show him up, I took the straw on the tray and sucked all the broth from the bowl with one sip.

"She's a sucker…quite the throat and jaw work, Dr. Carter. Good to know." We both laughed at his comment while I tried to swallow. He kissed my cheek and cleaned up the soup and the remaining trash. When he returned to the sofa, he handed me the medicine cup with the liquid. I downed it, then he handed me the Gatorade to chase it.

"Can see you enjoy shots as well. You took that with no problem."

"I've been living on that for two days; I'm a pro now."

He nodded and smiled. "Ok, well, time to detox tomorrow. You need to get up and running in time for Keysha's wedding."

How did he...Lorna!

"You're right."

Dolph looked surprised, then looked around. "Did the great Dr. Carter agree with me with no attitude. You must be sick or starting to see the bigger picture."

He was too much, and all his commentary warmed my heart.

"Whatever, Dolph. And it's Dr. Phillips, by the way! Let me get up, so I can let you out, so I can go get in my bed before these meds settle in."

"Don't worry about all that. Just rest. I'm here to take care of you. DJ is with my mom, so he's cool. She said to tell you to feel better."

This dude and mothers! How in the hell is it that he knows mine and I don't know his?

"Maybe you will meet her at some point, if you get some act right in your system."

Act right? Please! I got some act right for you, Dolph!

"Dolph, you a whole trip. You know that!"

I just shook my head and leaned it against the cushion. Dolph didn't move, just stared at me as he rubbed my head. The moment was intense and felt like it was made for us. I leaned into his hand, allowing myself to just be in the moment. Although I was sick, I wished he would kiss me. Dolph leaned towards my face, while still rubbing it, but before he could get in range to kiss me, my phone rang. He just rubbed my cheek and then went back to cleaning up the kitchen. While I answered my phone.

Clearing my throat and mid-sniffle, I answered the phone, which was a FaceTime call.

"Hello Robbie!"

"Bitch you look like hell hit with an ugly stick. What the hell?"

"I'm sick, heifer! Not really just a head thing." I grabbed a tissue and blew my nose while Robbie frowned in disgust. He was home relaxing with a cup of tea in hand and soft music in the background.

"You didn't have to blow your boogers into the camera, Sasha! Lawd, you would think Aunt Lorna raised you with the wolf pack. Why didn't you tell anyone you were sick, trying to be independent again?" Robbie's little comment caused Dolph to chuckle in the background. I rolled my eyes and sucked my teeth, then moved the camera closer to me.

"Fuck you, Robbie!" I was trying not to laugh as I coughed, then grabbed another tissue to wipe my nose.

"Keep fucking with me and I'ma mail you these snotty ass tissues. Besides, if you really loved me, you would come take care of me." Robbie sipped his tea and shook his head nope.

"Umm…please, I can't afford to be sick right now. But I could have at least sent you some reinforcements, a comb, some meds, a strip-a-gram, or something. Did you at least wash your ass today? You giving smelly puss and breath, Sasha, do better." Dolph chuckled again, and I lowered my head in embarrassment. Thanks to Lorna, I was clean and prepped, at least as best as I could.

"Why did you call me? All this emotional abuse is not helping my head cold, Robert-Bobby Winterford!"

"Bitch no, you didn't with my whole government! I should cast your ass to the wolves! You are no longer my favorite person for 30 seconds! Starting now!" Robbie looked at his watch, counting the seconds. I sighed and leaned my head against the sofa. We'd been through this before.

"Rob…"

"Aht aht, light still red! It's 10 seconds left, peasant. Wait for your turn to speak again." I looked over at Dolph, and he frowned while shaking his head. Once 30 seconds were up,

Robbie spoke again. I tried to move the camera away from the kitchen, where Dolph was still cleaning.

"Greenlight…now you know better than to…" When Dolph closed the cabinet and it made a sound, Robbie's antennas immediately went up. "What was that, Sasha? And don't hit me with nothing, cause I heard it. Turn the camera, let me survey the area. Your ass might have a Ph.D., but let's be real, you're a lover and not a fighter. No need to relive that catastrophe again."

Did he really have to go there? Punk!

Trying to deflect, I tried to change the subject.

"Robbie, so how's…"

"Aht, aht…let me see before I get ignorant and loud. I will spill all the tea to whoever you are trying to hide. You got till the count of 5." I quickly flashed the camera behind me and put it back on me.

"Umm…who is that beautiful brown Adonis in your kitchen? Here I am feeling bad for you for 2.5 seconds, and you got a whole sexy male hoe in your presence. Bitch yes! Have you…?" Before he could say anything else, I interjected and put a stop to it.

"No one. And please don't finish whatever your statement is going to be, PLEASE."

"Well, no one sure looks at home and obviously knows his way around your OCD cabinets." Dolph chuckled again while I frowned at the remark; my cabinets were not OCD. I just liked shit where it was supposed to be and facing front in a straight line.

"Robbie. I have to go, these meds are kicking in, and my OCD ass is tired." I was over the conversation and Robbie's meddling ass.

"Whatever, Sasha. You and nobody enjoy your night. Hopefully, he can unclog something else besides that snotty ass nose. I'm sure them walls are all vibrated out."

Why was everyone in my damn vag! Urgh!

"Really, Robbie! Urgh, you make it hard to love you sometimes."

"Might be hard to love, but you damn sure ain't gonna give me up. So, tell the duck to pull the truck and shut the fuck up! By the way, why didn't I get an invite to the freak-fest of the century?" I frowned, unsure what he meant.

"Oh, don't act like I didn't hear about Keysha and Kyle's co-bachelor party bitch!" I smiled slightly, thinking about the festivities. A giggle even slipped my lips, which caused Robbie to increase his tone and annoyance.

"Oh, so you were one of them bitches in them private rooms I heard about! You allowing niggas to suck and fu--" I hushed my tone as I spoke through my teeth and rushed him off the phone.

"ROBERT-BOBBY! First, I ain't do shit! Second, I can't account for others, but I didn't go into a private room. Third, I'm sorry. You were on set and off location, so you wouldn't have made it anyway. Now get off my phone. Love you, bye."

After I hung up with Robbie. I leaned my head on the sofa; the tiredness was taking over, and my head was starting to spin. Part of me prayed Dolph didn't hear Robbie, but I knew he did. So, I closed my eyes and hoped he'd let it slide. But I opened them when I felt a presence hovering over me.

"So, three things…" I let out a breath and waited for Dolph to say his peace. "I'm no one? So, that was the infamous Robbie. He's a piece of work for real. Also, what exactly happened at this bachelorette party?" A smile crept across my face again, thinking about the tent. I tried to hide it, but between the drugs and tiredness, I was in shit shape. So, why hide it? I smiled harder and stared at Dolph, who hovered over me. I grabbed Dolph's cheeks and gave him a serious look while I spoke like an old-timey preacher.

"You are somebody, Randolph." We both laughed as I gave in to the loopy feeling taking over me. I let his face go, then I busted into the song by the late and great Aaliyah. Dolph laughed and shook his head. "Are you that somebody? Tell your that somebody!" We laughed again, then Dolph spoke again.

"Can you answer my other questions so you can take your medicated ass to sleep."

"If I let this go…." I started to continue my terrible karaoke, but I quit as snot started to run down my nose. Dolph put a tissue to my nose and held it there.

"Blow"

"Randolph, I can blow my own nose, damn it!" Dolph didn't move; he just held the tissue and pinched my nose which caused me to sneeze. When I wasn't done, we did it three more times.

Urgh, I hate this! He's seen me throw up and blow snot! What's next, he'll be wiping my ass?

"Aww, the baby can breathe now, good job!" I rolled my eyes as he put sanitizer in both our hands.

"To answer your other questions, yes, that was the one and only Robbie. My Brother-Cousin-Baby. He's the best and the fucking worst with his rude ass." Mocking Dolph's voice, I added. "Maybe you will meet him at some point, if you get some act right in your system." Dolph shook his head and slightly laughed.

"Now tell me about this bachelorette party, Sasha." The request caused me to smile like a Cheshire cat, but no words came out. All I could think about was my masked gentleman and our tent antics. Part of me couldn't wait till the wedding in hopes he would reveal himself. Dolph watched me have my moment, then nodded as he got closer to my face and whispered. "So, tell me what happened, Sasha. Did you enjoy yourself the way Robbie described those other girls did?" I smiled and whispered as if someone else was in the room with us.

"I did enjoy myself, Randolph. However, it's not my story to tell. I was there, but someone else was being entertained." After I winked, Dolph raised an eyebrow, showing his curiosity for me to finish.

"Whose story is it, Sasha?"

"Candy. But, she doesn't kiss and tell." Dolph nodded, slightly laughed, and backed up a bit, but not before asking his final question.

"So, when do I meet this, Candy?" I laughed even harder, this time to keep my composure, knowing this conversation needed to end and now.

"Who says you haven't? We are imaginary playmates." After the words slipped from my mouth, I closed my eyes and started singing the song by René and Angela.

I heard Dolph go back into the kitchen while I vibed out to the music in my head. But I also started to feel kinda sour. The fuck up with Connor was behind me, but the outcome would still linger for a while. Too bad it wasn't Dolph; it wouldn't have been a second thought had it been him. Not wanting to allow myself to fall into the rabbit hole of regret, I turned on Pandora and let the *Mint Condition* station play. It sucked that I was sick, but the music soothed me. I decided to continue my terrible one-woman karaoke show. One song after another, I sang loudly and terribly until the emotions took over. When I was out of songs and breath, I was left with nothing but feelings of being overwhelmed. Although Dolph was just in the kitchen, part of me wished he were holding me as I pushed away the loneliness in my heart.

I closed my eyes and tried to sweep away the few tears that formed in my eyes, but a few escaped my quick swipes. Dolph walked over to me and touched my shoulder. I opened my eyes slightly; he motioned for me to sit up, then helped me up. He sat behind me and put the pillow on his lap, then I laid back down. He looked down at me as he rubbed my cheek.

"Sasha. Why do you do this to yourself?"

I didn't speak but frowned to relay; I wasn't sure what he meant.

"Why do you listen to music that makes you cry or get in your feelings?" It was true, I did do this to myself. However, it was also therapeutic. It helped me release and make room for what I knew was coming for me. Sometimes, I was sad, but most of the time I was happy, hopeful, and anticipated what I wanted most, which was love.

"It's hard to explain, Dolph, but it's release and preparation. One day it won't hurt so bad, I'll forgive myself for my mistake." From Dolph's face, he wanted to ask more, but he didn't. He leaned down and kissed my forehead. That was the last thing I remember before I felt him pick me up and place my head on his shoulder, then begin walking.

"Dolph…I"

"Shhh…just sleep, Sasha. I got you."

There was something about the whisper, but I couldn't decipher what it was. Part of me wanted to react and reply, but I was damn near comatose from the meds. I wasn't even sure if he was actually carrying me, but I heard and felt his words loud and clear. If this was a dream, I wasn't about to wake my ass up; shit, I'd see this to the end.

When I woke up, my eyeshades were on. I had no idea what time it was or even if there was any daylight. I slightly lifted one side, and it was still dark. The fan was on, but I was on the opposite side of the bed. I usually slept by the door, but I was by the window. I lifted my head and looked over my shoulder, and Dolph was on the opposite side. I was under my blanket, which I kept on the bed. However, he was under the comforter and sheets.

How the??

I looked again; he was dressed in an undershirt and had a rag on his head.

Did this negro bring a change of clothes? He really is comfortable.

I wanted to ponder what else had happened. But I didn't, I just laid my head back on my pillow, replaced my eyeshades, and closed my eyes. However, I opened them again and immediately removed my shades completely when I realized Black Vybes was plugged in on my nightstand.

OMG! He's seen Black Vybes, shit! My poor vibrating buddy has been exposed.

Feeling completely embarrassed, I tried to inch out of bed to put him in the drawer. However, when I opened the drawer, I saw my bible reading plan. It felt kind of weird putting him on or next to the Good Book or Workbook about the Good Book. So, I settled for putting him in the bottom drawer. Not wanting to get fully out of bed or wake Dolph, I inched closer to the nightstand and lowered my body to open the bottom drawer.

There was a significant distance between the drawer and the bed. However, I was determined to do it. I pulled the plug on Black Vybes and locked him to ensure he didn't turn on. When the light flashed twice, I knew I was good.

"Ok, buddy, be very, very quiet and don't make too much noise when you land, please!" I should have been ashamed talking to this toy like it would respond. But people talk to plants, and they didn't respond, whatever. When I heard Dolph move, I stopped until I was sure he was asleep again. When I heard him breathing again, I opened the drawer more and grabbed Black Vybes. As I was about to gently lower him into the drawer, I panicked a bit because my upper body was almost too far off the bed.

Fuck I'm too far. I gotta push myself back up. Shit shit shit!

I was about to ease back on the bed when I heard Dolph patting the mattress with his hand, looking for me. It was like my body sprang into action, and I used that as an opportunity to lunge myself back onto the bed. When I hit the mattress, Dolph put his arm around my waist. I was almost sweating and breathing rapidly. I was glad I put him away, partially. I could close the drawer when I got up. When I calmed down, I got comfortable and readjusted my head on my pillow while Dolph still held me.

"You ain't have to go *Mission Impossible* to put your little boyfriend away. I already saw him. We gonna discuss his retirement package in the morning."

I couldn't help but laugh. I knew he'd seen him. There was no point in trying to hide it. Dolph scooted back, and I got even more comfortable. When I was settled, he put his arm back around my waist and we went back to sleep. I slept even better than before. It was perfect.

In the morning, Dolph was already up when I woke up. He was in the shower. I had to pee, so I got up, closed the drawer, and went to the guest bathroom. Where I brushed my teeth and washed my face. When I came back, I laid back in bed and looked through my phone. The water was off, so I knew he was coming out of the bathroom soon. When he opened the door, a cloud of steam entered my room.

"Good morning, how you feeling?"

He asked as he adjusted the bath sheet on his waist, then he sat on the bench in front of my bed with his toiletry kit.

"I'm feeling 75% better, thanks for asking. How are you? Oh, Good morning to you as well."

"I'm good, slept great, ready to take on the day."

I nodded as I watched Dolph moisturize his body. He had a routine just like mine: body oil, moisturizer, and cream. It all smelled amazing, not too much, just the right amount.

"What you got planned today?"

I asked as I looked back at my phone while he got dressed.

"Make sure you good. Then run some errands and then pick up Little Man later. What you got planned?"

"Well…"

"The answer is nothing, Sasha. 75% ain't 100%, so the answer is nothing just resting."

Smart ass!

"Well, if you had the answer, why did you bother to ask Dolph?"

"'Cause I knew you were about to do the opposite of what I said."

I closed my phone, and he came and sat on my side of the bed. Dolph now had on sweats with a wife-beater. He looked at me, then at the floor, back at me, and laughed. I frowned and waited for him to speak.

"Yoo Doc, that's a long way to the floor from the bed. Good thing you had enough strength to pull yourself back up."

We both laughed; it was true. My bed was pretty high, and the bottom drawer was closer to the ground.

"Who you telling! If I had hit the floor, you we've caught me or at least made sure I was ok."

We laughed again, and he nodded.

"Yeah, I was awake, just wanted to see how far you were gonna go to hide your little boyfriend."

"Excuse me, Sir, he has a name, it's Black Vybes."

Dolph frowned and laughed. "He got a whole name…what else he got? Pull him out."

I didn't think he was serious, but he waited, then he opened the bottom drawer and pulled out Black Vybes. Dolph looked at the vibrator and then at me.

"So, Vybes got two sides, huh?"

He turned it on and went through the various speeds.

"What that button do?"

He pressed it, then the speed increased.

"Dang, I bet I know what speed you stay on?"

I laughed, and he continued to play with the speeds and modes before he turned it off.

"This is nice, does the job I'm sure…but no need to keep him for much longer. I don't go outta town too often, and when I do, he can keep you company till Daddy comes home."

Dolph winked and got up to finish getting dressed.

"Funny thing is you think you're replacing him. He was here first, sir."

I cradled Black Vybes as if Dolph hurt his feelings.

Dolph, who was now in the bathroom, eyed me through the mirror, shaking his head.

"Funny thing is you think I'm not. Shit, I slept in this bed, been in your house, and I know the most important people to you. You're the one who needs to catch up. But don't worry, I'll give you a little more time, then his time is up."

He finished in the bathroom and turned out the light once he was fully dressed, minus his shoes. So, I got up to freshen up. He sat on the bench, and I walked to the bathroom. Before I passed him completely, he grabbed my hand and motioned for me to sit next to him.

"Glad you're feeling better, Sasha. Next time or anytime, you need something, don't hesitate to ask me. That's what I'm here for."

I smiled and nodded, about to get up again, but he stopped me.

"You believe me, Sasha?"

I didn't know how to respond. I wanted to believe him, especially after yesterday. But part of me was still skeptical, so I shrugged. Dolph nodded and caressed my hand.

"Think about this, I did everything I did yesterday with no expectation. None. I still don't expect anything. I'm here because I want to be…I wanted to make sure you were good."

I appreciated his words but still had no response despite my heart yelling I was ready to be his.

"Look, I'm about to go make us some breakfast, then I'm heading out. If you need anything, I'm still here, Sasha. Maybe one day I won't be a phone call away, but even closer…more like a touch of hand if you learn to believe me. Go handle your business, I'll be downstairs."

Dolph helped me up, and I headed to the bathroom. When I closed the door, he went downstairs. Everything was going so well with Dolph, but there was always something stepping between us. The something was me; I wanted to be sure, but I needed more confirmation. So, I decided to wait until I was completely sure.

When I was clean from head to toe, I put on my leggings and shirt and headed downstairs. I washed my hair, so it was pulled back into a wavy bun on my head. Dolph had never seen my hair, or at least not like this. I usually had some extensions or a wig on. Maybe a hat when I went to the gym. He nodded at the natural version of me. The body oil and moisturizer I had on me caught his attention. He came closer to me as if to take me in.

"Damn, babe, you smell amazing."

I smiled at him and he kissed my cheek. Then he went back to finish preparing breakfast. Dolph handed me a plate, and we sat at the island to have breakfast. He prayed over the food, and we ate. We didn't talk; just ate the bacon, eggs, and fruit platter he prepared. It was just what I needed; all that was missing was my morning coffee. He kept glancing at me; he even touched the side of my hair. The touch made me feel safe, beautiful, and even more relaxed. I was becoming even more comfortable with Dolph. After a few moments, I looked around, confused.

"What you need, Sasha?"

"Coffee."

Dolph shook his head while he was chewing, then replied, "No."

Did he just say no to my coffee?

He acted as if I asked him a question. Better yet, responded as if he had the final say or something. Confused, I frowned and looked around as if one of my parents were in the room because he really lost his damn mind with this one.

"Umm…come again?"

He looked at me intently and then replied again, "I said No!"

Oh, he really done lost his mind. Maybe he the one sick cause I know he didn't!

"Ok, them fighting words, Randolph. First of all, I love coffee. We've been friends since I was in college. Second of all, we always have a breakfast date. Third of all …"

Dolph stopped eating and looked at me.

"I hear you, but coffee is the reason you're always running on ten. If you are not drinking coffee, it's tea. You always need something to keep you moving. So, no coffee or caffeinated tea today, try some water or herbal tea. You ain't gonna be running all over today anyway, so give your body the rest it needs, Sasha."

The fuck! Was he serious? It's over, we don't like you anymore, RANDOLPH!

I was unmoved by his speech and wanted him to move on. I folded my arms, staring at him as if he'd just called me a bitch or something derogatory.

"Look, you just finished being sick, just let them go for the day, let your body feel what it feels. Without the caffeine." Unconvinced, he added, "Please, one day for me."

For him? Was he kidding me! That shit is not gonna work!

I was about to tell him to go to hell. However, I thought about Dr. Kirk.

Invite love over for coffee Sasha!

I mocked her voice in my head and rolled my eyes in the process. I was inviting love over for decaf, which is equivalent to water. Giving in to his bullshit request, I displayed my brights annoyed smile then gave in.

"Fine, RAN-DOLPH! I'll forgo my beloved coffee and tea for one day. And one day ONLY."

He laughed, "Have the tea, no caffeine. Hell, even have de…"

"Don't you dare cuss at me with that D word. I'll never!"

Decaf in my opinion was water with brown food coloring. It should never exist next to real coffee, but I digress. Dolph raised his hands in surrender. He gathered our empty plates to place them in the sink. After he washed them and put them away, he packed up his things to leave.

"Thank you again for everything, Dolph. I appreciate it. I really do." I walked him to the door, and he sat on the step to put on his shoes.

"You're welcome, Sasha, anytime you need me, I'm here."

Part of me wanted to say the same in return, but I hesitated. So, I smiled and he stood up to leave. He put his arms around me and held me.

"Make sure you get some rest. I'll be checking on you later. And lay off that cough syrup." I laughed, "Don't wanna have to put you in rehab. Been away from you long enough as is."

His words were like his hug, everything I needed at that moment. I looked up at Dolph, and he looked down at me. I leaned in to kiss him, and he came closer, but his phone rang, and I moved back, although he didn't.

Dolph answered his phone while still keeping his eyes on me, while he held on to me.

"Hey Buddy, you miss Daddy?"

When he spoke, I let him go. However, he didn't let me go completely. He used his free hand to put the phone on speaker.

"Dada, I watch Bluey."

The sound of his son was like a shock to my system. But not in the way he thought. My breathing became labored, and my chest became tight. I completely removed myself from Dolph's embrace to hide my face as I fought to keep tears back. When he tried to turn me around, I moved out of his reach. I needed more time to compose myself.

When I turned around, Dolph didn't say anything, but his eyes displayed his hurt. He didn't understand, and it showed. I didn't have the answers at least ones I wanted to reveal, yet. He nodded, which said everything he didn't. In that moment, I should have stayed with him. Let him see me fall apart if necessary. Then explained as we held each other. This could give him assurance that I was ok with his world. I was willing to be a part of it. But instead, I pulled away again at the mention of his son. Dolph sighed and shook his head while he walked out as he continued to talk to his son. Little did he know, I pulled away as I thought about what happened with Connor. I terminated my chance at having a son because I was reckless with a man who I wished was him. I knew I would love his son and he would love me if we ever met…but at this rate, that wouldn't happen. Neither would Dolph and me.

Chapter 11

Days before the wedding, everything was quiet, and two weeks had passed since I heard from Dolph. Keysha was only working half days so she could mentally prepare. I was glad she helped me out since she would be off for two weeks after the wedding. Things were really in full swing. It was around lunch time, and my next appointment with Maria and Dexter wasn't until 3:00 pm. Keysha ran out to handle an errand while I added some new books to the bookcases in the lobby. I was so caught up in my organizing that the doorbell chime scared the shit outta me. When I checked the camera by Keysha's desk to see who it was, I almost didn't answer.

"Fuck is he doing here? Urgh!" I wasn't in the mood for bullshit. The day was going seamlessly, and this interaction was not what I needed. The bell chimed again, and I stared outside of the mirrored glass while he attempted to look in.

"Sasha, I see your car outside. Please let me in."

I wanted to shout *like hell I will,* but I didn't. That type of attention in this suburban neighborhood would garner too much attention. So would some random guy yelling at my door. So, I hit the button and let him in. When he entered, he smiled as if I should be the least bit happy or even appeased by his presence, but I wasn't. If anything, I wanted to maul him over with my truck and make him disappear right then and there.

"Sash…"

He started to come near me with flowers in his hands. However, I put my hand in the air and motioned for him to stop. Without saying a word, I waited for him to speak again because, of course, he wouldn't leave without saying his peace.

"How are you? You look great, babe."

When I didn't say anything, he attempted to smile again, then continued.

"I got you these; they're beautiful, bright, and full of life like you, babe."

He can cut the bullshit with this babe talk! Fuck him and them funky ass flowers. Why did he even think this was ok?

"Sasha, look…I know I shouldn't have come, but you haven't answered my calls or texts. I didn't know how else to reach you. I mean, beyond calling Lorna, but I'm sure she doesn't want to hear from me."

Damn skippy she don't! You fucking coward. She knows you broke my heart, asshole.

He attempted to come closer again, but I stepped backward, and he stopped.

"Babe, it's me…you don't have to be afraid of me. I'm still the same person. The man you love…or loved."

And that's the problem… you're still the same! Further, you think I am too. As if I still even remotely love you, which I don't.

When there was still no response, he looked disappointed. He set the flowers on a nearby table.

"Babe, I came to tell you somethings…I just need you to hear me out. Please. I know you're mad and you should be…hell, can't even blame you if you hate me."

He came closer, and I backed up again, only I had backed myself into the wall. This gave him the opportunity to get closer than necessary to make his last request.

"You haven't said a word since I've been here, and I get it. I swear I do. But I need you to do something for me, please…just one thing."

I frowned and glared at him, the audacity of him to ask me for shit. I didn't owe him a fucking thing. However, he owed me his life in this one and the next for all the bullshit he put me through. As he stared, it was like he was reading my thoughts.

"Meet me at our spot, let me clear some things up. Then I'll leave you alone. Please."

I sucked my teeth at the request and damn near laughed in his face. It took everything in me to not unleash the beast inside. So, I called his bluff. I softened my face and smiled at him like I used to. He fell for it immediately; I stepped closer to him and sized him up. Then I grabbed his hand, he looked at it, then me, and smiled.

"Come with me…let's go."

I whispered close to his face. In my former life with Blue, that was a green light for some adult activity, no matter where we were. He let me lead him to the front door, while he followed closely behind. Not enough to touch but enough for me to know he was ready to fire all cylinders, if I was down. I unlocked the door, then turned to face him while he intentionally tried to cop a feel on my ass.

"Damn, babe…you look and smell amazing. It's been way too long."

Blue attempted to sniff my neckline, but I opened the door and stepped back. He smiled and rubbed his chin as if we were playing a game. However, he didn't move, just waited for my gaze to meet his. When it did, my face was blank, letting him know whatever he thought was about to happen wasn't. Blue wasn't one to give up. If anything, this intrigued him, and he would work harder to force me into submission. While I held the door, Keysha and Sarye had just entered the parking lot in separate cars. When Keysha spotted Blue, she got out immediately, and Sarye followed, sensing the urgency.

They both approached at the same time. Neither said a word, but Keysha cleared her throat and clapped twice to get Blue's attention. When he looked at her, she gave him *the get the fuck outta here* face. Not wanting any more of Keysha's smoke, Blue made his exit and walked past her and Sarye. When he was in his car, he yelled.

"Babe, I'll be there at 7:30 pm. Just give me 15, please."

Keysha glared at him, then walked into the office, followed by Sarye. I closed the door and locked it.

"Fuck is he doing around here?" Keysha said as she threw the flowers in the trash. I wasn't mad, if anything, I was glad cause I was about to do the same thing.

"Umm…who was that? He's cute, but from y'all faces, he on that bullshit. So, somebody fill me in."

Sarye got comfortable and opened her lunch container to eat.

"Yeah, he is Mr. Bullshit. Calling him a Fuckboy is a compliment. Better yet, they haven't even invented a word for the scum that is Blue." Keysha almost seethed as the statement came out. I went to my office to grab her some water, then came back. As I handed it to her, she looked at me.

"Sasha, you haven't even said a word. What did he say? Are you good?"

Sarye and Keysha waited for me to respond. I hadn't realized I was silent beyond the few words I said to Blue.

"He said his usual. No need to rehash it. I'm fine. No need to worry about me circling the block. We good this time, Key, we REAL GOOD."

Keysha nodded with assurance that I meant what I said. Before there could be any more discussion. I went to my office and closed the door. Knowing I needed a moment, no one interrupted me. I lay on my recliner chair and slid it all the way back to close my eyes. Blue was no longer the problem he "intended" to be. I'd done enough work to make sure of that. However, the proof of his existence was always there mentally, just void of pain and agony it once caused.

Imagine being in an art gallery. Walking around, enjoying the historic art pictures of whatever…pick something. Then, sitting on a bench to admire one particular picture. Its color, context, imagery…all that fancy shit. You see yourself staring into the image and marveling at…can't take your eyes off it. Then you blink and it's a completely different image.

At first, you can't make it out. However, as you blink more and it comes into focus then eventually becomes clear. It's an image that looks familiar; it's something you haven't seen, but you damn sure recognize it. You want to look away, but it's a harsh truth you didn't want to see; it is holding your eyes hostage. As soon as you look away, the image is on every canvas in the room. It's now blown up and plastered on every wall. You can't cry or even react; all you can do is just look. You want to close your eyes, but

*you're afraid…what if there is more? How could there be
more? But your eyes can no longer resist looking or
recognizing the truth in front of you.*
*When you finally close your eyes and open them again,
you're no longer in the art gallery. You're in a bedroom,
standing at the foot of a bed, only it's not your own. He can
see you, but she can't. She's snuggled under him while
you're forced to watch.*
*When he finally acknowledges you, he smiles, even blows
you a kiss while he cuddles you as if he's done nothing
wrong. Again, you can't react or cry can't even utter a
word. There's no reaction for you, only relief for him that
his secret is out. He smiles and kisses her forehead, then
says, "We're still good, Sasha, this doesn't change anything.
We're still going to have the life we talked about, I
promise."*
*After those words, the tears finally came down while he held
her closely. I am unable to move as I think about how
everything we had was a lie. It was all right in front of me;
how could I not see it?*

That was the dream I had when I first began to suspect
that Blue was married. Apparently, my gut, subconscious, and the
universe couldn't take any more. A few weeks later, I found the
evidence in black and white, a wedding announcement from five
years prior. Funny thing is, I looked for it, I mean, really searched
for it…but it never came up until after the dream. Talk about fate
and a much-needed reality check. When I confronted Blue, it took
a few days before he responded. All he could say was sorry. We
eventually spoke and he performed a one-man show of *I fucked up*.
He tried to justify it, I cried, then yelled and swore off him for
good. There would be no house, no marriage, and no kids…the
Kool-Aid I drank now tasted like sewage, and I wasn't interested.
We did our dance for another few months before I ended it all.

When my personal phone vibrated, I got up from the
recliner to answer it.

"Yes, Lorna. How are you today?"

"Is that how we address our mothers these days? These new-age tendencies are too much for me."

Knowing she was feeling some type of way, I started again.

"Oh, dearest mother, how art thou? How goes it, your world-th?"

I tried not to laugh as I woke up my computer to check my emails. Knowing Lorna, she didn't call for a quick chat. She had some chatter in her today.

"Really, Sasha! Well, since you asked, I'm good. Life is great. My world is fine. Just enjoying the outings with my church ladies. But, enough about me."

Lorna, hurrying past, talking about herself, only meant she was about to start in on my life. Not only would she start in, she would make herself comfortable with her nosey butt.

"How are you? Have you talked to Randolph yet?"

Since the day WE met Dolph, he was her favorite conversation piece. Apparently, the boundary I set went out the window. No surprise. They still talked at least once a week and she intentionally told me all about his doings. Then she apparently told him about all of mine; despite my telling her not to. She didn't listen, so there was no need to get mad anymore. I always sighed and hoped she would move on from the conversation and eventually him.

"No, mother, I have not talked to Dolph."

"Well, I have, and he's doing well. Did you know his business…"

Lorna proceeded to give me the rundown of all his dealings as I checked my email. I barely listened. There was no beef, but why did I need to know what was going on in his life? However, when she said the next words, she had my attention.

"We're going to lunch next week. He's meeting me at the Senior Center after my bridge game."

Was she kidding me? Lorna Lorna LOOORNNNNA! Talking was one thing; outings was a whole different ball game.

Feeling like this Dolph obsession had gone on long enough. I wanted to put a stop to it; she needed to move on. We were done, so she was done too!

"Lorna, now I'm calling your name on purpose. Why do you still talk to him? What is the point? Matter of fact, why are y'all having lunch?"

"I like him. He's a nice young man, Sasha. I don't know why you won't give him a chance. He calls me every week to check in. He even sent me flowers and helped me find a new gardener. You know that old one wasn't worth squat. Oh, and his little boy, Sash, you would…"

Knowing Lorna was set in her ways, I was done with the conversation. If they were happy together, she could have at it. However, I was done, and that was cool with me. They could be mother and son. Hell, at this rate, I'd see him at every major holiday and family function we could take turns picking her up and dropping off. Lorna kept talking, but I was done and ended the conversation.

Fuck it, I give up! I'll put myself up for adoption and they can have one fucking happy family!

"Lorna, you enjoy your imaginary son and grandson. I have work to do. Glad everyone is well. I'm sure our paths will cross soon. Love you, bye."

Before I could hang up, Lorna cleared her throat, daring me to hang up on her. When I was silent, she said her peace.

"Sasha, look, I don't want this to be a problem. It shouldn't be. But, if it is, I'll let it go before you say the words. You know I always got your back, that won't ever change. Look, I'm going to say this one last thing and then I'm done."

Famous last words from all mothers!

"You've dedicated your life to your profession and to that loser Blue. I heard he came slithering around today."

Fucking Keysha, did everyone have a group text to alert them when bullshit followed me? Note to self, fire Keysha.

"Now, I know you're good. I've seen the change in you, and I'm so proud of you. I really am."

Thanks, Lorna, I needed to hear that—I really needed that reassurance. Love this trouble-making lady.

Hearing Lorna say those words completely tumbled the frustration I felt. My attitude didn't have anything to do with her or even Dolph. The fact that I was that reactive meant I needed to reset and quickly. Lorna was and always had been loyal to me. She wanted the best for me always. Sometimes, I was short-sighted and didn't see it but I knew the truth.

When Blue and I broke up, I tried to shield the happenings from her, but she knew. It wasn't until years later that I told her everything that happened. Of course, she said she knew he wasn't the one for me. And vowed that if she ever saw him on the street, she'd run over him with her car or the church van. When I was silent, Lorna took a breath and continued with her sentiments.

"Look, long story short, look at his reappearance as the permission you needed to move forward. It's time to get back out there again."

You know she's right; it's beyond time!

"Now I'm not telling you who to choose or move on to."

Of course you wouldn't…not you, Lorna!

"However, there is a man with a sweet baby who's waiting for you. What happened the day you got sick?"

Not wanting to tell Lorna about the abortion, I stayed silent. She took my silence as a cue to move on and continued her story.

"By the way, (DJ) he's so cute. I saw him on that FaceTime thing. He calls me Lor-Lor, and he's my DJ, such a sweet boy. I just know—…"

Palm to face, why is she FaceTiming people? How does she know about that…note to self: take Lorna's phone.

"He's being patient with you whether you see it or not. But don't expect him to be patient and available forever. You know that heifer at the gym is just waiting to prance on him."

How did she? Never mind! Ok, conversation over!

"Thank you, Lorna, I mean, mother. I appreciate it, receive it, and will consider it. I will."

"That's all a mother can ask from her daughter. Love you, bye."

Lorna was a whole trip. She got on my nerves, but I wouldn't trade her for the world. The only time I really thought about Dolph, that I cared to mention, was when she brought him up. Which was every time we talked. We hadn't seen each other since he left my house. But part of me was glad Lorna kept up with him. He was truly a man of his word and treated her with respect, so what else could I say or do? Respect their relationship and leave it alone.

Too bad we couldn't work out.

If Lorna had already adopted his son, then he was really in the family now. She didn't like other people's kids; she mostly tolerated them, especially boys. She felt they were smelly and would create booger motifs around her house. I don't know where that idea came from. However, she liked 'DJ', so that meant he was set for life.

Maybe you should…Nope! Things to do, Doc, clients in 30 minutes.

Shaking myself back into reality, I prepared for my appointment. As I mentally tried to center myself, I couldn't stop thinking about him.

Focus, Sasha…we need to!

"FUCK!!!" I let out my frustration and scrapped the centering exercise. I picked up my phone and clicked the number. It rang a few times, as I was about to hang up then the call connected.

"We need to talk, see you at 7:00 pm tonight. Don't be late."

When I hung up, I felt relieved. I needed that to happen. I was exhausted more than I cared to say. Now was the time to revamp and reset. This was the first step.

Chapter 12

"You got this, Sasha. It's been a long time coming, and now it's finally here. We are more than ready for whatever happens on the other side of this conversation."

I sat in my truck and prepared myself to exit. I could see him waiting for me in the distance. He looked so nervous but also calm. His hands were placed behind his back as he mumbled to himself. Almost as if he were practicing his words. At 6:59:59 pm, I got out of my truck and made my way towards him. I walked with confidence and pride; I was ready. It was time. It was now or never. When he saw me, he smiled and extended his arms so I could embrace him with a hug.

"Babe, you made it. Thank you so much for coming."

Blue smiled and breathed as if he was relieved by my presence. I didn't respond but kept my hands behind my back.

"Tell me you at least got some words for me," he said, then bent slightly to see what was concealed behind my back, "And not just the flowers I gave you earlier."

I handed him the flowers, but when he didn't take them, I set them on the picnic table behind him. I didn't come to reunite with Blue but to finally let him go. Along with anything else that belonged to him, which included the flowers.

"Can we at least sit down, talk a bit, babe?" I sat down on one side of the bench, and he sat on the opposite side. "Look, Sash…"

"Before you say anything, Blue, let me go first. Please."

He nodded, then waited for me to finish.

"Thank you for coming today. I didn't know I needed to see you until I saw you today."

Blue wasn't sure if he should be honored or not, so he waited for me to finish.

"I spent days, nights, weeks, months…a lot of years trying to heal from what happened with you. I know you already apologized and went through your spill of why you concealed that you were married. But truthfully, none of that made me feel better. It further twisted the knife you left in my heart. But all that's done now. I've finally healed, and I'm so much better now than ever before. Every day, I wake up and I marvel at the woman you see before you. A woman who is truly living her best life, loving, breathing, and living with true happiness. So, if you feel like you need to apologize or say anything to relieve yourself from the past…don't. Those words are for you, not me. I've already moved on; there's no need to talk about the past or the future. I don't drink Kool-Aid anymore; these days, I pop champagne and expensive cognac. So, with that said, I have to go. Peace. Blessings. Love. Healing. Wish you the best as always."

Blue just stared at me, as if he didn't believe it was over. However, I walked away. Blue followed me, then started talking as we walked.

"Sasha, I'm divorced. I've been for years. I went to counseling; I did the work, too, babe. I finally got my life together. I'm ready to give you everything you deserve and more. Just please stop walking away from me. Give me a chance."

I didn't stop walking but slowed up. Blue grabbed my hand to hold it, but I moved it from his reach. He pinched the end of his nose but then stopped me.

"Look, I tried to make things right a while ago, but you didn't answer my calls. I called Lorna last week and she hung up on me. But not before telling me a few non-church lady words and that she already had a son and a grandson. What that mean? What, you dating a nigga with a kid or something?" Blue laughed at his remarks.

Ha! The one thing Lorna failed to mention while going on with her Dolph rants! How funny. Bet he wished he didn't make that call.

It was then that I couldn't have been prouder of Lorna for opening her big mouth. For once, it had done me some good. Right as I was about to respond, a toddler came running past with his father in tow. He smiled and laughed as they were engaged in a game of chase. When his father scooped him up, he squealed and smiled, showing a mouth full of teeth. His father kissed his cheek and ushered the baby towards a woman who waited for them. When they reached her, the father and son kissed her cheek, and they all smiled at each other. I was so wrapped up in the couple and child; I forgot Blue was there and awaited a response.

"So, you gonna answer my question or not, Sasha. You dating someone?" Blue said with a bit of frustration.

"Look, Blue, it doesn't matter what I'm doing or not. That's none of your concern, now, nor will it be EVER AGAIN."

"Can you just answer the question, please?" Blue said a bit calmer.

"If Lorna said it, then it must be so. Hell, she knows everything. Plus, you know she doesn't just claim anyone, so take a hint." I continued towards my car, and Blue followed.

"Sasha, that ain't even you, nor your style. What can a dude with a kid offer you that I can't? Hell, I ain't even got no kids. But we can change that as soon as…"

Having had enough of his arrogant, disrespectful attitude, I turned to Blue one last time so I could leave.

"So, he got a kid, what does that matter? He's the sweetest, kindest, sincerest guy I've ever met. You know what, until today, I've been depriving myself of being with him because I couldn't see him. Nope, let me stop lying…I was afraid to see him because I was afraid, I wouldn't be good enough for him…them. And another thing, if that baby is half as handsome and charming as his daddy, then I'm already sold. I'd take them all day, every day before I ever considered taking you back."

"Please, Sasha, you ain't ready to be no one's momma. You always dreamed of being in St. Barts, shopping, and living it up after your weight loss. Well, you accomplished that shit finally, damn shame to give that shit up now to play mommy to some brat."

That was a dagger; he definitely didn't have to bring my weight into it. When Blue and I dated, I was 75lbs heavier than I am now. With all the stress of life, our relationship, and my health problems, I could gain weight but losing it was tough.

"Blue, let me tell you something. I am different than you remember. However, losing the weight hasn't changed who I am…that's a lie, it has. I'm better than before, 1000 times better.

I'm that bitch! But I digress. Yeah, I do still want those things and damn it I'll definitely have them. So, I don't care if I gotta strap that baby to my back, get a fancy stroller, or hire a nanny… we're going to those places and more. My man and our baby."

Blue clapped and laughed as I got into my truck. Once I started it, I rolled down the window.

"Good luck with that shit, Mommy/Nanny 911. I know you, Sasha, you gonna be bored and tired of them soon. Your ass will be back!"

I smiled and laughed.

"You might be right or wrong…who knows. But it beats going back to your broke, bullshitting, lying ass. Oh, and by the way, it's Dr. Mommy/Nanny 911, bitch."

I sped off and laughed as Blue stood there watching my taillights.

I had to slow down as I realized I was speeding through the neighborhood. I hit the button on my stirring wheel.

"What would you like to do?" The car replied.

"Call da Negro."

The car responded, "Calling da Negro."

As the phone rang and I prayed he would answer. We hadn't communicated since he sent me the text about us meeting up. But I needed him to answer now. However, it went to voicemail. When the phone chimed, I left a message.

"Dolph, it's Sasha. When you get a chance, call me, please. We…need to talk."

I hung up the phone and hit the call button on the stirring wheel again.

"What would you like to do?" The car replied.

"Call Lorna."

The car responded, "Calling Lorna."

But she didn't respond either.

"Da fuck is everyone at today?" I said, frustrated as the call went to voicemail.

"Lorna, mommy…it's Sasha. I need to know where Dolph is…we need to talk. Call me back, please. Love you, bye."

When I got home, no one had called me back. For the rest of the night, my phone was silent, but my thoughts were loud.

Where are you? What are you doing? I need to tell you I'm ready…I hope it's not too late. I'm ready, Dolph. I'm really ready.

The next morning, my phone rang and woke me up outta my sleep. Still asleep, I reached for it immediately and put it to my ear without looking at who was calling.

"Hello."

"Sasha, it's after 7:30 am and you're still sleeping. Get up, girl. You know Keysha is out of the office today for her appointment."

Keysha was ready to be barefoot and pregnant. So, she and Kyle had an appointment with her doctor.

For once, I wasn't annoyed about Lorna's early morning phone call. I was glad about it. However, she had some explaining to do and my voice reflected as such.

"Mother, could you at least say Good Morning, hello, anything before you start fussing. Did you get my message? Why didn't you answer the phone when I called?"

"Well, look who's lost her manners. Sheesh!"

Lorna was right, my tone was a bit aggressive so I calmed myself. However, I still anxiously wanted answers to my questions.

"I'm sorry, Good Morning, Mother. Oh, happy day!"

"Whatever, doesn't count since I had to tell you."

We both laughed at our running joke.

"But to answer your questions. Yes, I know where he was. And I didn't answer the phone because we were at Bingo last night. He called the numbers since Sista Agnes had bronchitis."

What the entire Fuck! Why didn't I go looking for her, urgh!

I tried not to sound anxious because I wasn't ready to tell Lorna I came to my senses yet. So, I tried to mask my energy with sarcasm as if I didn't care. Which was a damn lie!

"Lorna, he was with you last night. I thought y'all were going to lunch this week or something."

"We were, but he and DJ are going to the Carolinas to visit his grandmother and great-grandmother. So, he came to bingo last night and were going out in a few weeks."

Fuck now I gotta wait a week! Great, just fucking great! Never can be easy with this guy!

I let out a breath, frustrated. "When will he be back?"

Lorna chuckled a bit as she replied matter-of-factly. I knew her ass was smiling and excited that I'd come to senses although I didn't say it. Again, women's intuition.

"Oh, in a week or so. He doesn't get good service there, so he said he would check in sometime soon."

I could hear her satisfaction in my frustration. But I didn't care she earned it.

Great! Out of town and unreachable, just great.

Hearing answers that didn't help my cause but made me tired. When I looked at the clock, I realized I was running extremely late.

"Ok, great, thanks, Mom. I'll call you later today. I need to get going."

"Everything ok, Sasha?" I felt Lorna smiling through her statement. I could have just told her, however, where was the fun in that. I needed to get something outta this. Plus, I knew she had a big mouth and would tell him before I could.

So, I sighed, then responded. "I'm good. Just processing the day. But I'll call you soon. By the way, you have a ride for Saturday, right?"

"Yep, I got a car coming to get me. I'll be dressed to the heavens with my good hat. Earline is gonna press my hair too."

Miss Earline was Lorna's right hand. Where there was one, the other followed.

"Well, great, I look forward to seeing you both. Love you, bye."

I ended the call and stared at the ceiling fan.

He's gone till next week. No service. No contact Sasha. It's ok boo, let's get through this weekend. We will circle back when he comes home. He is coming home and I'll be waiting... for both of them!

After the incident with Blue, I called Dolph for days to say I was sorry for our interaction. For how I acted and to explain my reaction. I'd left several messages, but he never called back. I knew Lorna said he was out of town with bad cell reception. However, I still called; at least he would see my efforts. Maybe that could soften whatever he might have thought or felt, which I was still uncertain about. But I was sure of one thing…I was ready. I just hoped he would take me back.

Chapter 13

The day of the wedding, it was beautiful chaos. Thankfully, the suites for the Bride and Groom were on the same floor as the wedding hall. There were screens to block the views from guests, which was good since things were off to an interesting start.

"I'm the queen, you bitches do as I say." Keysha said as she filled her sister's glass again with champagne. We were all tipsy (some more than others), per Keysha's orders. She was in charge for the day, so we did as she said. I heard the Queen, but I was no jester; someone needed to be sane. So, I moved away from the round of drinks. I also needed to help Keysha not self-destruct her wedding.

"Ok, Queen Keysha, you're right. Pour it up, one last time. But let's chase it with water and some nosh because we want to be sexy and functional so we can cut loose at the reception." Keysha nodded at my request, then put the champagne bottle down. It was like my word took the needle off the record and she sobered up immediately.

"Yeah, someone tripping and falling at my wedding is not the move. Sober up bitches, and I mean now." We laughed at Keysha's drill sergeant attitude as she sat in the make-up chair. She was definitely power hungry, but who could blame her? We all knew it was nerves and excitement. Marrying the love of your life will make anyone crazy.

After her make-up and hair were done, Keysha went from drill sergeant to nervous wreck. On the verge of a meltdown, I took her to a private room to relax her nerves.

"Sasha, it's almost time. Nothing is ready; the girls are all over the place. What if Kyle doesn't show up? I will cut his balls off and shove them down his throat. If he ever..."

Keysha was going off the deep end on some shit that hadn't happened. So, I needed to reel her in quickly.

Wonder where she gets that shit, huh, Doc?

"Key, Keysha…Kyle is going to show up. The girls will get it together. Everything is right on schedule…we have an hour before everything starts. So…what are you panicking about, love? We good. You're beautiful and will be even more polished once you're in this dress. Now you relax. Here's a drink."

We both laughed, and Keysha downed the drink. When she shook off her emotions, I knew she was good.

"Ok, Doc. I'm ready, we're ready…let's do this."

Keysha's mother and sister helped her get ready. Once she was done, she made everyone leave, and I had strict instructions to come for her in 15 minutes.

In the meantime, I was instructed to check on Kyle. Keysha was worried since his Best Man was still MIA. Fully dressed, including hair and make-up, I went down a few doors on the opposite side of the hall and knocked on the door that held the Groom's men. When one of them answered, he sized me up and motioned for me to come in. I entered and found Kyle immediately, while passing the five other men in the room.

"Hey Handsome Groom, I came to check up on you per your Wife's request. You good?"

Kyle was calm, collected, and looked as if he was sure of the decision about to take place within the next hour.

"I'm great, Sash…is she ready? How does she look? Can I at least talk to her, hear her voice?"

His words were like music to my ears. Keysha told me to call her only if he asked. So, I reached into my pocket for my phone. While I found her number, I asked Kyle a question.

"Wait, Kyle, before I hand you this phone. Please tell me your Best Man has appeared!"

Kyle smiled and reached for the phone.

"Yep, he will be here in 10."

Relieved, I handed him the phone and breathed a sigh of relief.

"Hey Key, Key, how are you doing?"

Kyle and Keysha talked for a few minutes, while I stood at the window to admire the city view. We were on the top floor of an expensive hotel. A perfect view of the water, the George Washington Bridge, and the Ferris wheel, lit up in various shades which included white, red, and yellow in honor of Keysha and Kyle. The sun was high, but it would make its way down soon. In time for the vows to be exchanged during the sunset. Today would be perfect, so far it had been nothing less.

"Sash, I'm done."

Kyle broke my thoughts when he spoke and handed me my phone. I smiled and adjusted his tie and pin.

"Perfect. Now I'm off to see the Mrs. I'll see you soon."

Kyle smiled and nodded. I turned to walk away but stopped and faced him again.

"Kyle, I couldn't have picked a better man for our girl. Thank you for making her life complete. I love you both. I also can't wait to be an Auntie, so make that happen soon."

Kyle laughed, "Love you too, Sis. Glad to be a part of the family. Oh, and we about to get on that ASAP, sis."

I headed out the door down the hall. There was a wall that intentionally separated the Bride and the Groom's suites. When I passed the elevator, it opened, but I kept walking. Someone got off and walked in the opposite direction. However, I didn't turn around. My mission was to get everyone in the hall so they could line up and head down the aisle. However, I wouldn't have to do much because the pushy wedding coordinated was on our asses. Consistently straightening or primping each of us in her reach. Every time I passed by her, she asked, "You know what you're supposed to do right? And where is the best man? You are supposed to be walking with him. Does anyone know where he is?"

Each time she asked the same damn questions, I'd nod yes, smile and shrug. She'd get frustrated all over again. Then her mood changed instantly as if she'd come back to life.

"Good, I don't have to worry about you. If you gotta walk by yourself, just strut your stuff beautifully. Glad you ain't like these other drunk heifers, barely functional and drunk! If one of them falls, keep me near the cross." Then she'd swipe my hair as if it was out of place before she moved on.

She had one more again to ask me that shit. And, if she touched my hair one more damn time it was about to be a problem.

Trying to stay calm, I began avoiding her.

Keysha and Kyle decided to take the nontraditional route and do something unorthodox by walking down part of the aisle together. Everyone else in the bridal party would walk down together before them, the last people being the best man and maid of honor, the Groom, and then the Bride. Kyle would wait for her at the end of the aisle while Keysha was escorted by her Father and Stepfather. That was something different but special, it would allow them to take their walk to the altar together, of course, after her fathers agreed to give her away.

When everyone lined up in the now screen-split hallway, Keysha requested that I stay with her until it was my time to walk. She was almost nervous yet excited.

"Key, you look amazing, love. I can't believe this is finally happening."

I adjusted her veil as I tried to move the mandatory long, straightened hair out of my way.

"You look great, too, Sasha. Everything turned out amazing. I can't wait to exchange my vows and then show out at this reception."

I was about to respond, but the music started, letting us know the Bridal Party was beginning to head out.

"It's time, love!"

I smiled at Keysha and lowered her veil.

"Let me head out. See you soon."

I was about to leave, but Keysha grabbed my hand.

"Sasha, wait! There's something I need to say first…before we walk out."

"Key, we don't have time for this love…we have to."

"It's my wedding, they can wait for me. Look, Sasha, you are my best friend and I love you. Hell, you're more than my friend, you're my sister with your bossy ass. But I just wanted to say thank you for all that you've done and been to me. I can't wait for whatever the next part of our journey is, Sis."

I dapped my eyes and attempted not to smear my makeup.

"Key, stop. We got pictures to take. All this sentimental crap is…"

Keysha hugged me tightly, and I did the same. She was my sister; I didn't have siblings, and beyond Robbie, she was closer to me than any biological sibling. Keysha kissed my cheek. When I tried to pull back, he drew me closer.

"You're my sister, Sasha. I just want you to be happy."

I leaned back and checked her face. She smiled with a hint of uncertainty. I was about to ask her for clarification, but the coordinator came in.

"Ok, ladies, it's showtime, let's go."

I smiled at Keysha and walked towards the door.

"Sash…wa…" Before Keysha could finish her statement, I walked away.

There was now also a screen outside the doors of the wedding hall. It kept people in the wedding hall from now seeing into the hallway. The bridesmaids were to enter from one side of the screen and the groomsmen from the other. Then the doors would open and they'd walk down the aisle. Again, this was Keysha's bright ass idea. Yet another "revealing moment". First, it was the masks at the bachelor/bachelorette party; now it was these damn screens. This was stupid as hell, but again, it was her day. I could see a silhouette of a man waiting for the wedding hall doors to open. From behind, he filled out the black suit tailored to fit his body. I stopped by the mirror to adjust my hair and then walked up.

"Ok, maid of honor, hurry, the doors are opening soon. Remember big smiles and happy thoughts." The wedding coordinator hurried my steps.

This bitch is getting on my damn nerves. I'm walking as fast as I can.

As I walked up before even getting to the other side of the screen, he extended his arm as if to cue me to take it. Before I entered the other side, I smiled brightly and imagined a happy thought of smacking the wedding coordinator. Then I walked around the other side.

"You must be the…OMG!"

I couldn't believe it. This was unreal; it couldn't be. I stopped dead in my tracks, not even getting close to the best man. When I looked at the other side of the curtain facing the bride and groom's rooms, I saw Kyle and Keysha checking to see my reaction. They couldn't see each other, but both showed a nervous reaction; the jig was up, and everyone had some fucking explaining to do. The coordinator ushered me closer to the Best Man, which included hooking my arm in his and giving me my flowers. He didn't look at me, but I couldn't take my eyes off him. I turned to address him; however, the doors opened up and I sprang into action. Facing forward, smiling slightly, walking smoothly, while mentally kicking everyone's asses.

We made it down the aisle flawlessly. However, on the inside, I was on the verge of throwing up, and my knees felt weak. How the fuck could this happen? When we got to the end of the aisle, on cue, I curtsied to him and he lifted my left hand, then kissed it. Only then did he make eye contact with me. His kiss was warm, but his eyes were distant. I couldn't get a read on him.

When Kyle came down behind us, he smiled and nodded at Dolph before stopping to wait for Keysha so they could walk to the altar. Dolph quickly went over to straighten something on his tux, and they exchanged a brotherly hug. He whispered something to Kyle, then returned to his place. When it was Keysha's turn, everyone stood and turned in her direction except Kyle. However, he smiled anxiously waiting to see his future wife.

When she and her fathers were right behind Kyle, they stopped. The music lowered, and the preacher asked, "Who gives this woman to this man?" Both Fathers responded, then they kissed her cheeks. It was then that Kyle could turn and view his bride. He immediately cried, and Keysha was already in tears, so they shared a moment. She took Kyle's arm and they walked down to the altar together with her fathers behind them.

As the ceremony got underway, I took Keysha's flowers so she could hold hands with Kyle. I tried to concentrate on the union taking place, but I couldn't help but steal glances at Dolph. He looked in my direction a few times, but his face was straight. Part of me couldn't believe he was here.

If he was the best man…that meant! What the entire fuck!

The more I thought about it, I started to get pissed off. The questions started to fill my head, and frustration started to engulf my spirit.

Had she known him from day one? Did Lorna know? Was this all one big setup? Da fuck is this bullshit? Has everyone been playing me for a damn fool? Not now, Sasha…but we're gonna get some answers, trust and believe!

Remembering it was Keysha's big day, I tried to hide my frustration by smiling; however, my smile was becoming an angry glare. I kept mentally recentering myself throughout the ceremony, which included my facial expression. Before I knew it, the preacher was announcing the bride and groom. The ceremony, from what I paid attention to, was beautiful; everything from the vows to jumping the broom reflected the love between Kyle and Keysha. When the ceremony concluded, it was time to walk back down the aisle again. Dolph and I fell in line and walked up the aisle arm in fucking arm. As we walked, in the 3rd pew, there was Lorna and Miss Earline.

Of course, she knew he would be here. Lorna knew everything.

When Dolph saw Lorna, he smiled as she blew a kiss towards him, and Miss Earline snapped our picture. Of course, we both smiled, only his was genuine, and mine was a fake, sarcastic smile in response to their makeshift mother-son relationship and the fiasco of our interactions.

Urgh, can't get up this aisle fast enough. What else don't I know…Apparently, I don't know shit!

When we made it to the end of the aisle, I let him go immediately and headed in the opposite direction from him.

Dolph didn't say anything; he began to converse with people around him.

I went to the bathroom and composed myself and returned to the hallway where everyone was now gathered. We stood on separate sides of the wall. We didn't even look in each other's direction, just waited for the newlywed Mr. and Mrs. Miller. When Kyle and Keysha were in our vicinity, I put on my best smile and hugged them both.

"Congratulations, Miller's."

Kyle hugged me immediately, then Keysha. She held me close and whispered to me. Her voice sounded weary, almost unsure about my reaction.

"Thanks, Doc. Are you…"

"Not, now, Key, let's just get through these pictures and the rest of this day."

Keysha nodded and smiled as I kissed her cheek. She had nothing to worry about. I'd never ruin her day, but she was gonna hear this shit later, that was a promise.

Chapter 14

After a few pictures in the wedding hall, we all headed back to our respective rooms to prepare for the reception. Before the reception, everyone agreed to meet in the groom's suite to enjoy refreshments while the guests attended the cocktail hour and were seated. Being anywhere near the gathering was the last thing I wanted to do, knowing I'd run into Dolph. So, I took my time getting to the Groom's suite. Thank goodness, the hotel rooms were on a separate floor than the hall. I could at least be away from guests and other annoyances for a moment.

Arriving at my suite, it felt good to close the door behind me and be alone for once. Although it would be short-lived since Keysha was enroute, so I could help her get into her reception dress. Plus, I knew Sarye and Monet were coming as well. So, I decided to get comfortable. The suite was large enough for at least 5 to 6 people. It consisted of two bedrooms, two bathrooms, a living room, a dining area, and a breathtaking view of the water and local scenery. However, it was mine alone. And I couldn't wait to get back to relax and do nothing, ALONE.

I immediately abandoned my shoes and skirt, leaving on the top of my bridesmaid's dress and putting on some cut-off jean shorts. I plugged in my flat iron and checked my makeup in the mirror. The bathroom in the master suite had a large glass shower, tub, private toilet, and huge vanity. As I admired the white porcelain and tan marble décor, my excitement to return to my suite increased. This reception couldn't be over fast enough.

When I heard a knock on the suite door, I knew it was Keysha since she had texted, she was on the way. So, I headed to the front door, opened it, and walked away. I returned to my bathroom and started to flat-iron my hair. Keysha still hadn't said anything, but neither did I. Part of me wanted to wait to interrogate her, but I needed at least some answers now. So, I just started talking loudly from the bathroom.

"Umm, I know it's your wedding day and all…but when were you gonna tell me Dolph was the best man. We're not gonna get into all the specifics today, but ummm, you could have given me a heads-up, Key. Like, way before we were about to walk down the aisle. Don't get all silent Bob on me now, let that shit out."

When there was no response, I stopped doing my hair to check on her. I tried but failed at being calm in my tone; I worried I'd hurt her feelings or that she was crying. I couldn't be a complete asshole on her day.

When I stepped outside the bedroom, he was leaning against the wall.

Oh fuck! Not Key…sha

"Real smart opening the door and walking away, Sasha."

Really dude!

I folded my arms and waited for him to speak. However, Dolph just stared at me as if I owed him an explanation.

After a few moments, when neither of us had spoken, I broke the ice. I wouldn't yell or scream at Keysha. However, he would get a taste of my frustration because his ass owed me an explanation as well. So, I came closer to him and stood in front of him so we could truly be eye to eye. Being in his space, my hands began sweating, so I crossed my arms and held my elbows so I could speak confidently.

"Look, Randolph, I know you're mad…at least I think you are. You haven't called me back, so I'm guessing you are. Which is fine, I can respect it. But I need you to know some things…in reference to what happened the last time we were…you were at my house. But I also need you to clear some other things up."

As I spoke, my thoughts and words failed me. My frustration reflected nerves, causing me to stumble and extend them.

Epic fail, Sasha. You should have let him speak first. Good job, Doc!

Dolph still didn't say anything, just leaned his back against the wall and waited for me to speak again.

"Dolph, I…"

Before I could finish, the door to my suite opened and the ladies came in talking loudly.

"Doc!!! We here, girl!" Sarye yelled as I heard them bringing items through the door.

There was a slight hallway before entering the living area of the suite, so they couldn't see Dolph and me standing on the other side of the wall in the living/dining room area near the entrance.

"Yeah, where you at, boo. We need to talk about that fine MF who walked..." Monet yelled but stopped when she saw us. "Oh shit...my bad." She smiled and nodded, which prompted Sarye and Keysha to come see what she was looking at.

When Dolph saw Keysha, his expression finally changed. He smiled at her and the other ladies.

"Hey, Dolphie, I'm so glad you made it. You scared me when Kyle said you might not come." Keysha swatted at him and gave him a hug.

Did she just call him Dolphie? How well does she know this dude?

He hugged her tightly and chuckled.

"You know I wasn't gonna miss my cousin's big day. Me and Kyle been tight since we was youngins. That's my brotha, and you definitely my sis now."

Oh really now...fucking family reunion around this bitch! Oh, I got something for both of them.

I guess my thoughts reflected my face. I nodded and frowned at the interaction between Keysha and Dolph. Keysha's face was remorseful as she knew she had some explaining to do. Dolph glared in my direction before he addressed Sarye and Monet with a smile.

"Hi, ladies, I'm Kyle's cousin, Dolph. It's nice to see you all again."

Oh, these heifers were in on this shit, too! Bet!

I looked at Sarye and Monet, who looked confused, then at Dolph clarified.

"We met at the bachelorette party. I was the gentleman with the full mask on with the lights on it."

He was the damn masked mystery man from the tents. Another fucking plot twist.

I shook my head and walked away. Every time I thought I knew something, I didn't know shit. I walked to the window to look at the view while everyone else talked. The ladies nodded and discussed how they met him at the party. Kyle introduced them to Dolph before they left the party. He never took off his mask, but the ladies were intrigued that he had a mask that disguised his voice. I was no longer in the "reunion mood", so I returned to the group with the intentions of asking everyone to leave once Keysha was in her reception dress.

"Oh shit, we took a bet that you were ugly or some shit, that's why you had that mask. Damn, I lost $5.00." Monet said, then handed Sarye some bills from her purse.

Everyone laughed, but I didn't. As I was stuck since a lot had happened in the past few minutes.

Everyone around me has known about him all along. How the hell? Keysha, Lorna, Kyle…he's been everywhere. Yet, I feel like I don't know shit about him.

As my thoughts continued, I kept looking left and right as if I was putting all the pieces together. When I noticed everyone looking at me, I snapped out of it.

"Umm…Sash, you good, boo?" Monet asked, unsure of what my reaction would be.

Before I responded, I took a breath and smiled. I intended to remain calm, but my frustration took over as I turned my attention to Dolph and Keysha.

"So, was lunch planned too?"

No one responded.

"So, Key was he the 'date' when y'all tried to hook me up? What was he a swap out? Is that how I got stuck with…"

Still no response.

"So, let me back up even further…was it a coincidence that you showed up at the gym when we first met? Oh, let me guess, the lunch date was part of y'all's plan too?"

Still no response.

"Oh, and let's not forget what happened in the tent?"

Monet mumbled to Sarye, "What happened in the tent?"

Dolph never changed his face or stance, but Keysha looked sad and was on the verge of crying.

"Never mind, forget that. Was Lorna in on this, too?" I tried to regain my composure, as this was Keysha's day. However, their silence was not helping my mood.

Monet was invested, her face displayed her trying to put together the pieces. When she finally caught on, she yelled. "Yo, this is throw up, bae? Get the fuck outta here."

Sarye tried not to laugh, and even I shook my head. This was a hot ass mess, but the comment helped lighten the mood some. Dolph frowned, unsure what she meant until he caught on, then he shook his head as well. Tears came rolling down Keysha's face, which made my heart break. This was her day, and she shouldn't be sad, only crying tears of joy.

"Sash…I'm sorry I didn't tell you." Keysha sniffled as tears fell from her eyes.

Damn her tears! Now I can't be mad, urgh! Now I gotta console her crying ass.

"Keysha, relax. I'm not mad, we good for now."

Keysha wasn't buying it, so I handed her some tissues and pulled her close to hug her.

"For real, all is well, Key. I'm just a little caught off guard."

As I rubbed her back, Keysha rested her head on my shoulder. Dolph rubbed his forehead, then the back of his neck, before he spoke up.

"Look, I'ma get outta here let y'all talk. Nice meeting you, ladies."

Dolph made his exit and didn't even wait for me to respond. But he wasn't getting off that easily. We still had unfinished business, and I wanted to say my peace now.

"Rye, give me your key. I'll be right back, ok."

Sarye handed me her key, and I rushed out the door.

Dolph was halfway to the elevator when I entered the hallway. Not caring about making a scene, I yelled down the hall to get his attention.

"Hey! We not done yet."

He turned around and looked at me as I headed in his direction. When I got closer to him, I grabbed his hand and led him to Sarye's room. I unlocked the door and motioned for him to go inside. Once we entered, he went to the desk chair and sat down while I sat on the bed.

"Look, Sasha…"

"Just stop. I didn't get to finish what I was about to say. After I speak my peace, you can say what you need to."

Dolph leaned back in his chair and waited.

"You've had the upper hand all this time, Dolph. In everything, from how we met, interacted, everything. I was left in the dark about everything. I didn't get a choice in anything, how is that fair? I feel like you played me or something. What was your plan exactly? You came into my life, got all comfortable with my people, who apparently you already knew."

He didn't say anything.

"You know everything there is to know about me, and yet I know nothing. Or feel like I know nothing. Like I've been led around under your spell or whatever you call this bullshit you pulled on me."

Dolph took a breath and pinched the bridge of his nose.

"You want me to just accept you, your world, and whatever comes with you just because you say so…how am I supposed to trust you or just give in to your requests when I don't even know you."

"Because you know your people, Sasha. It ain't rocket science. It's called falling in love and trusting the other person to catch you."

"Falling in love, Randolph, are you serious?"

Negro please! Only thing I'd love is to smack the shit outta you for this mess.

When his stance didn't change, I knew he was serious. This was deeper than I imagined, which didn't make things any better.

"The last time I did that you're talking about, I ended up heartbroken because some guy who was already married he wanted to sell me on a dream that was never going to come true. You're running around here practically doing the same thing with this façade of love or whatever you call yourself doing. This is bullshit, I deserve better than this."

As I spoke, a few tears came down my face. I wiped them quickly and tried to keep my frustration at bay. This speech was not going the way I planned. I'd gotten completely off topic; if anything, it was becoming heated and not in a good way. I felt myself getting angry as I thought about all that had happened.

"First, what does what he did got to do with me? I been trying to show you who I am. However, you're so busy with your internal bullshit that you can't even see me. So, the question is, why are you running around acting like you're ready for love? You are constantly pushing it away. Why? Is it because it doesn't look like what you 'envisioned' or some other bullshit? Looks like you are wearing the façade, Sasha, not me. So, why even waste my time, huh?"

Damn, he got you there.

What was the point? I didn't have one at this point. So, I was about to get up to leave, but Dolph wasn't done and continued.

"And let's be clear, I ain't married. All I got is a baby, which I told you about up front. But for some reason that's a problem for you…you've made that clear on more than one occasion."

Fuck it…time to come clean since we are here!

This was not the conversation I wanted to have, nor how I wanted to have it. However, here we were, and it was no turning back. I took a breath and, in a calmer tone, I responded to Dolph.

"Your son isn't and hasn't ever been a problem."

"Bullshit, Sasha, you keep saying one thing then…"

Dolph waved me off and sat back in the chair, further calling bullshit on my statement.

"I had an abortion, Dolph. I fucked up my chance to have what you already have. An amazing little baby who calls me to tell me he's watching TV or just to hear my voice. So, yeah, that day at my house, I had to turn away because it was still fresh. I didn't want you to see me fall apart over the decision I made on one wreck less night with an asshole who pretty much told me to kick rocks when I told him I was pregnant. So, there you have it. It was never about you being a father to DJ. I respect the shit outta you for that. He sounds like an amazing little boy; Lorna seems to love him, and she don't even like kids. Her ass barely likes me. But I digress."

I checked my watch, and it was almost time to go. So, I wrapped up my speech.

"Look, I don't even know what else to say about this or whatever the fuck has happened. It doesn't matter anyway; we gotta go, time for the reception." I stood up and headed towards the door.

"So, that's it, Sasha? You don't have nothing else to say?"

Without turning around, I replied.

"No, RAN-Dolph, I don't. Today ain't the day for this bullshit anyway. Let's just get through the rest of this day."

I headed out the door as his footsteps followed me. I went back to my room, and the ladies and I got ready to head down to the reception.

After meeting the requirement for us to enter the reception hall together. Dolph and I stayed on separate ends of the room, the rest of the reception. We didn't interact or make much eye contact. While everyone mingled together, we mingled separately. We were in a few pictures together, but always with other people. When I saw him talking to Lorna or Kyle, or Keysha, I stayed away. If we happen to be talking to anyone in proximity to each other, I found a reason to exit.

On the dance floor, we danced with other people, far from each other. Just to be petty, I made sure to dance with all the men who approached me. Including a groomsman who danced a little too close to me while Juvenile's *Back That Thang Up* played. But who could blame him? I was doing as the song stated. However, I noticed my dancing with this one particular gentleman seemed to piss Dolph off as he kept making annoyed faces in our direction. So, I danced with him the longest, four songs to be exact. The gentleman caught on to Dolph's mood, which caused him to smile harder, which pissed Dolph off even more.

When it was time to prepare the suite for the newlyweds' first night together, I went alone. This was supposed to be the responsibility of the maid of honor and the best man, but I didn't care. Sarye offered to help, but I declined as I needed the time alone. I missed the bouquet and garter toss, but the time alone was worth it. Monet caught the bouquet, and the Groomsman I danced with caught the garter. Apparently, she got felt up and he got a date for later, so both were happy.

By the end of the night, I was exhausted, but my mission was complete, and the day had gone off flawlessly, almost. When the reception was officially over, I was beyond glad. I rushed to go upstairs to shower, enjoy my two pieces of prepackaged cake, and watch trash TV while continuing to enjoy my time ALONE. There was one more event the next day, the bridal party brunch. Then I'd be rid of my duties and would be free until check-out time on Monday.

On the way to the elevator, I slid past family and friends corralling in the lobby, hoping no one would stop me. I was almost home free when a voice spoke behind me.

"You could have waited for me or let me know you were going to decorate the room. I would have helped you, Sasha."

Without turning around, I spoke nonchalantly.

"No biggie. I enjoyed the time alone. Now I'm going to do it all over AGAIN. Too bad you won't do the same since this is your family reunion or WHATEVER!"

When the doors to the elevator opened, I rushed in and closed the doors, not even looking in Dolph's direction. He managed to slip in a few words before the door closed.

"Yeah, whateva, Sasha."

I was glad that was over; at least I'd be rid of him and anyone else for the rest of the night. Sarye would be entertaining Curtis. Keysha would be making me a Godmother. Lorna's ass went home, thank goodness. Monet mentioned she may drop by, but given that she'd found a new friend, I was sure she'd likely be busy. Everyone was accounted for, and I was glad for it.

When I got to my room, I immediately took off my shoes and slid on my slippers. I rushed off to the bathroom to use it. Then I mentally prepared to take my shower. Getting out of this princess dress was going to be one of the highlights of my evening. Thank goodness this was a one-time thing; it was surely going to Goodwill or someone's donation box asap. When I came out of the bathroom and prepared to undress, I heard a knock at my door. Part of me wanted to ignore the door, hoping the person had the wrong room, but when there was another more aggressive knock, I knew I couldn't not answer it.

Dragging my feet and my patience along, I grumbled as I made my way to the door.

"Urgh, who is it? I'm over people today."

I swung open the door without looking through the peephole.

I know you fuckin' lying!

"That's the second time today you didn't check the peephole or ask who was at the door and just opened it," Dolph said as he walked past me with his bag in his hand.

I know he lost cause umm…Sir!

I stood with the door open for a second as if he was coming right back. I leaned outside the door to check my room number because clearly one of us made a mistake. But it wasn't me. When he didn't come back, I stood a few more seconds, almost dazed.

"You can close the door; I'm not going back out."

Was he serious? Umm…why is he here? We just spent the past couple of hours avoiding each other. And I said my peace…yet here he is again! Fuck!

I huffed, closed the door, and walked into the living room area. Dolph was sitting on the sectional sofa, rummaging through his bag. Feeling annoyed and slightly disrespected, I addressed Dolph and his presence in my room.

"Umm…can I help you, Sir? You realize this is my suite…the living room, dining room, bedrooms, bathrooms, fruit basket on the table, mini bar, decorative soap, shampoo, conditioner…all mine, that I paid for." I put my hand on my chest to further emphasize my point.

Dolph grunted as if I was bothering/annoying him. He looked up from his bag and made eye contact with me.

"Yeah, yeah, yeah, I know all that. The hotel is booked because of the wedding, so I need a place to stay."

He returned his attention to his bag, continued pulling out his toiletries and his lounge attire as if it was nothing. I folded my arms and leaned over the sofa further as if to get his attention.

"Umm…hello again! Is there something I'm missing? Apparently, you got family and other people you know here…but you came to my suite. How interesting. Can't you stay with one of them? Better yet, ain't the bride's suite available? Keysha staying in Kyle's room. So…."

Dolph grunted again and stood up along with his things, for the shower.

"I could, but why would I do that?"

I can tell you $450 a night worth of reasons, why you could….

Appalled, I was about to tell him how and why he could, but he spoke up again.

"Look, Sasha, it's been a long ass day. All that you are attempting to say or not say, just don't. I'll take the shower over here."

Dolph got up and walked past me into the spare room and closed the bathroom door. I stood stuck.

Did he just invite himself to not only my suite but the shower and to spend the night? He never answered my question about the bridal suite. He never gives a damn about what I say; he just gets comfortable, and I gotta suck it up. Does he listen to anything I say, EVER!

When Dolph came out of the bathroom, he was partially dressed in an undershirt with a towel around his waist. I still stood in the same spot as before. Still dressed, arms still folded, still pissed. Again, he walked past me and shook his head before he returned to his bag.

"So, you gonna stay in that princess dress all night? I mean, it's nice." Dolph stopped and shook his head, then spoke again. "Fuck it…it's really not, but you make it look somewhat cute. But, I'm sure it's uncomfortable by now."

Dolph grabbed his suit bag and put his clothes inside. Then he put his things away in the front closet. As he moved, I just watched him, still frowning. Before returning to the sectional, he stopped behind me.

"Here, let me help you."

He pulled the string to my top, which was the second part of why I was still in this dress. I instantly let out a breath as Keysha insisted on stuffing me into the top. My plan was to cut the string and pray it fell to shreds, but this worked too.

"Now, can you please go shower and change so we can relax. And before you say anything else, please don't, Sasha. Let's put the bullshit aside for tonight, please and thank you."

Bullshit, this is your damn fault, Sir! And here we go again with that WE shit! Why does he insist on believing he is spending the night? And did he just shush me? Why has he not considered the bridal suite? The shit is free! What the hell, urgh!

I didn't say a word; I just went to my room and slammed the door.

"Can you also change your attitude before you come back out, too! Ain't nobody trying to deal with that shit and pay for shit because you are having a tantrum." Dolph yelled from the living room. I could have run into the living room and give him a front row seat to my damn tantrum. However, it wasn't worth it, so I decided I'd ground myself in the shower. Have a whoosah moment; hopefully, the water and cleanliness would help rejuvenate my tired spirit and pissed off attitude.

When I finally got into the shower, it felt like life. All the preparation, duties, and bullshit of the day fell off me. I closed my eyes and stuck my face under the water. It felt so good I could have fallen asleep. However, I needed to resolve a few things about the happenings of my evening, which now included Dolph. First, he wasn't leaving, so I could give up on that. Second, he didn't care about my little speech earlier, which was his "walking papers." He metaphorically tore them up and torched them in my face when he walked into the suite with his shit in hand. Third, I was exhausted with no more fight in me for today. Even if I had to spend the entire night in my room alone, I'd survive because his ass was gone tomorrow. I'd still get my night alone one way or another. However, I still planned on saying my peace to him, Keysha, and Kyle's ass soon. Tonight, I'd let I go so I could decompress and rest, just me and my cake, fuck Dolph.

He'd better not ask for none because I'm not sharing, damn it.

Still enjoying the water on my face, I felt a cool breeze, which let me know the bathroom door was open. I opened one eye with my head still under the sprayer.

You've got to be kidding me! Why didn't I lock the door? Fuckity, Fuck, Fuck!

"Sasha!" Dolph yelled as he entered the bathroom with something in his hand. He didn't look up but focused on the object he possessed.

Of course, he came to interrupt my shower. Why not? He's comfortable. He might as well see me naked, or better yet, invite himself in. He welcomed himself everywhere else; what's the point of hiding now?

Not responding immediately, I removed my face from the sprayer and wiped my eyes.

"Randolph! You're in my bathroom while I'm in the shower, naked."

Dolph didn't say anything; he just looked up, nodded, then looked back at the object. Seeing he was unmoved, I huffed and continued.

"…how can I help you, Sir?" I mumbled, slightly annoyed.

"I'm about to order some wings and fries. So, we can watch the fight. You want something else?"

Who said I even like boxing? The only boxing I was interested in was him boxing his shit up and leaving. And now he's ordering room service, of course, he is. He'd better have some damn money. Freeloading ass!

When I thought about it, the reception food had worn off, and now I was starving.

Fuck it, I'd indulge this part of Dolph's game for a bit.

"Make mines all flats, if they can. Please have them fried hard. Also, ask them to make the fries fresh. Oh, can you add a ranch, and do they have honey lemon pepper?"

Dolph looked at the menu before he replied.

"Yeah, they have it. I'll order it now, so when you get dressed, it should be here."

He was about to leave and close the door, but not before he said one last thing.

"Glad you're over your salmonella phase."

I sucked my teeth and rolled my eyes. He added one last thing before he left.

"Throw up, bae? That's some funny shit."

Dolph chuckled, and I shook my head.

"Whatever, Ran-DOLPH! And thank you."

"You welcome, babe."

He closed the door, and I returned my face to the water.

Get on my damn nerves, and why does he insist on calling me babe? I didn't agree to that shit. But what had I agreed to? The answer is nothing! He just does whatever, urgh. It's all going to be fine, Sasha, just get your food and come back to your room and close the door, and this time, lock it.

When I finished my shower, I got dressed in a navy-blue, pin-striped, oversized night shirt. I tied a scarf around my head and put on my furry slippers. When I entered the living room area, Dolph was sitting on the sofa with his head back, eyes closed, with his arms spread across the top of the sofa. The food had not arrived yet. So, I sat on the opposite side of the sectional.

When I sat down, he lifted his head and looked in my direction.

"Feeling better?" He asked as he yawned while looking in my direction.

"Yep, much better."

I put my feet under me as I got comfortable. I planned to engage in small talk while we waited for the food, then I'd ghost his ass.

"Why you sit all the way over there. You can't even see the TV really good. Come sit with me."

Now he's pushing it. We are only cordial at most, Sir. You better not, Sasha!

"Sasha, can you stop all that internal dialogue and just come sit with me, please!"

He doesn't know us or the voices in our head. Bet Lorna told him I did that... she's a snitch for real.

Sucking my teeth, I didn't respond; I just got up and sat on the cushion next to him.

"Nah, closer man, this ain't our first time, let's cut the shit."

I slid closer to him, and he put one of his arms around my waist. Then I leaned my head on his shoulder.

"That's better."

Sucker! He got you now! Enjoy your night with Dolph, Doc!

He kissed my temple and cradled me even more. It was nice to just settle in and relax. I was exhausted, although I planned to be alone, this was nice and what I needed, apparently.

After a few minutes, the food arrived, and I moved to get the door. However, Dolph motioned for me to relax.

"Nah, you ain't dressed for company. I got this."

I couldn't help but laugh; he was really playing house tonight. We weren't together, and still, he was insistent that another person not see me "unproperly dressed." When he came back with food, he set it on the coffee table in front of the sectional. Everything was fresh and piping hot. I grabbed a pillow off the sofa and tossed it on the floor and slid onto it.

"So, we're sitting on the floor to eat dinner?" Dolph said, looking at me from the sofa.

Laughing at his remark, I replied sarcastically.

"I'm sitting on the floor; you don't have to."

Dolph shook his head and followed my lead, placing a pillow on the floor and sitting down closer than necessary to me.

"How you gonna share your fries if you can't feed them to me?"

I laughed hysterically.

"Umm, Sir, it's three things I don't play about my money, my business, and my food, specifically my flats and fries."

"Sasha, we've already been through this…you gotta learn to share. So, you gonna come up off them fries and some of them flats."

I laughed and shook my head, then he spoke again.

"Besides, your list is a bit out of order."

I pondered for a second, then he said, "It's God; your man, money, business, food."

He had a point, but of course, I couldn't just let him have one, so I responded.

"Dolph, I can agree with adding God first. However, I don't have a man, but I do have money and a few businesses."

He laughed, then got closer to my face, as he smiled.

"The night in the tent, all that changed…I touched it, so it's mine."

Then he kissed my cheek. We both smiled at the memory. The bachelorette party was a turning moment for us, even though I had no idea it was him. When I didn't say anything, Dolph prayed, and we started eating. He turned on the pre-show for the boxing match while we ate. For a while, there was nothing but silence between us as we devoured our food.

"How's your food, babe?"

I rolled my eyes and then responded.

"It's really good…everything is cooked to perfection."

He nodded, "Cool, can I have one of those wings and some fries?"

I laughed again because he, too, had wings and fries. However, his wings had buffalo spice rub on them.

"Dolph, you have your own wings and fries."

He turned his face towards me and waited for me to give in. So, I lifted a single fry from my container and handed it to him.

"Nope, feed it to me."

He was pushing it, but again I gave in. I fed him a few fries, and he smiled while he acted like mine were better than his. When it came to the chicken wing, I made him pick his own. I drew the line at holding it and waiting for him to bite it. He didn't push back for once; he just said we'd work our way up to that.

Of course, he believed that shit.

"Damn, I should have ordered us some drinks or something."

He was right, a nice mixed cocktail would have been great. We continued eating and watching the pre-show when his phone rang, and he answered it. Dolph continued his conversation while I ate, wishing I now had a mixed drink or two to sip on.

"Hold on."

He pressed the mute button on his phone, then turned his attention to me.

"Hey, babe, the fellas and some of the ladies from the wedding are going to the bar to watch the fight and have some drinks. You wanna go down for a bit? We don't have to…"

"Nah, it's cool. Let's go."

Dolph unmuted his phone and told the groom's man we'd be down in an hour.

After dinner, we both got dressed to go downstairs. I put on a tangerine tube dress and some slides, along with another head scarf around my head, letting the weave flow down my back and shoulders. Dolph had on a white shirt, black shorts, and white socks—the end.

When I added perfume, Dolph chuckled.

"Sasha, we're just going to the bar to have a drink and watch part of the fight real quick. You could have thrown something on."

I laughed, "I know. This is just something I threw on."

Dolph sized me up, "Well, ain't no vacancies around here, let's be clear on that."

Part of me wondered if he meant the hotel room or something else. But I didn't bother to ask. Dolph put on his shoes, and we were out.

While we waited for the elevator, I checked my lip gloss in the mirror in the hall. Dolph watched me from the opposite side of the hall near the elevators.

"They juiced enough, just so you know those belong to me too."

Funny how men get territorial quickly before even asking us to commit to a relationship. When the bell dinged, I turned around to head into the elevator without responding to Dolph's comment. However, he didn't care and grabbed my hand to kiss it as he selected the floor with the bar. This was another pet peeve of mine. But, once again, he didn't care.

At the bar, everyone from the wedding was downstairs, including the bride and groom. The place was crowded, so Dolph stayed close to me (still holding my hand) as we navigated to the back of the bar, where our people were.

"Hey, look who arrived together, the Maid of Honor and Best Man. Where was this unity a few hours ago?" Everyone laughed at Sarye's comment, including us. She winked at me as she sat in Curtis' lap. Sarye made the introduction between Curtis and Dolph. They dapped each other up, and Dolph took a seat next to Curtis while I stood and talked to Sarye.

"Where's Monet?" I asked, not seeing her in the crowd of people.

"Girl is probably getting her garter chewed on. Sash, you missed it, the way them two were showing out on the dance floor after he put that garter on her, you would think they were newlyweds."

I laughed, knowing she wasn't making it up. I just hoped Monet was ok and safe.

When the newlyweds approached us, they both acted like they were about to brace for the impact of my wrath.

"Is it safe to approach?" Kyle asked as Keysha peeked behind him.

"Nope. Get the hell on!"

They both frowned until I laughed, then they both hugged me while Keysha acted like she was going to kiss me.

"Whatever, both of y'all get on my nerves. Get away from me, I don't know what you've been doing. Besides, what y'all doing down here anyway? Letting all my hard work go to waste."

Keysha kissed Kyle and sighed.

"Your hard work wasn't in vain, Doc. We enjoyed some of it a few times before we came down, and definitely going back for more. Thanks to you, there's so much to do and explore."

We all laughed, and Kyle joined the fellas while the ladies talked.

Dolph motioned for me to lean down, and he whispered in my ear.

"What exactly did you do, Sasha?"

I smiled devilishly at him, then replied.

"I gave them the full experience."

He raised his eyebrow as he nodded.

"So, what is that? And how do I get the experience?"

I smiled but didn't respond to his questions. Dolph laughed, then I walked off as Keysha motioned for me to follow her to the bar.

"So, you not mad, Sasha…for real?"

Keysha asked as she leaned her head on my shoulder.

"Key, I'm not gonna lie. I don't know how I feel about all this. It's still fresh and a lot to process. And to be honest, I don't understand it…any of it. But for now, let's not think about it. Let's just enjoy the moment and have some fun. Today is about you and Kyle; everyone is having a good time, so let's just focus on that. Deal?"

Keysha smiled, and we chilled for the rest of the evening. She introduced Sarye and me to her family, and we mingled with other guests. We'd been downstairs for so long that the main event was about to occur. Some people retreated to their rooms, and I wanted to do the same, as I was tired.
I found Dolph in the back of the bar, where I left him with Curtis and Kyle. When he saw me, he got up and approached me.

"Hey, I'm going to head up, kind of tired. But stay, enjoy yourself, you got the key. I'll see you later." I turned to walk away before he could respond. However, Dolph grabbed my hand, then he turned to the fellas.

"Hey y'all, we're about to head up. But I'ma see y'all on them courts in the morning before brunch."

The fellas said their good-byes, and he said, "Lead the way, babe."

Confused, I addressed him, "Dolph, you didn't have to leave. I'm…"

Dolph didn't even respond; he just started walking while still holding my hand. While we waited for the elevator, he turned to face me and addressed me.

"When you go upstairs, I go upstairs. When you go to bed, I go to bed."

I didn't understand his logic, and my face reflected as much.

"Things happen when we go to bed together, Sasha. Fun things. Get used to it."

It was no point in even responding, so I didn't when the elevator doors opened, he moved aside, and I walked in first.

When we finally made it to the room, the main event was just getting started. I headed to my room to change, and Dolph headed to the spare room to do the same. When I came out of the bathroom, back in my night attire, Dolph was in my bed with the fight on. I busted out laughing and just stared at him.

"Dolph, you just have no problem making yourself at home, do you?"

He looked from the TV then at me.

"Nah, we're gonna end up in here anyway so…"

"Oh, was that gonna happen?"

I leaned against the wall and waited for his response.

"Yes, Sasha, now can you please just get in bed so we can get comfortable and watch this fight?" He said it like it was nothing and I was tripping.

I laughed again and cut off the bathroom light and crawled into bed. Dolph immediately pulled me close. As the fight started, he explained what was happening. I didn't watch boxing and had no clue what was happening. However, as the rounds went on, he broke it down for me. We even counted the punches that landed to see who was closer. When the event was done, I found myself a boxing fan.

"That was crazy! Goodness, who knew boxing was so intense? That last two-piece combo took that dude out. Damn." I said as I sat up in bed to stretch my back.

Dolph smiled at my interest and excitement.

"Dang, I'm glad you enjoyed that, babe. Something else we can do together."

Dolph kissed my cheek. I shook my head, then turned back to the TV.

"What, Sasha? Why do you shake your head when I call you babe? What you don't like it?"

I couldn't help but laugh. I didn't know how to explain it. So, I just said it.

"Because, Dolph, you are so comfortable. Like you're in your element and always have been."

Dolph nodded and looked up at me.

"Why shouldn't I be? Yeah, things have been crazy between us, Sasha, but we are where we are supposed to be. That's all that matters, right?"

I didn't have a response and went back to watching TV. However, I could feel Dolph looking at me as he rubbed my leg. When I yawned, he reached for the remote and cut off the TV and motioned for me to lie on the pillow next to him.

"Let's get some rest, babe. Been a long day, got an early start tomorrow for brunch. What are you doing after that?"

Dolph asked as we both got comfortable.

"Not sure yet, I got one more night here. So, I might go to the spa after brunch. Then come back and crawl under my bed, I'm sure. Been a busy weekend."

Dolph nodded as he looked at me while we rested on our pillows. He touched my face, pinching my cheek.

"Yeah, it has. I should take off Monday too, and we can sleep in together."

I rolled my eyes, "There you go again, Mr. Comfortable."

I laughed, and Dolph leaned forward and whispered, "You're right, I am." Then he kissed me, showing me just how comfortable he could get pressing his body against mine. "So, stop fighting it and join me…been long enough, Sasha."

He gripped the small of my back so we were even closer. When he found the slit along my sleep shirt, he caressed my thigh slowly. I couldn't help but let go. Why not get comfortable with the inevitable, which was about to happen?

"I can stop if you want, Sasha."

I leaned my head back just like in the tent, giving him the green light. However, he pulled me forward so we were eye to eye.

"Get on top and give me the full experience, babe."

I smiled and whispered, "And what do you think you know about the full experience, Randolph?"

He glared as if he didn't understand.

"You think you're comfortable now, your ass won't ever leave if I did all the things I think about doing to you while my little boyfriend entertains me."

He smiled and lay flat while putting his hands behind his head.

"Well, in that case, give me the full workup Dr. Carter."

I nodded and leaned forward so we were face to face, then smiled.

"Ok, Dolph, the doctor will see you. Just know I don't have all my tools, so this is a partial experience. But I can definitely make do with what I got."

Dolph raised his eyebrow then smiled. As I smiled back, I finished my statement.

"This time you have to wear the blind fold."

He was hesitant at the request and wanted to resist. However, when I slid my eyeshades over his eyes, he went with it.

"Now, relax, let me do all the work…I mean, you can reply, of course, matter of fact, I'd really like that. Wait right here."

"Sasha, what are you…"

"Shh…it's Dr. Carter, remember. Only words from you are those of pleasure, got it."

Dolph smiled and relaxed while I gathered a few items from the living room. When I got back, I closed the door and turned on my *Big Girls Vybes* playlist. If you don't know what that is, get one. They are perfect for moments just like these. I returned to the bed and straddled Dolph, purposely sitting above his dick. It was waiting and ready. I could hardly contain myself, we'd see if he really stood a chance against Black Vybes.

"So, Mr. Carter, where should we start, hmm?"

"Wherever you choose, Doc, I'm at your mercy."

"Hmmm…I like those words. They make me very happy."

I leaned closer to his ear and kissed it while I spoke into it.

"Keep that same energy you gave me in that tent. I want you everywhere, Dolph. Make me lick it, suck it, take it…make Candy drip her sugar, Daddy."

Dolph went to take his hands down, but I stopped him.

"Nope, take it like a man until it's your turn. Then you can touch and explore whatever you want, got it?"

He growled in disappointment, but that only turned me on.

"That's right, Daddy, let me hear and feel that frustration. It only pushes me to let loose more. Now, where were we, hmm?"

Dolph's breath increased as I licked the side of his face.

"Oh yes, I was about to do something."

I sat up and unbuttoned my night shirt, then hovered back over him. I purposely let my breast rub against him, which caused him to grunt again. Although I had on my bra and panties, he didn't care; the thought alone excited him.

"So, tell me, Dolph, what are you thinking about…remember, don't be shy."

I took a nearby strawberry and ate it while I waited for him to respond.

He cleared his throat and attempted to adjust his position.

"Dr. Carter, I'm thinking about how I'm going to make you pay when it's my turn. I know you're practically naked, and I can't see you, and it's fucking with me. I can't wait to ravage

Candy and watch you devour my dick with those beautiful ass lips."

"Hmm…I like the sound of all of that. I do."

"Fuck a drip, I'm going to make her weep for all the time she spent away from us."

Did he just say what I thought he said? Jackpot!

Looking at the strawberry in my hand, I got an idea.

"Dolph, do you enjoy strawberries?"

He nodded yes. That's all I needed to know. I'd hate him to break out in a rash or hives from what I was about to do.

"Ok, Dolph, open slightly, baby."

He did as he was instructed, I bit the other end of a small strawberry and put my mouth to his. We kissed while strawberry pieces fell between our mouths. When it was done, I decided to try something else. Still kissing him, I took a sliced strawberry and rubbed it all over Candy.

"Ok, Dolph, now open wide, tongue out, baby."

Then I put it between my teeth and fed it to him, purposely rubbing the strawberry up and down his tongue before allowing him to eat it. When he recognized the difference, Dolph lost it.

"Fuck this, babe, that shit tastes good as fuck. Come on, stop teasing me! I need to talk to my Candy now."

He went to move his hands again, but I wouldn't allow it.

"Nope. I'm not done yet. You have to wait for your turn. Keep making me lose my track and I'll stop altogether."

Dolph grunted once more in frustration. His facial expression was not happy, and I was enjoying it, maybe a little too much.

"Now, where was I again?"

Dolph was anxious and replied annoyed.

"You were about to do that shit again, fuck!"

I laughed at his frustration, and he smiled, then spoke a little calmer.

"Babe, can you at least do that shit again? I love the taste of my Candy, Sasha."

Yep, I knew this would happen. One taste and he's hooked!

"Your Candy Dolph?"

I laughed and kissed his lips, but he wasn't laughing.

"Please, I touched it, and she responded. Once I stick my tongue in her and she drips on it, we go together. Once I fuck her, it's a wrap; she's mine. No takebacks. She's off the market and so are you, so what else is there to discuss?"

I laughed; he was so serious and aggressive. It was exciting.

"Oh, yeah, who said you get to do either RAN-Dolph?"

Dolph leaned up but didn't take off his mask.

"I meant what I said last time. Everything is coming off tonight. I'm definitely filling her up, multiple times, and that's just tonight. So, get used to that shit. But don't worry, you'll be getting on board by the end of the night, that's a promise."

I kissed his lips and smiled.

"I was just playing, relax, let me help you back down so we can continue."

His face was still tight as I helped Dolph back onto the pillow.

"Now, let's see what we can do to change that frown to a smile."

I continued to work my way down Dolph's body. Not missing a spot to kiss, bite, or lick. He seemed more relaxed and pleased with how things were going. However, when I reached his boxers, he couldn't take it anymore.

"You gotta let me take this off. I want to see you take it."

I laughed as I eased back off him and sat on the bed.

"Hmm…I could, I really could, but where's the fun in that, Dolph?"

He grunted, "Sash…"

"Aht, ath…"

He corrected his words while he grunted.

"Dr. Carter, come on, babe, I've been waiting to see you take that shit since I met you. Come on, please. At least a peek, fuck."

"Aww…the begging is so sexy, Daddy. But I can't just give in. What are you offering in exchange?"

Dolph frowned and thought about it.

"Shit, tell me what you want…let's make a deal."

I laughed; he was willing to bargain; this was so cute. So, I had to play fair, a little.

"Fine, Dolph, I'll let you take a quick peek. You can watch me suck the tip for ten seconds. Then the blind fold goes back on. Deal?"

Dolph laughed and shook his head nope.

"Nah, I want to see the whole thing. What I'm supposed to do? Imagine that shit? Fuck that. I want my front row seat."

"Then I'm not doing it. Enjoy the blue balls, Sir."

He snatched off the eye mask and stared over at me like I had called him another name. When Dolph saw my shirt open, he tried to touch me, but I moved his hand out of reach. He tried to give me a sad face, but that shit didn't work either. He stared at me while I glared at him, waiting for him to give in. When he didn't, I folded my arms as if I didn't care. This was my game, my rules; he followed them or I quit—those were the only options. He tightened his lips while he flared his nostrils. Then he mumbled through his teeth.

"Fine. We will do it your way. But remember, payback is a mothafucker. Believe that Dr. Carter."

I smiled and kissed his cheek.

"Ok, great. Now stand in front of the bed and drop your boxers, let's see what you're working with."

Dolph, still annoyed, did as he was told. I grabbed a pillow and dropped it in front of him while still looking up at him. His face was still tight, but I liked it. I couldn't ignore the massive object in front of me, but I had one more thing to say before we were properly introduced.

"Ok, Dolph, I'll make you a deal."

He was unmoved and motioned for me to spill it while he purposely leaned forward, causing his dick to slightly brush my face. I laughed at his petty antics, and so did he. Then he leaned back while he crossed his arms.

"You don't have to put back on the blindfold."

Dolph's face lit up like I offered him some money. However, I wasn't done yet.

"You can get a 15-second window, but once it's done, you can only look at the mirror in front of you. And you can't look down, or I'll stop. Deal?"

When he frowned again, I chuckled.

Not surprised he hated that idea.

"No, I don't like that shit either."

Trying to reason with him, I continued to make my case.

"Why not? You can still see my head move, you have access to your hands…you just can't look down. It sounds like a great deal to me."

I licked my fingers and touched his balls. It was then that he breathed deeply and changed his attitude a bit. Dolph closed his eyes and leaned his head back. He moaned as my hands continued to graze him, then he mumbled.

"Sounds like some bullshit, but I'll take it."

I smiled at him, then stopped. He opened his eyes and looked down at me.

"Good, cause I'd be disappointed if I didn't get to taste him. So, let's get started."

Dolph glared at me as I finally gave my attention to the object in front of me. I felt excited and ready for the job ahead of me.

"Hello there, glad we get a chance to finally meet. I'm your Dr. and you're my new client. I want to test your reflexes."

I looked up at Dolph.

"Now be sure to tell me where it hurts or needs some extra attention, ok."

He nodded as he tried to control the urge to shove his dick in my mouth.

"Now be sure you're watching my fingers, because after 15 seconds I will stop every time, you peek."

He growled at me, and I began. I bent down and caught the tip with my mouth. Dolph let out a loud grunt and gently rubbed all over my head as I worked him.

"Fuck, babe, you fuckin' with me already."

I used my free hand to begin my countdown, only I counted slowly. I slid Dolph in and out of my mouth slowly while he moaned and guided my head. When he looked away, I stopped counting and continued once he looked back at me.

"Damn, Sasha, urgh, keep working me."

Although it started slowly, when we were at 13 seconds, I sped up.

"Babe, I'm almost outta time, slow up, fuck."

At 15 seconds, I let loose on him, humming and letting spit drop. Then purposely let him have it. It must have felt good because his knees were starting to buckle. When I caught him looking down, I stopped and eyed him while still holding his dick in my mouth. He grunted and closed his eyes, then leaned his head back. However, when he tried to peek through his eyelids, I purposely let his dick slide out of my mouth. When he no longer felt my mouth on him, he looked down instantly. Dolph was annoyed; however, he knew the rules. I wouldn't start again until he looked away. Speaking through his teeth, he mumbled.

"Ok, ok, ok, sorry, babe fuck, my bad, my bad."

This time, he turned his gaze to the mirror, and then I started again. Tasting Dolph was like eating a ripe piece of fruit; it was a pleasurable feeling, my mouth filled with his juices, and I couldn't get enough of him. After a few minutes, I was done fucking with him. I was focused on the job at hand, and so was he. When his knees buckled again, I stopped.

My poor baby is weak in the knees. Time to put him out of his misery.

"Lay back, babe, and let me finish the job."

Dolph didn't respond, just plopped back and opened his legs. I couldn't help but laugh, then I went back to work. When he found strength again, he finally rested on his elbows, then used his hands to grip the back of my head. He finally got a full view, and when our eyes locked, I could tell he was pleased.

"Sasha, babe, I'm about to let loose. Fuck! If you don't wanna catch a mouthful..."

However, when I showed no signs of stopping, he gripped harder, and I angled my head to let him slide down my throat.

"Shit, babe, that's my Doc…urghhhhhh! Fuck!"

The feeling of him filling my mouth was ecstasy. I'd gladly let him fill my spaces anytime. When he was finished, I made sure to suck him dry while he caught his breath.

"Damn, babe, if I didn't know any better, I'd swear y'all were made for each other."

He sat up and helped me off the floor. I winked and went to the bathroom to clean up.

"I want the other half of my experience, Sasha. If that's half of it, I'ma be looking for that shit all the time."

Dolph yelled from the bed while he rested on it. I came back to wipe him down. While I cleaned him up, he just stared up at me intently without saying a word.

"Well, did you enjoy yourself?" I asked as I smiled.

Dolph didn't respond, just grabbed my arm and helped me to sit on top of him.

"Sasha, I'm a little weak in the knees now. But in about an hour or so, it's my turn. I got two words for you babe…PAY BACK."

He let me go, and I rolled off of him to put the washcloth back.

When I came back, Dolph was under the covers, snoring. *Mission Accomplished.*

I got back into bed and turned on the TV. After an hour or so, I started to feel tired myself, so I turned it off. I grabbed my eyeshades and slid onto my pillow. When I rolled over on my side, Dolph slid closer to me.

"My turn. Time to pay up, Sasha!"

The sound of his voice brought me back to that night. The words from the whisper, I wasn't sure what or who I heard. And here he was—here we were. No mask, no disguises, just us. He rolled me over and took off the eye mask while he gently kissed me, slightly smiling. The lights were off, but something else turned on.

Dolph made good on his promises; he licked, kissed, and fucked the shit out of Ms. Candy and every space available to him. I thought I had given him the full experience, but he showed me up. Time and time again, Dolph had me gripping the sheets, digging my fingers into his back, and holding on for dear life as he worked my entire body. What really did it for me was all the shit talking the entire time. He'd beat me at my own game and made it known. Dolph had me begging and pleading for him to give me more pleasure. I could kick my own ass for staying away from this man and his dick for so long.

Dolph had me bent over the bed while he controlled us from behind. He hovered over me as he gripped my hips, controlling our movement. He asked while he bent me over while holding my hands, thrusting into me like a madman.

"Now, Doc, what was all that shit you were talking about earlier? You still single, Sasha? You letting someone else taste MY Candy?"

Dolph purposefully put emphasis on the "my candy" part. Trying to regain my composure from the euphoric experience, I tried to answer, but I couldn't get my shit together. So, I hurried the words once I found them.

"No, no, Dolph. Fuck!"

He laughed at my compliance, then continued.

"Oh yeah, so who's Candy is this?"

He pumped so hard, I almost fell forward.

"Yours, babe, only yours I swear."

Feeling satisfied, he eased up. Finally looking up, I could see him in the mirror; he smiled.

"Good, now that we've got that straight. Let's not discuss it again."

He smacked my ass, and I nodded. He'd proven his point, and I was in total submission to his plan.

I was about to let loose when Dolph stopped abruptly. Part of me was disappointed until he leaned his face closer to mine while looking at me through the mirror.

"You ready to stop running from me now, Sasha?"

Gathering my breath and my wits, I prepared to answer him while he kissed my cheek and shoulder slowly.

"I'm ready to stop running!"

Dolph nodded, then he asked another question.

"You finally comfortable, Sasha?"

I smiled and looked over my shoulder, putting us eye to eye.

"I'm comfortable, Randolph, I'm finally comfortable, babe."

Finally calling him babe, caused Dolph to smile and kiss my lips slowly.

"Good. Because I'm not going anywhere. Things started off kinda fucked up and got outta hand. But we can talk about that later. Just know I wasn't gonna let you go, Sasha. No matter how many of them, *Independent Woman* bullshit antics you pulled. I meant it when I called you Dr. Carter. A man knows when he meets his wife, and you're mine, Sasha."

I wanted to laugh at his independent comment, but I was on the verge of tears. He kissed my lips once more. Dolph kissed me once more, but this time I didn't let him ease up. I gave him the most passionate kiss with what little energy I had left in my body. There was no mistaking it, he loved me even if he hadn't said it yet. Everything in me felt it, and I felt the same way.

"Now that we've got that shit out of the way. Let me add some more filling to my Candy so we can get some sleep. Fuck, we're gonna have to do this shit often. Daddy is going to need his Candy on tap; I don't give a fuck where you are, I'm coming to your ass!"

Even Houston or Dallas?

Dolph and I picked up where we left off with no problem. More shit talking and more pumps, Dolph and I exploded at the same time. We were both out of breath and beyond exhausted. Part of me couldn't wait for his ass to run outta steam. I was tired as fuck, at least his ass had a nap. I barely had enough energy to get up and pee, but I managed to roll out of bed. Dolph got up after me, and I could tell his knees were beyond weak; his ass walked like he had a charley horse. When he came back to bed, we both lay on our backs.

"Fuck, babe, I ain't gonna be worth shit in a few hours."

Dolph smiled and rolled over to his side to look at me.

"Yeah, but that ass is definitely gonna be sitting higher. I'm sure it will look even better in whatever tight ass dress you're wearing to brunch."

He was right, I not only had a tight ass dress but some high ass heels that I now regretted.

"Just hope my legs hold up in the heels I brought."

"Don't worry, babe. If your feet hurt, I'll rub them for you…but only if you agree to put the heels in the air tomorrow night."

He winked, and I cradled up next to him so we could get some sleep.

At 6:30 am, I was asleep when I heard movement in the bathroom. Too tired to care, I rolled over and pulled the covers over my head. A few minutes later, I was slightly awakened by the smell of body wash and a hand rubbing my back. My face was covered except for my lips and nose, so I could breathe in fresh air.

Of course, Mr. Comfortable is awake. Why is he up so early? Is he just looking at me?

"Good morning, Babe. I know you not sleep. You comin' out them covers so I can see your face before I leave?"

Dolph was sitting on the bed with his back towards me.

"Good morning…why are you up so early?"

I mumbled as I slowly removed the covers from my face.

He turned around to look at me and smiled.

"Going to play basketball with the guys before brunch, remember?"

I nodded and closed my eyes again.

"Ok, have fun. Don't break anything or hurt anyone."

Then I rolled over to go back to sleep. However, Dolph was not done and rolled on the bed, positioning himself right behind me.

"Can I at least get a kiss before I go?"

Urgh, he's one of those morning people. Are we really doing this?

I leaned back and pecked him slightly on the lips and rolled back over. I attempted to pull the covers back over my head, but he held them.

"Nah, that wasn't good enough. Try it again."

I hated morning kisses, especially before brushing my teeth. To me, it was rude and not hygienic.

"Dolph, it's too early for all this. Ain't you gonna be late?" I mumbled through my teeth.

"Yeah, I'm going to be late because my lady is slacking this morning. But it's ok…I'm going to show you how I like to be greeted with a kiss, so next time there won't be a question."

Is he serious? This is too much; I haven't even had my coffee yet.

Before I could reply, Dolph kissed me passionately like he did the night of the bachelorette party and last night. Slowly, gently, not missing any part of my mouth. Just exploratory, as if he knew his way around. When we finished, I was no longer tired, and something else wasn't asleep either.

"I gotta go, babe. But get some more sleep, you deserve it. I'll see you when I get back or at Brunch. Come walk me to the door."

I'm glad I brought Black Vybes because I need him right about now.

I got up and followed Dolph to the living room. When he sat down to put on his shoes, I excused myself to the bathroom to spruce up a bit. When I came back out, I stopped at my bag to grab Black Vybes and plug him in. We were going to have a "discussion" so I could go back to sleep. Dolph was standing and waiting at the bedroom door.

He laughed, "I see you brought your little boyfriend along."

I smiled, "Yeah, he's like Visa, don't leave home without him."

Dolph smiled and nodded, "Well, he can hang out a little longer, but he ain't allowed in Daddy's house, so leave him at home, deal?"

I laughed, "I could never, he's been so good to me. I value loyalty, and he's been nothing but a good companion." I picked up Black Vybes, then kissed the tip of him and held him closely.

Dolph laughed again, "I can respect that I can."

Then he came and put his arms around my waist. He took Black Vybes out of my arms and laid him on the dresser. Dolph pulled me closer to the swollen version of him.

"But after last night, your loyalty is to us, remember?"

I smiled, and then he rubbed his hand down the front of my shirt. He stopped in front of Candy.

"Besides, she and I already got an agreement. Also, you already gave me full access multiple times. So, it's mine now."

I rolled my head back as he pressed harder against me with his hand and body.

"Go ahead and enjoy Black Vybes while I'm gone, 'cause we both know you're gonna be thinking about me."

Dolph backed up, and I refocused my attention on him. He took my hand and led me to the front door.

"See you later, babe." Before Dolph could say another word, I fell into place and kissed him like he taught me. When we finished, he smiled. "That was perfect, babe…let me get outta here before you lure me back into that bed. Enjoy your nap. Be sure to save some for me later."

He opened the door quickly and slid out. When I locked the door, I was dazed. Whatever was "happening" with me and Dolph wasn't just a fantasy, but it was real. I couldn't fight it any longer, despite feeling scared in the pit of my stomach. Everything was finally on the mend; I didn't want to go back. Whatever was next, I just hoped we could tackle it together. Part of me hoped he didn't turn out to be a disappointment. Shaking the negative feelings from my thoughts, I headed back to bed.

For the next hour, I tried to ignore the thoughts and feelings I attempted to release with the help of Black Vybes, but I couldn't; all my thoughts went back to him. Everything centered around Dolph; I tried to stay focused on the positive. His words and movements were etched into my mind and body; I could feel him even when he wasn't there. Every time I encountered him, the night at the tent, the night I imagined him, us lying in bed last night. I could even imagine our future sessions, the possibilities. Each time I released or uttered a word or moan, it was all for him. However, what really put me over the edge was the vision of Dolph asking me to marry him. The image alone sent the second-best orgasm I ever experienced through my body. The loud sound that shot through my mouth shocked me. I lay there for a few minutes, letting it all seep from my body, not wanting to waste the moment. When I was finally done, I was exhausted but re-energized. However, it was time to get ready for brunch. So, I set a 15-minute timer and caught a quick nap. When the timer went off, I was ready for brunch and whatever else the day had for me…for us.

Chapter 15

Brunch was in full swing; the theme was: Hats and Sundresses, Bowties and Suspenders. We all looked like Black Excellence in the dining hall, which was draped in adornments that included various flowers and cigars to tie everything together. This was the last gift to the Bride and Groom from their parents before they went on their honeymoon to the French Riviera. There was a live band, various tables, an open bar, and food galore. I was thankful we were inside because outside it was steaming hot. Some of the guys went outside to smoke their cigars under the tents, which consisted of large fans and other items to keep them cool. I was grateful I didn't need to do anything but show up.

I went to the bathroom to do a quick mirror check before I sat down for the remainder of the event. There was a dance floor and music; however, thanks to my pre-game, I was in no mood to do anything but eat, drink, and be merry while waiting for Dolph to arrive. As I adjusted my diamond studs, I admired my form-fitting jade green halter dress. The green in my dress perfectly matched the ribbon of my khaki hat, which had a large brim. I pulled my hair back so it fell down my shoulders, adjusted my strappy heels, and went back inside. Dolph was right, my ass looked amazing in the dress. However, my legs felt like spaghetti, so I prayed the lines were short so I could sit down.

After I greeted a few people, I made my plate and found an empty table that was meant for two people, then sat down. I also happened to get my hands on a newspaper, so I planned on reading and grooving to music while I waited for Dolph. When I came in, I ran into Keysha, who was whining about the guys being late due to playing another basketball game. Her whining to me was cut short when her sister came to alert her to another looming crisis. I used that to make my exit. Coffee was calling me, and I dared not ignore my morning bestie.

When I finally sat down, I was so excited. I prayed over my food quickly and marveled at my coffee.

"Finally, it's me and you, boo."

I smiled at my coffee as if it would respond. I picked a random section from the paper and started to eat. While everyone else swirled around me, I was in my zone. When my coffee was low, a waiter came by to refill it without my asking. It was like a little piece of heaven. Halfway through my meal, I heard a gentleman clear his throat. I lowered my paper, lifted the brim of my hat, and looked up to make eye contact with him. He was older, with salt and pepper hair, dark skinned, tall, slim, with a great smile. I felt like I'd seen him before, but I couldn't place him.

"Seems like you got the best seat in the house. Mind if an old man joins you?"

As long as you don't talk, flirt with me, or touch my coffee…rest your bones, old timer.

I smiled at him and motioned for him to sit down. He placed his plate and coffee cup on the table.

"You got the right idea, ain't nothing like coffee and the paper to start the morning, especially after a conversation with the man upstairs."

The waiter came by with more coffee as well as cream and sugar. The gentleman took his first sip and closed his eyes. It was the same thing I did after my first sip of the day. When he finished, he addressed me again.

"I'm sorry, where are my manners. My name is Del, and you are?"

"I'm Sasha, it's nice to meet you, Del."

We shook hands, he prayed over his food, and we began to get to know each other.

"Del, can I offer you a section of the paper?"

He smiled brightly, "Absolutely, my dear, thank you for sharing your space with me. I was sure some gentleman was occupying this seat. But when I didn't see one, I had to come claim it."

"Well, it must have been fate. I'm glad you came to join me."

Del started to eat, but I couldn't help but interrupt him again.

"Del, I'm sorry to interrupt your breakfast, but do I know you?"

He laughed and smiled, "No interruption, ask and talk as much as you want. I'm holding space with a beautiful woman, so I'm all ears. But, to answer your question. You don't, but you do."

I wasn't sure what he meant, so I just looked at him curiously.

"Well, you do because we did share a dance or four yesterday."

I nodded, "Yes, we did! We cut up to the Whisper's *The Beat Goes On*"

He nodded, and we toasted our coffee cups.

"Yep, while that angry dude off to side, eyed us. Guess he wished it was him."

I laughed because I was sure he was talking about Dolph. We never interacted at the wedding reception, but I did notice him giving me the eye a few times. So, I purposely danced with any guy who asked and even ones who didn't.

"Well, if the spirit moves you today, Del, I say we show out one last time. What do you say?"

Del raised his cup again, and I raised mine.

"Well, I'll drink to that...here's to showing them how it's done."

We clicked our glasses and went back to eating and reading our paper. We both grooved to the smooth jazz that was played by the band.

"Sir, can I get you or your wife anything else?"

The waiter asked, we both smiled at each other, to be funny, I added.

"Well, honey, can he get us anything else?"

Del pondered for a second, then said.

"Well, love, do you think we should have another coffee or a Mimosa?"

I sat and thought for a second, but before I could respond, someone said.

"Neither I'm sure y'all already had two cups of coffee. Alcohol is the last thing y'all need. Can you bring them two waters?"

We both leaned back to look behind the waiter, and Dolph stood behind him. It was then that I finally made the connection. The waiter moved to the side and watched our interaction.

Del looked at me, and I looked at him.

Del looked back at Dolph, then he addressed me.

"Do you know him? Because I don't."

I shook my head nope, then frowned while looking at Dolph.

"No, honey, I don't know him either. Can you please leave me and my husband alone, Sir?"

Dolph frowned at us both, then pulled up a chair. Del and I laughed while Dolph mocked our laughter as he shook his head.

"I see you've met my father. Waiter, can you take these coffee cups and bring three waters?"

The waiter cleared the table. I looked at Del and Dolph; they were a splitting image of each other. Both equally handsome and charming. How I didn't make the connection yesterday was beyond me.

"Why you gotta come bust up our groove. Me and my wife were enjoying ourselves until you arrived. Urgh, never thought I'd raised a player hater."

Del said as he looked at his son.

"Pops, no one says that anymore. Plus, I put in all the work, and you take the credit. Ain't that some shit. How you gonna replace me already, Sasha?"

I laughed, "Just testing out the older model to see if the younger one is worth the ride."

I winked at Del, who applauded my response, while Dolph just shook his head.

Dolph laughed, "Thought I proved that last..." When Dolph realized Del was waiting for him to finish, I chuckled.

Feeling slightly embarrassed as my face was slightly flushed, I moved us on to the next subject.

"Besides, weren't you the one fawning over Lorna yesterday?"

"Whatever, Lorna is one of my favorite girls. Besides, someone wasn't checking for me until now…took your ass long enough."

I rolled my eyes; the only reason I was talking to him at all was because he refused to leave. Plus, he still had some explaining to do. But that was a discussion for another time. Dolph and Del continued to catch up while I returned to my paper. When Del was finished, he got up to leave.

"Husband, you are leaving me?" I said and pouted.

Del came over and took my hand.

"Never, my love, besides you still owe me a dance. I'm just going to mingle a bit, but I'll be back for you. I promise."

He kissed my hand and winked at Dolph, then left us at the table.

"Dang can't leave you anywhere. How you just gonna go marry my pops and not tell me?"

"Well, technically, you got what you wanted…my last name is Dr. Carter, according to you. Only I'm married to another Carter man."

I laughed as Dolph mocked my laugh.

"Whatever, SASHA! You know who you belong to."

Dolph kissed my cheek and got up to get his plate while I returned to my paper.

After a few minutes, he came back and sat in Del's chair. He prayed over his food, then began eating. I decided to put the paper down so we could catch up.

"You look very handsome. A bowtie and suspenders look good on you. Funny how it matches the khaki in my hat. Coincidence, I think not."

He smiled and adjusted his bowtie.

"Thank you, babe, you look great as well. Naw, it's no coincidence; I made sure I matched my babe. Can tell your ass is sitting higher."

Dolph winked, and I giggled.

"Did you get your nap out?"

I smiled at the comment and took a second before responding.

"Barely, but yes. Thank you for asking and the mental stimulation."

Dolph smiled, "Glad I could assist you."

We engaged in small talk about the basketball game and other happenings in the room before we were silent again. Keysha approached the table; she looked calm yet nervous.

"Hey, y'all, Sasha, can I borrow you for a second?"

I could tell she had something urgent to tell me, so I got up while Dolph looked at us. Keysha hurried me from the table across the room towards the nearest exit. We were about to leave the door when a gentleman approached us.

"Excuse me, Sasha?"

My back was to him, but I didn't need to turn around; I knew who it was, and so did Keysha. Her face was now ten shades of pissed. I turned around and looked at Connor, who smiled.

"It's been a long time. How are you?"

He reached to touch my hand, but I moved it out of reach.

Of course, it has, sorry bastard…problem is it hasn't been long enough.

"Damn, you couldn't just stay put. How you just gonna roll up on her like that! I told you to let me tell her first, fuck." Keysha mumbled in frustration.

"I didn't mean to intrude; I just wanted to say hello. See how you were." Connor said casually.

"You said your peace, keep it moving." Keysha meant business; she tried to whisper but failed miserably, plus everything in her demeanor said pissed. This alerted Kyle, so he made his way over to us. When Dolph saw the gathering at the door and Kyle headed in our direction, he made his way across the room as well. Seeing them heading in our direction, I tried to defuse the situation.

"Key, calm down, all is well. Kyle and Dolph are headed in our direction." I said, looking at her, trying to assure her I was good. She glanced at me, and I turned my attention to Connor.

"Look, thanks, I'm well…but please go. This is not the place for any of this."

Connor still didn't move and further displayed his remorse.

"Look, Sasha, last time you called me I was …I heard what you said but…"

Connor was stumbling over his words, which was odd for him. However, I didn't care; he just needed to leave without making a scene. This was slowly becoming the case as more people were watching our interaction. Everything remained calm until Connor instantly became frustrated.

"Wait, did you say Dolph? So, that nigga is real?"

OMFG! Please don't make a scene and get the fuck on.

I didn't answer Connor as I was looking for Dolph. However, Connor was unmoved and wasn't leaving without answers. I didn't owe him shit; he didn't matter to me, but Dolph did. When I searched the room again, he was less than 20 feet from us with his sleeves already rolled up.

"You gonna answer me or nah, Sasha?"

Connor said a little too loudly for my comfort.

Before I could answer, Dolph slightly moved me out of the way and stepped between me and Connor.

"Keep it moving before we have a problem."

"Dolph, it's cool," I said from behind him.

When Connor heard me say his name, he immediately looked passed Dolph and then raised his eyebrow. With his hand, Dolph gently moved me back even further.

Connor, being the ass he was, stepped aside from Dolph to address me. When Dolph went to move, I stepped in front of him. This wasn't his fight; I'd dug this hole, so I needed to get myself out and keep him from jumping in it.

"Wow! So, this is the original, huh? So, what was I, a stand-in Sasha?"

Connor's words now had the entire room's attention as he was almost yelling. Kyle came and stood next to me. Then he addressed Connor.

"Connor, look, we've always been cool. But you are disrespecting my family, and I ain't having that. So, you need to leave." Kyle said, then Dolph added, "Yeah, before we help you leave."

Connor quietly walked towards his table, but then he walked back towards us. Then he whispered loud enough for people close to us to hear.

"So, you tell him about what resulted from our night together, huh?" What made it worse was when Connor said "our," he pointed at himself, Dolph, and me. "I can see you ain't keep that shit. Wonder who you would have nam…"

Before he could finish, Dolph went to lunge towards him and warned him again to get the fuck out. Luckily, Kyle and another groomsman caught him. Kyle lured Dolph away while the other groomsman made sure Connor left. Connor didn't say another word, just backed away like he was hurt. He walked towards the young lady he was with, whispered something to her, and they left.

Keysha and I walked out into the hall. I felt like all eyes were on me. The last thing I wanted to do was be in the dining hall. After a few minutes, Kyle and Dolph reappeared while Keysha and I sat on a bench in the hall. They went inside the dining hall while we continued to collect ourselves. She was visibly upset, and I was visibly humiliated. This was not how I wanted things to go or be ingrained into the family. Feeling like I had a Scarlet S on my chest for Slut, I wanted to retreat to my room until checkout time. However, Keysha refused to let me hide.

"Sasha, my bad, I tried to get him to leave or at least let me give you a heads up. Fuckin' ass hole wouldn't wait."

"Key, it's good love. Let's move on, today is about you and not whatever that was about to be. Now go mingle, do newlywed stuff."

Feeling terrible for ruining her brunch, I tried to calm Keysha down. But I was failing miserably. Her sadness manifested into frustration.

"You ain't do shit wrong! Fuck anyone who judges you or bats an eye of shade your direction. I'll smack a bitch, family or not, Doc. You, my sis, and I stand with you regardless. His ass was wrong for that shit, and he's a bitch for trying to call you out. He should have had all that care and shit when it mattered. But, no, he bitched up and now him trying to pull the victim card, my nigga please!"

Kyle walked up on us to check on his bride. Only he was alone, meaning Dolph was somewhere inside, likely waiting for some answers. Although I'm sure he put the story together.

"Kyle, please go make her do something else. Make her smile again, please. No more tears today, Keysha, unless they are tears of joy. Ok."

Kyle nodded and whisked Keysha away while he mumbled something that made her smile. When she did, I was glad and hoped she didn't give the clusterfuck another thought. However, someone else wasn't going to let it go so easily.

Biting the bullet, I headed back inside. Everyone had returned to mingling and eating. No one was paying attention to me; however, I felt like I had a target on my back. I saw Dolph sitting back at the table. I kicked myself for not grabbing my purse before I left the table. If I had, I'd already be upstairs. But I didn't, so I had to go back. As I made the dreaded walk to the table, someone grabbed my arm from behind. I turned and smiled at the familiar smile.

"Sasha, my love, are you ok?" Dell asked, and he gave me a fatherly hug which almost brought tears to my eyes. Holding me, he whispered in my ear. "That fool ain't do nothing but make an ass of himself. Don't you worry about anything. As you already saw, you were protected. If Dolph hadn't reached him, I was almost there. I only had a butter knife, but I would have spread him like Parkay butter if he said one more word."

When Dell let me go, he kissed my cheek.

"Thank you, Dell. I appreciate that and you."

I kissed his cheek, and he shook my hands before he left.

When I got back to the table, I sat down and took off my hat so I could face Dolph head-on. He was back to eating his breakfast and hadn't said a word. I decided to wait silently until he spoke. When there were no words, I went to grab my phone from my purse, but he finally decided to speak.

"Who was that, Sasha?"

Dolph was visibly frustrated but calmer. He knew the answer to the question, or at least some of it, but he still asked. So, I reached across the table and rubbed his arm, then slightly smiled to help ease the situation.

"A mistake that led to another mistake, which caused regret. That led to a vacation and my revival. Now it's nothing. So, we are good, let's move on."

Although I slightly laughed at the end of the statement, Dolph didn't and was not satisfied.

"Yeah, I hear all that, but you ain't said nothing. And from Keysha's reaction, that was more than nothing. So, let's hear it in plain English, Sasha."

I took a breath as Dolph was about to get up. However, I motioned for him to sit down and he did.

If he wanted the truth, he was going to get it.

I told him the truth—all of it, including the pieces he didn't know. Dolph listened intently as I told him about Connor, the date, our interaction (his part in it), Connor's reaction to the baby, the abortion, and the aftermath. He didn't interrupt, just continued eating and kept his eyes on me while I spoke. When I finished, he pinched the bridge of his nose before he spoke.

"Cool. Thanks for being honest."

That was it? All that I said, and this was his reaction. Something's not right.

"That's all you have to say?"

Unsure how to process his words, I waited for Dolph to respond.

"What else do you want me to say. You said, The truth...or your truth."

Dolph sipped his water as he looked at me. He said one thing, but his face read something different. I tried not to read into it, but my gut called bullshit. We could table to conversation now, but we'd definitely be circling back to it. He stood up and gathered his plate to place it on an empty table.

"You need something while I'm up?" He asked plainly, when I shook my head nope, he left the table.

I closed my eyes; he was either angry or disappointed. Either way, he wasn't ok. Brunch was almost over, and I was glad; I wanted to truly clear the air with Dolph and whatever would be, would be. The rest of the brunch, we acted like we did at the reception. Barely speaking, looking at each other, just existing on opposite ends of the room.

Once Keysha and Kyle left, I made my exit. I found Dolph outside smoking cigars with some gentlemen. When I approached him, he didn't even say anything. However, everyone just looked at me as he did while he blew his smoke in the opposite direction.

"Hey, I'm leaving, going upstairs."

He just nodded and turned his back towards me. So, I left and tried to prepare myself for the inevitable once he came back to the room.

If this was all it took for him to leave, he could be gone now.

When I got back to my suite, I took off my hat and shoes, putting them back in their boxes. I pulled my hair back into a bun and began to take off my jewelry when Dolph finally came in. He didn't say anything, just entered the living area as I came out of the bedroom.

"Say it, Randolph." He didn't move or respond just looked at me. "Whatever you couldn't say downstairs...just let it out. You obviously have a problem with what happened, so let it out. I can take it."

Dolph chuckled to himself and leaned against the sofa.

"You're right, Sasha, I got a big ass problem with what you told me. The whole thing was fucked up, and yeah, I'm pissed. Better yet disappointed in you."

Me? Urgh, whatever. Fuck it, let's get this over with.

"Well, out with it…let's get this shit over with."

Dolph came closer to me so we were face-to-face.

"Let me tell you why I'm pissed. First, you let your girls push you to go on dates with two basic ass dudes. For what, Sasha? You ain't need that shit."

Dolph was right; by then, I'd already met him. I wouldn't have needed to go on those dates had I handled things differently with him. Everything always seemed to come back to Dolph. Talk about signs and wonders, consistently ignored. Although I hated it, he deserved to say his peace whether I liked it or not.

"If I'm not mistaken, you were one of those dates, right, Dolph?"

Dolph laughed in my face, which hurt. But I got it.

"Yeah, which is why I ain't go. That is some bullshit and I ain't want nothing to do with it."

Feeling a little taken aback, I responded a little annoyed.

"So, why even agree?"

Dolph laughed again and walked away from me towards the sectional, then leaned on it.

"I didn't. That shit is for weak ass females who are desperate. First, I didn't know it was you. And, I would have never taken you as one for agreeing to such bullshit."

Keysha hadn't told me that. Guess she didn't want to hurt my feelings. But my feelings were hurt now from his reaction.

"Keysha kept pushing, but I wasn't interested, especially in some woman willing to sell herself to whoever said yes."

His words crushed me.

Is that what he thought about me and what happened? Damn.

"Continue…there's obviously more…"

Frustration was getting the best of us; however, it was too late to turn back. We were about to either work it out or fuck things up.

"I heard what you said about your little interaction with ole' boy. About missing me and shit, but still you…y'all…were reckless and you got pregnant, Sasha, then you had an abortion. Shit, part of me understands why ole boy was in his feelings. That's some fucked up shit, Sasha."

His defense of Connor really hurt. I definitely couldn't let that slide. Had he not heard the part about Connor being an ass to me when I told him I was pregnant? I walked up on Dolph like he was a random dude off the street. We stood face to face; I folded my arms while he gripped the back of the sofa.

"Oh, so you're defending that bitch ass nigga? He didn't even want the baby; that shit downstairs was for show."

Dolph didn't say anything, just waved me off. However, his silence was enough, and I walked away. After a few moments, he spoke again.

"I'm not judging you…"

Now standing on the opposite side of the room, facing him.

"Like hell you aren't Randolph! Fuck it, if you are, you are. I can't change that shit or what I had to do."

Dolph let out a slight chuckle. He walked away towards the front closet and got his bag.

Knew this shit was coming. Hopefully, he will make this shit quick, then leave.

"You didn't have to do it, Sasha."

Feeling really pissed off, I walked to the sectional, getting closer to Dolph but not in his personal space.

"Excuse me, you don't know shit."

Dolph looked me in the eye and we continued our conversation.

"Oh, I do know shit. You could have kept it."

"Then what?"

"Raised it. So, the fuck what if ole' boy left or wasn't interested."

Tears were now coming out of my eyes. His judgment hurt more than I cared to acknowledge in the moment.

"Oh, so would you have still been interested if I were pregnant with another dudes baby, Randolph?"

He didn't say a word, just took in air and pinched his nose. That was enough for me; the answer was clearly no.

Fucking hypocrite!

"You're being unfair, Randolph. You get on me for allegedly judging you for having a son…now you're judging me for not having one. Make that make sense."

"The difference is my son is alive. And yours…"

Wow! I can't believe he just said that to me.

Dolph might have stopped before he finished. However, it didn't matter. The fact that he thought it was like a dagger to my heart. From his facial expression, he instantly regretted it. However, the damage was done.

Almost sobbing, I yelled, "Go to hell, Randolph." Then I went into the bedroom and slammed the door shut. I hoped he would just leave, but he didn't. When Dolph opened the bedroom door, I regretted not locking it behind me. I was standing at the dresser when he entered. A mirror stood before us, but neither one of us looked into it. Dolph tried to touch me, but I snatched away from him. He let out a sympathetic sigh and stood behind me.

"Look, Sasha, I'm sorry. I apologize for what I said. It just…"

Sniffling and wiping my eyes, I then replied.

"You said what you felt, so don't apologize. It is what it is. I fucked up, and now I live to regret it every day. So, look, let's just call this a wrap. This was fun. But obviously, you don't respect me for my decision, and I get it."

I was expecting Dolph to leave at that moment. However, he didn't; instead, he stepped closer to me and put his hands on the dresser.

"Sasha, let me ask you something. Be honest with me, if I got you pregnant, would you have an abortion?"

Why did he have to ask that question? What does it matter anyway?

The question caught me off guard. When I didn't answer, he continued.

"We did a lot of reckless shit last night, Sasha. So, if you are pregnant, are you going to get rid of our baby, Sasha?"

When he put his hands on my stomach and began rubbing them over it. I closed my eyes and breathed deeply.

"Dolph…"

Dolph leaned closer and put his head on my shoulder.

"I can't move forward with you if we can't expand our family together, Sasha."

When I finally spoke, I whispered the answer to his question.

"It was different, you've got to understand that."

"Tell me how, Sasha, explain it to me so I can understand, please."

He whispered back, still holding on to me. Dolph continued to rub his hands against my stomach again, and I felt butterflies, but still had no words.

"Your situation hasn't changed. The only difference is I wouldn't leave you; I'd be there for and with you every step of the way. We'd do it together. So, the real question is, are you ready to be a mother? At the end of the day, it's truly about you."

He lifted my head to the mirror in front of us so I could meet his stare.

"Are you ready to be a mother, Sasha? Because I'm ready to introduce you to DJ and have as many kids as we can afford."

I wanted nothing more than to be a mother. My whole life was based on being a wife and mother; I'd prayed for it and awaited the day it was answered.

"I never wanted to do it alone, but…"

Before I could finish, Dolph kissed my neck and squeezed me tighter.

"I wouldn't leave you, babe…"

He said between kisses before he turned me to face him.

"Answer my question, Sasha, would you have my babies?"

Dolph waited for my response as he looked into my eyes. So, I spoke honestly.

"Yes, I'd have your babies, Randolph."

That was all he needed. Dolph kissed me passionately, showing me his pleasure in my reply. We kissed so much, my mouth hurt, but I couldn't stop. There were no words, just a feeling of relief that we survived our heated discussion.

I stopped kissing Dolph so I could say something that pained my heart. Even if he didn't acknowledge it or understand it. I had to say it. Dolph looked at me as he rubbed my cheeks.

"I'm sorry, Dolph," I whispered between kisses. He stopped and looked confused at me, waiting for me to explain. "I'm sorry I let you down…but…" tears came down my face as I processed my words. He wiped my face as I continued, "You have no idea how hard that was for me…What I went through after. It almost broke…" He held me closer to him while I let it out. "I couldn't be tied to him…I did what I thought was best." Dolph just nodded as if he finally understood. Which made me cry even harder. When I finally settled down, he led me to the bed and we lay down while he held me.

"Sasha, you, ok?"

"Yeah, just tired…exhausted."

"Go to sleep, babe."

What if you're not here when I wake up?

Almost as if he could read my thoughts, Dolph replied, "I'll be here when you wake up."

I closed my eyes, but there was still one question left to ask. I had to ask. If he said no, I wouldn't be mad at him. If anything, I'd understand and count it as punishment for my decision.

"Dolph?"

"Yeah."

"Do you forgive me?"

"Yeah. I forgive you."

"Promise?"

"I promise, babe. Get some rest."

With that, I fell asleep in his arms. I expected him to pull away at some point, but he didn't. He held me tighter, and I completely relaxed into him. Maybe this was real, and I could relax. I loved Dolph, and he loved me. Maybe that's all we needed.

Chapter 16

When I woke up, I wasn't surprised; if anything, I expected this outcome. The warmth of his body was gone. The bed was cold, felt like it had been for a while. Although I dreaded it, I rolled over, and he was gone. His side of the bed was made as if he never slept in it. I went into the living room to search for a trace of him. But there was nothing. I even checked the spare bathroom and front closet, but everything was gone. Dolph had left. Nothing but his cologne lingered in the air. I tried to hold back the tears that streamed down my face due to the harsh reality in front of me. But it was no use. He changed his mind about me, and he had every right to do so.

Frustrated, I went back to the bedroom and screamed into the pillow until I damn near suffocated. Then I let out a loud cry, better out than in. After a few minutes of crying, I finally collected myself and tried to settle on what to do next. Dolph was gone; I was still reeling from the incident at brunch. What else was there to do but cry myself back to sleep? Hopefully, more rest would give me a reset to consider next steps. As I closed my eyes, I pondered what life should be like going forward. I hadn't told Keysha yet, but I was interviewing soon for the position in Houston. If I got it, I was really considering taking it, especially since things with Dolph were over. I didn't have to move, but what else was left for me in the DMV? She would be pissed and likely shun me, but it may be best for her, especially now that she was married.

Urgh, too much to consider…let's get some rest! Why couldn't he have at least told me goodbye?

When I heard my phone chime, I sucked my teeth and rolled my eyes. The last thing I wanted was to talk to anyone. However, something told me to check my messages. I rolled over towards the nightstand and grabbed my phone. When I looked, I saw a message from Dolph.

da Negro: *Sasha, I want to believe you…I do. But I don't know if you're ready for what I want…for us. Until I'm sure, I can't introduce you to DJ until I'm 100% sure you're all in. A man builds a kingdom for his Queen. I'm sure that I want to build multiple houses for you. Maybe we need more time, should get to know each other more. But don't mistake it, this doesn't change what I feel for you or about you. I don't play about the most important people in my world, which includes you. The hotel bill is taken care of. Call me when you wake up, let's figure out how to move forward.*

MDSCarter: *I get it. No worries, no harm, no foul. You take care, Randolph. Peace. Love. Blessings.*

Dolph called me, and instead of ignoring his call, I answered. I could barely answer before he started talking. He wasn't yelling, but he definitely wasn't happy either.

"Did you not read anything I wrote? Come on, Sasha."

My voice was hoarse from crying and screaming. So, I tried to clear my throat enough to sound normal enough to reply. However, I failed. As soon as I said his name, I started to cry again.

"Dolph, I read it and I get it. And you're right, maybe I'm not ready."

"No! You are just using that as a cop out. Come on, stop that shit, Sasha! You might need more time, but you are ready."

Feeling perturbed that he even called me out. I spoke directly and intentionally to Dolph.

"Says the man who left me without even saying this to my face…"

Dolph sighed. If I knew him well, and I did, he was shaking his head or pinching his nose.

"My mother had an emergency, so I had to get DJ, Sasha. If that hadn't happened, I'd still be there. Hell, if I knew you were ready, I'd bring him back with me now. I ain't some bum ass dude, who leaves when shit gets tough. I'm a man about mines."

We were quiet, which was likely a great thing to let us both cool down. When we spoke again, we were both calmer.

"You're right, and I'm sorry for even saying that. Funny thing is that's one of the things I love about you."

Damn, didn't hold that in for very long. Sheesh woman!

The phone was silent, which caused my heart to race. Part of me hoped the line went dead and he didn't hear me. I hadn't meant to say it, not out loud at least. But it was too late; he heard me loud and clear.

"You love me, Sasha?"

Dolph sounded uncertain when he asked.

"Yes, Randolph, I love you. I'm not saying it because of what happened. I've felt that way for a while now…just was afraid to admit it. But…"

"No but's babe…"

"But I don't want to waste your time or mess this up. Well, any further than I already have…I love you, Randolph. Maybe you're right, we should take more time and revisit us later."

"Sasha, that's not what I…"

"Randolph, please…let's just give it some time and see what happens."

"What does that even mean?"

"I don't know. I don't know. But I know I don't want to hurt you or lose you. I need you more than you know, maybe even more than I care to acknowledge. I can't risk losing you or whatever this is. Give me some time, please."

He was quiet, surprisingly; he usually had a quick rebuttal. Then he sighed and finally spoke.

"Fine, Sasha. Let's do things your way. But know I'm glad you said you loved me…because I love you too. I'll be waiting, babe."

He ended the call, and I went back to sleep.

When checkout time came, I was more than ready to put the wedding events behind me. Thanks to Dolph, the bill was taken care of. All I needed to do was leave and head back to reality. As I packed my things up, I heard the front door open. I was thankful I was dressed in a navy-blue button-down shirt that tied in the front, jeans, and some navy-blue slide-on sandals. I had my phone in hand, ready to dial 911 as I couldn't see who was coming down the hall.

"Umm…hello? I have a gun and pepper spray." I yelled.

I didn't have either, but maybe that would send the perpetrator away. When Dolph came around the corner, I breathed a sigh of relief and closed my phone.

"Why didn't you say anything? I could have…"

Dolph looked at me unfazed, "First of all, why isn't the lock on the door? And what were you gonna do, Sasha, we both know you don't have a gun or pepper spray. What were you gonna do, call 911 and then lock yourself in the room under the bed until they arrive? Please."

He was dressed all black, in a short-sleeved button-down, jeans, and shoes. As always, he looked and smelled amazing. I was a bit surprised to see him, but glad he came.

"Look, I know you're about to check out. But we need to talk first, have a seat."

I sat down on the sectional without a word. He sat on the arm of the sofa. Dolph grabbed my hands and held them while looking at me.

"Sasha, look, I've been waiting for you to say you loved me from the first day I met you. What you don't know is that when Keysha first mentioned you, I didn't tell her, but I thought you were dope. She spoke so highly of you and all you'd accomplished. I knew instantly I wanted to meet you. Then, when Kyle happened to show me your picture. I was blown away. You were/are beautiful. I knew right away I wanted to get to know you. Hell, if I'm being honest, I wanted to marry you then.

Meeting you at the gym was on purpose. But not how you think, I asked Keysha what gym you went to and around what time. She told me that you were a creature of habit. So, I came to check you out. I didn't mean to run into you literally. However, when I did, I knew it was meant to be.

When I brought you lunch, I told Keysha in advance so she wouldn't blow my cover. I didn't want you to feel pressured to like me since we had people in common. I kinda hoped you saw my sincerity, especially when I stayed to clean up your little puke fest. I hadn't seen that much throw-up since Little Man was a baby.

But anyway, when we had that misunderstanding, the first one. I'll admit, it made me fall back a bit. When you approached me that day in the parking lot, I was still pissed. So, I brushed you off. But days went by, and I couldn't stop thinking about you. I felt like I was giving up on us too soon. When I finally reached out to Keysha and Lorna, you'd left for vacation and were unreachable. However, they began to tell me more about you. I made a promise to myself I'd find a way to reach out when you returned. At first, when you didn't answer, it bothered me. But the night I saw you at the gym, I knew it was fate. I wanted to give us another try.

At the party, when I saw you in that little ass bathing suit, I watched you all night from afar. Everything in me wanted to go to you. But I didn't know how you would take it if you found out how I knew Kyle and Keysha. Part of me worried you would react how you did after the wedding, and I wouldn't get a chance to explain. I hadn't intended for you to see me in the tents. But I had to make sure you were good. There were a lot of dudes talking about pushing up on you, and I wasn't having that shit. Babe, when you took my hand and told me to follow you, I almost gave it all up then. I wanted to take you home immediately. Part of me hoped you knew it was me and that I'd be back for you.

When Lorna called me and told me you were sick. I couldn't wait to help you get better. Caring for you, putting you to bed, holding you even when you tried to hide Black Vybes. I knew I wanted to be with you and hoped we'd get our chance moving forward. But we hit another roadblock. I wish you had told me what you felt at that moment. Maybe we could have fixed things. But, then again, maybe we wouldn't have or things would have gotten worse, I don't know.

When you finally called me while I was back home visiting my grandma, I couldn't wait to get home. The reception is fucked up there, but I got every call and message. I listened to them several times. I knew you really cared for me. I hoped you were ready for me, us. I even talked to her about everything. She called me a mule for not returning your calls sooner. She encouraged me to go to town and call you. But I wanted to wait till the wedding. My grandma told me I'd be a fool to let my wife get away because I was being a jackass. Calling you wasn't enough; I knew I'd be walking you down the aisle, for the first time, but hopefully not the last time.

I asked Kyle, Keysha, and Lorna not to tell you because I didn't want you to find some reason not to show up or something. I could handle it if you were mad, but not if you didn't come. When you saw me, you were shocked. Although I didn't look directly at you, I was happy to see you, touch you. I missed you so much. But, when you 'attempted' to give me my walking papers before the reception, I was pissed. Sasha, I wasn't going to let you get away that easily. When I came to your door, I was prepared for you to slam it in my face. Or worse. But when you opened it wide, I just came in and didn't leave. That's how I feel about us now. Sasha, you opened up the door to your heart when you told me you loved me. And I'm not walking back out… we're not giving up on us. Let's figure this shit out; we wasted enough time. Come on, babe, tell me you're on board with us."

Wow! That was beautiful. He really was all in. Now so am I, but it will take more time.

Hearing Dolph lay it all out for me made me cry. It all sounded like a romantic, dramatic love story when it came together. I'd never had someone love me and work so hard for my love. No matter how foolish I acted or attempted to pull away. I pulled Dolph close to my face and kissed him deeply. I was ready to give it all up for him. However, I knew he still wasn't ready to give himself fully to me, and I understood. After we stopped kissing, I smiled at Dolph, and he smiled back.

"Randolph Carter, you are the most amazing man I've ever met. I've never had someone love me the way you do. I'm ready to give my all to you, babe, I swear. Whatever we can do to fix things, I want to do it."

Dolph's face lit up, and it brought joy to my heart. However, there was more, and I knew his light would dim a bit.

"But, baby, you're not ready, and I get it."

Dolph instantly dropped his head and let out a breath, then grunted.

"Sash…"

"I'm not saying I'm going anywhere or that I'm giving up because I'm not."

When Dolph still hadn't looked at me, I guided his face towards mine. Then I held it so he could keep his eyes on me.

"You have to protect that precious little brown baby, and I get it. I want you to be 1000% sure about him meeting me before you bring him around. I'm here and I'm ready. I'm not going anywhere, but you have to be sure, Dolph. I don't plan on being someone in his life who disappears. When I meet him, I want to be there forever. I love children and I always wanted one, even if I didn't birth one."

Dolph sighed again and rubbed his head. So, I finished up so we could head out, as it was almost checkout time for real.

"When you're ready, you have my word that I'll love him, protect him, nurture him, guide him, and support him like he is my very own. He will be in good hands with me, whether you're around or not. Randolph Jr. will be a priority to me, just like you are. You have my word, Randolph."

Dolph kissed me, and I stood up. We both knew it was time to go. He stood, grabbed my bags, and we headed out. Neither one of us said a word; we just held hands all the way to the lobby. When the valet brought my car around, Dolph put my bags in the car but had to rush off to a meeting.

Before he left, we spoke our last words.

"What do we do now, Sasha?"

I smiled and rubbed his cheek.

"Well, babe, we allow space to happen, but knowing that when the time is right, we are gonna be back together."

Dolph nodded and held me close. He kissed my face and whispered.

"I love you, Sasha."

"I love you too, Dolph."

He squeezed me tight as if to indicate he didn't know when we'd touch again. I understood. He looked at his watch, kissed me and then left. We never discussed when we'd talk again or even see each other. However, I wasn't worried; this was only temporary. I had faith in us and that this was the best move.

When I got into my truck, the clerk knocked on the window and handed me an envelope.

"What's this?"

"It's your spa package, madame. Your husband got it, but unfortunately, you weren't able to use it, so we put it on a gift card for you. Come back and see us soon."

I took the card, and the clerk left. I opened the envelope and it was $500 for spa services. It also had a personal message written by Dolph.

> *To my new undiscovered best friend. Thank you for making my*
> *Dada so happy!*
> *Enjoy the relaxation! ~ Love DJ*

I couldn't believe he was so thoughtful, but the message from DJ was icing on the cake. I texted him immediately.

> MDSCarter: *Thank you so much for the gift card! Please give DJ a big hug and kiss from me. I love you both.*

> da Negro: *You're welcome, Doc. We love you too.*

I headed home prepared to decompress. Tomorrow was a new day, and my clients awaited my return.

Chapter 17

Two Weeks later...

Fridays were quiet days in the office. Clients were not scheduled; it was our catch-up day. It was Keysha's first day back in the office. We had some loose ends to tie up before our busy season, which started next week. So, Keysha handled appointments, insurance claims, networking events, and other duties. I worked on client notes, external material, focused on board and committee duties, and any other personal appointments.

We agreed to work for half a day. Keysha needed to handle personal stuff. Instead of going out for lunch, I ordered breakfast. We agreed to work and be out of the office no later than 2:00 pm, if not before. At noon, I stepped away from my computer to ask Keysha a question. I was glad I dressed down today. Thanks to Sarye, I was enjoying my expanded wardrobe, and the new pieces made it easier to get dressed. Which included today's fit. A cut-off black T-shirt with the Looney Tunes on it which tied in the back. A cute pair of slim, tight-fitting jeans and some black and red sneakers to match. I added some silver hoop earrings and a monogram necklace with the letter S in rhinestones. My hair was straight and flowed down my shoulders. It was the same sew-in from the wedding, only refreshed. I not only looked good, but I felt even better.

I handed Keysha a file, and we began to discuss it while I hovered over her to show her some data points. When someone knocked at the door, we both looked up. The door was glass, but you could only see out and not in. It was him. I hadn't heard from Dolph since we talked at the hotel. He didn't call or text, which was fine. I knew there'd be some distance. However, I hoped he would call or come around when he was ready. And here he was today, knocking on the door.

Before I could say anything, Keysha hit the button by her desk to let him in.

"Key…"

"What Doc? He came to you…that's something."

It was. I didn't know what he wanted to say; it had been weeks. However, part of me was glad to see him. Dolph grabbed the door and held it open.

"Come on, Man," he said as he waited.

Moments later, Dolph ushered in a mini version of himself. The toddler held his sippy cup to his mouth. With the other hand, he brushed everything in his path. I couldn't take my eyes off him. He was adorable, a spitting image of his father. Only he had corn rolls, bright eyes, and, of course, he was small. His face was one I had seen before, very vividly. It was no mistake or question now who he was or what they both meant to me.

"What's up, Keysha, Sasha?"

Dolph said as he hovered over his son, straightening up his shirt. The toddler was mesmerized by the office. He likely sized up what else he could touch while he sipped his cup. Which was fine, I didn't mind it. Hell, he might fix or improve something. Little did he know this was his domain. I'd gladly make space for him in it. Dolph may have been looking at me, but I was focused on the toddler. Seeing him brought a smile to my face and an ease to my heart I'd never felt before. When Dolph or I hadn't spoken for a while, Keysha broke the ice.

"Hey, Dolphie, what's up, handsome man! Remember me?"

Keysha said as she looked at his son.

"This is Little Man. Say hi, man. You remember Keysha?" Dolph said as he tried to remove the cup from the toddler, but he wasn't having it. He moved out of his father's reach and stood closer to the fake plant in the corner.

I couldn't take my eyes off him. Everything about him made my heart hurt. I loved him as soon as I saw him.

Why did he do this? Why now? If this goes left, it's going to be a problem. But it won't…I've seen it. Better yet, I've seen him clearly.

My hands started to feel clammy, so I rubbed them against my jeans while I still watched the toddler.

"Sasha?" Dolph whispered as if to get my attention.

I finally looked in his direction. He smiled and nodded, as if he could read my mind. I partially smiled back but didn't say a word. Dolph's eyes held some hope and remorse. Mine did the same. I didn't realize how much I missed him until today.

When Little Man rustled the leaves on the tree, it broke our focus.

"Hey, leave that alone. Come over here, man," Dolph ordered, and Little Man came to him. He picked him up and stepped closer to me.

"Can you say hi to Doc and Keysha?"

Dolph rubbed his son's stomach. Still holding on and drinking from his cup, he lowered it and smiled.

"OMG, Doc! Look at his little face," Keysha said as we both fawned over the full smile on the toddler's face.

"He's beautiful, Dolph, just absolutely awesome," I said, looking at the bashful toddler. Those were the only words I'd spoken since they arrived. Dolph smiled at me, then he replied.

"Thanks."

Dolph kissed his son's cheek. I was about to say something when Little Man finally spoke, then laughed.

"Dock't"

It was the most beautiful sound I have ever heard. He couldn't say Doc so it had a K sound. I was won over officially. He could have everything I owned if I could hear that little voice say my name again. Dolph smiled and kissed his cheek again, which caused Little Man to play coy. I wanted to hold him but didn't want to move too fast. So, I rubbed my hand against my arm as I gathered my words to speak.

"You know my name, huh?" I smiled at him.

He turned away and then laughed again.

"Don't act all shy now, she heard you." His father said as he laughed at him.

I was so excited to hear him call my name. However, I was even more thrilled when Dolph told us the reason for his visit.

"I've been showing him your picture and talking to him about you. He'd also seen your pictures at Lorna's house when we visited a few times. But I showed him one of you that Keysha sent me from the wedding. Every day, I asked him if he was ready to meet you. Most days, he would laugh or just go back to playing with his toys. But today I asked him he nodded yes. I thought it was a fluke, but he grabbed his cup and headed to the door. So here we are."

Little man turned around and then reached out for me. I looked at Dolph, and he extended the toddler towards me. Once he was in my arms along with his cup, it was like he never left. Little Man lay his head on my shoulder, and I rubbed his back. His little breath against my chest was everything. When he raised his head, I held him on my hip, and he just stared at me. When I smiled, he did as well, then turned his attention to the characters on my shirt, rubbing his hand on each one.

"Aye, stop being fresh rubbing on her like that," Dolph said, smiling slightly embarrassed.

"He just likes the characters," I said as I stared at the toddler, then kissed his little cheeks, which caused him to laugh.

While he pointed, I told him about each character.

"Bunny, can you say Bunny?" I said

He smiled and pointed at the next character.

We went through the rest of the characters in our own world like old friends. While Keysha and Dolph just looked at us. When we finished, he held onto the charm on my necklace, laying his head on my shoulder again. After a few moments, he shook his cup as if to say he was out of juice.

"Would you like some more juice?"

He nodded, yes, and we headed to my office.

"Let's see what I have," I said, and sat in my chair and rolled over to my fridge.

Dolph stood in the doorway of my office and stared.

"I have one last apple juice; can you have that?" I said, asking Little Man, but looking at his father.

Of course, Little Man nodded yes, then Dolph nodded that he could.

"Dang, you got her last with no attitude; she really likes you."

Dolph came in and sat on the other side of the desk.

I smiled as I thought about the lunch fiasco. I attempted to put Little Man down so I could wash his cup out. But he wasn't having it.

"No, Dock't. Up. Up."

So, we headed to the sink to rinse his cup. When I turned on the water, he couldn't resist putting his hand under it. We laughed and washed our hands along with his cup.

"Dang, I should have introduced y'all earlier. Maybe we could have been married with another one on the way by now."

Dolph joked as he watched me wipe out the cup.

"Very funny, Randolph."

I sat down and refilled the cup with apple juice and diluted it with some water.

"He ain't gonna drink that. You put too much water in it." Dolph said as if I made a rookie mistake.

"I bet you he will." I didn't know if I was right, but he challenged me. So, I couldn't back down now.

Dolph leaned over the table and extended his hand with his thumb up. Knowing we were about to make a bet, I did the same.

"If I win, you spend the rest of the afternoon with us."

"And if I win?"

Dolph thought about it.

"I'll take you on a date anywhere you want."

We touched thumbs, shook hands, and we both sat back to see who would win.

I handed Little Man the cup, and he took a sip. Then immediately frowned and handed the cup back.

"No, Dock't. No want it."

Dolph and I laughed. He definitely was not going to finish the juice. So, I poured out some of the contents and added more juice. It was then that Little Man not only drank the juice. But then he lay his head back on my chest and put his little feet on my desk. When his father went to correct him, I waved him off. He was comfortable and wasn't bothering anyone.

"So, Dock't what time you get off. We got a few more places to hit." Dolph said as if he had accomplished something.

"I'm off now."

Dolph smiled while Little Man kicked his feet on the desk. He wasn't fooling anyone, so I called his bluff.

"And let's be real, this bet was set up for you to win either way."

Dolph laughed and nodded, "Yeah, it was. I owe you for not calling you back sooner." I nodded, then he continued. "Plus, I don't think your new best friend is gonna let you go anytime soon. So, you're stuck with us now."

I laughed, "Yeah, well, you can drive us around. I mean, since you gotta be there or whatever."

Dolph laughed, and so did Little Man as if he got the joke.

"Dang, it's like that? Shoot first, my father gets more action than me, and now my son. Maybe I need to take some lessons from them. I can see DJ speaks Dock't very well." Dolph was quiet, then spoke again. "Matter of fact, when you saw him, you were sold."

He was right and he knew it. I also didn't negate it, just smiled in his direction. Dolph stood up and came to my side of the desk to help me stand up while I still held Little Man. While we were face-to-face, he added, "But that's ok. We just need to be reacquainted. Maybe we will sell each other on something more, especially since WE not going nowhere."

Dolph kissed my cheek. Not to be outdone, Little Man kissed my cheek as well and returned to his apple juice.

"Hey, don't be kissing my woman, brah."

When I kissed Little Man's cheek, I looked at Dolph and laughed.

"Oh, that's what we're doing, Sasha? Ok, cool."

Dolph nodded as if he needed to muster up a plan.

"Dang, the baby is getting more action than me on the first day. We're gonna have to fix that."

We headed out since Keysha was already gone.

Dolph drove, so we spent the rest of the day running errands, which included lunch, a trip to the park, stopping by one of his barbershops, a Costco run, and dinner before he dropped me off at the office. When we arrived back, it was almost 7:30 pm. Little Man was asleep, worn out from all the running around. Truth be told, so was I. I couldn't wait to shower and crawl under my bed.

"Thanks for hanging out with us today, Sasha. Glad I finally worked up the nerve to come talk to you. See your face. Let you meet Little Man. It had been on my mind since our discussion."

"I'm glad you came by, too. I have to admit, after meeting him, I regret delaying things for so long. I really do understand and commend you for protecting him, I really do. I really am sorry, again, Dolph, that I doubted you."

"No need to apologize. I believed you were ready the last time we saw each other in the hotel room. I guess, I just didn't know how to move forward."

"I get it. Everything happened for a reason."

I unbuckled my seatbelt and was about to exit his truck, but he grabbed my hand.

"Sasha, if you're free this weekend or soon. Can we meet up, have dinner, or something?"

"Sure, call me."

Dolph smiled, then he frowned before he finished.

"You still got my number? Or can you at least unblock me and shit."

I laughed; I hadn't thought about blocking him in forever. Besides, I was the one waiting for him to call me. Although I hadn't changed his name in my phone yet.

"Dang, you really didn't call me. But yes, I still have your number and it's still saved."

Dolph smiled, "What's it saved as?"

"Right now, it's *da Negro*." He laughed loudly, then I added. "But now, I'll change it to *Package Deal*."

He kissed me, and I smiled, then got out. Dolph waited for me to start my truck and head out before he left.

As I opened my door, his back window rolled down. Little Man was awake and waved.

"Tell her bye-bye, Man."

"Bye, bye, Dock't, bye," he yelled.

I smiled as his little hand waved frantically. I waved back and blew him a kiss, then he blew one back.

"Hey, y'all gonna stop leaving me outta these kisses." Dolph fussed jokingly.

I blew him a kiss and got into my truck, then pulled off.

Today was perfect. I couldn't have asked for a better ending. Fuck, I'm a goner! Both father and baby have my heart in a chokehold. This was scary. I just hope no one let's go.

When I got home, I finally got cleaned up and slid into bed. I looked at my phone and then updated Dolph's name to *Package Deal.* I included a picture of all of us at the park as his face card. The three of us smiled while Dolph held my phone up.

MDSCarter: *Enjoy the rest of your evening. Thanks again for today.*
I sent the picture from the park.

Package Deal: *You're welcome. Today was perfect. Thank you for seeing me. I've missed you, Sasha. Sorry it took me so long to say it, never again.*

Package Deal (replied to the picture): *Look at that…Our Package Deal! Good night, I'll call you tomorrow.*

Chapter 18

*"Because he loves me," says the Lord, "I will rescue him; I will protect him,
for he acknowledges my name. He will call on me, and I will answer him; I
will be with him in trouble, I will deliver him and honor him. With long life,
I will satisfy him and show him my salvation." Psalm 91:14-16*

I ran across this scripture during my morning routine.
Every day when my eyes open, I immediately give thanks. Sending
prayers up for my current and future loved ones. Covering them
for the day and thanking God for his provisions and guidance. I
always make sure to send a personalized prayer for my future
husband. Ensuring that God knows I am intentional about his
safety, the plan for his life as an individual, and our lives
together—whenever that happens. But always first and never
least, I cover myself. I wasn't a Bible thumper, might be far from
it. But I did pray and listened to the word, or read my bible daily,
giving. The least I can do is give the Lord at least 15 minutes. On
Sundays, I was intentional about listening to the word (online)
and spent the rest of my day taking it easy. Self-care Sunday is a
must in my profession. Sometimes, I needed a day in the middle
of the week, depending on how I felt.

After my morning coffee, the rejuvenation of my spirit. I
usually made breakfast, cleaned up the kitchen, and then sat
quietly while I made a list of duties for the week. After my list, I'd
put on my *Sounds Only* playlist, then began to write. That was my
routine until the words stopped flowing in between changing
playlists and preparing dinner at some point. It was perfect, my
little oasis, until it was time to put out trash and get ready for bed.
Just me and my thoughts, which eventually the world would read.

Around 2:00 pm, I stopped to take a quick mental break.
My phone rang, and it was a FaceTime call from Dolph.

*There's no way I'm answering this phone. He will not see my R&R
look. Sorry, Dolph, not today!*

I ignored the call. However, he wasn't giving up that
easily. He called again, this time not on FaceTime, so I answered.

"What's up, Dr. Carter? Why didn't you answer my FaceTime call? I wanted to see that gorgeous face. Did I catch you at a bad time?"

He was always determined to get his way. Not today, Sir!

"Good afternoon, Dolph, how are you?"

Although he didn't see my face, I smiled at the thought of our day together. Since then, I was smitten with Dolph and Little Man. Watching Little Man play on the playground, helping him down the slide. Him sitting on my lap while Dolph pushed us on the swing. While in Costco, he let me push him in the cart while he ate snacks. It was all good until he tried to mother bird me. I liked him, but not enough to eat drool-filled snacks. We all laughed, and I nicely slid the snack into the trash. At dinner, when he was tired, he let me rock him to sleep while Dolph and I caught up. It was all perfect. So perfect, I almost didn't want to leave them. But I knew it wouldn't be long before I saw them again.

"I'm great. I wanted to see my lady, but she won't answer my video call. What's up with that, Sasha?"

He's not going to let up, Sasha. You might as well give in.

I sighed and cut my eyes as I whined, hoping he would let it go. However, I knew better.

"Dolph! Sunday is my rest day. So…I look like I'm resting, you follow me?"

He laughed before he responded.

"Sasha, I don't care about that. Head scarf, bonnet, eye boogers, whatever…I know you're beautiful. You don't even wear make-up like that. So, stop playing and let me see you."

I contemplated his request, then I heard my FaceTime chime again.

Did he just hang up and call me back? He's a trip.

I answered the phone, only I didn't get on camera. Not immediately. I had washed my face and brushed my teeth, but I needed to adjust my scarf and re-gloss my lips. My oversized nightshirt was open, so I buttoned it more. Then I finally picked up the phone. He smiled and nodded in approval.

"What's up, beautiful? By the way, that's a face I definitely want to wake up to every morning."

Dolph winked and we both smiled.

"I know you didn't call to just make me smile. So, what are you up to on this fine Sunday?"

The sounds of Anita Baker flowed through my home. As I sipped my second cup of coffee and waited for his response.

"Nothing. Wanted to see if my lady had time for me today. But looks like she's chilling, got a whole ambiance going with music and whatever is in that cup."

"Sundays are usually my chill day."

I told Dolph about my Sunday routine. He seemed impressed as he nodded while I explained.

"I like that you take a day to relax and care for yourself. You deserve it, Sasha."

Glad he understands. That's refreshing.

"You deserve a break, too, Dolph!"

He didn't respond to the remark, just chuckled, then spoke again.

"I definitely don't want to interrupt your rest day. If anything, I hope you will show me how or allow me to join you one day. If it's not too much trouble."

It wouldn't be. I welcome the company; glad you seem interested in my world.

"Sure, I'll teach you how. What do you typically do on Sundays?"

Dolph thought about it before he responded.

"If I have Little Man, it's breakfast, cartoons, maybe go to the park, then dinner at Mom's. Then we come back home, get ready for the week, and then bedtime. If I don't have him, my sister or Mom's got him. I just sleep until it's dinner time."

"Well, that sounds good. And somewhat relaxing? I think it's dope that you have dinner with your family. That has to be a lot of fun."

"Yeah, it's cool. Everyone comes together: Mom, Dad, Sister, Her Boyfriend, Cousins, and their kids, spouses, or whoever usually comes by. We cut up a bit. Then everyone heads home. It's usually chill until somebody gets on that oil. Maybe one day, I can convince you to join us."

Meet his family? Was he serious? Can't say I've ever gotten that far with a guy.

My face indicated uncertainty about his statement.

"What, Sasha? Or should I say Dock't! You met some of the most important people to me…why not meet the rest of them?"

I nodded. He had a point, but I wasn't sure if I was ready for that just yet. So, I switched the subject.

"Speaking of my buddy, where is he?"

Dolph nodded and followed my lead, moving on from the conversation.

"He's at my mom's. I'll pick him up later. You know he can't stop talking about his 'Dock't.'"

He was exaggerating, but it was cute.

"Aww! Well, tell him hello for me. And blow him a kiss."

I giggled while Dolph shook his head.

"I'll do that. Only I think he'd prefer to see you in person. You've spoiled him already. Sure, he can't wait to lie on you, kick his feet up with his apple juice again."

"Well, I ordered a whole case of juice for him. It arrives on Monday. So, whenever he's ready…tell him to come on by."

"Damn. Can I get a case of Tea or Clear Canadian in your office?"

"You are a trip, Dolph."

"What?!? Better yet, I want something else like the other half of my full experience."

I cracked up laughing at his shenanigans. Dolph laughed but spoke more melodic in his next statements. "I want to hold you in my arms again, while I listen to your day or whatever is on your mind. Just be, know you're at peace, you deserve it, Sasha. It's been too long, babe. Time for you to come home to us."

You ain't said nothing but a word!

He was too smooth; his words had me locking my knees and searching for some air despite being in an open space.

"Dolph, let me ask you something."

"Ask away, Sasha."

"Why?"

"Why what?"

"Why me?"

Dolph looked away from the phone; then he spoke.

"Sasha, I don't know how to answer that question without it sounding like bullshit or something. But I care about you. I've learned a lot from Lorna, Keysha, and I'm sure I'll learn more from Robbie. But from what I know, I can't wait to get to the point where you tell me more—yourself."

I didn't know what else to say. Or even how to feel. But I did feel something.

"Look, Sasha, I don't go around introducing Randolph Jr. to everyone. I take being his father very seriously. I wouldn't have made that introduction for nothing. I'm just asking you to meet me halfway, and let's see where this will go. You already know that I love you, and I know you love me too."

I wanted to agree immediately, but something hesitated in my spirit. Dolph sensed my feelings and decided to end the call.

"Take as long as you need. We're not going anywhere, just please don't take too long. Been away from you too long, babe. Enjoy the rest of your day, love."

Dolph ended the call.

Did you really just let him hang up? Stop it right now!

Looking at the blank phone. I realized I didn't need a minute. I was the one tripping. So, I called him back on FaceTime. He answered on the first ring.

"Sash…"

"Let's try a first date and go from there."

"Hell yeah, Dr. Carter, let's do that!"

He was killing me with this Dr. Carter mess. But he didn't care, he was standing on business and his feelings. Dolph stopped and then sighed.

"Look, Sasha, I got Little Man all week so…"

"Bring him."

"Huh?" He raised his eyebrows as if to question my response.

"Look, if this 'works', this will be our norm. So, we all might as well get to know each other more."

Dolph smiled, knowing I was now ten toes down.

"How about dinner on Tuesday? Next week gonna be crazy. I don't get off till 6:00 pm, but we can order in or something…"

"Perfect. I'll bring the apple juice and tea."

"Cool. But when we put Little Man to bed, can I get some attention, please? Tired of feeling like a third wheel on the bestie's playdate."

It was true, Dolph was more of a third wheel when Little Man was around. His son wanted all the attention, and his "Dock't" didn't spare him.

"Ok, I'll make you a deal, you can play with us, Dolph. Then after our first solo date, I promise to give you the other half of your full experience, deal?"

"Cool. I can't wait to get that Doc experience again. I definitely need to give my Candy some attention in return…been too long."

He smiled and winked. I ended the call and pondered my decision. I was going to give Dolph a shot. The thought of it excited me; I just hoped he was worth it.

Chapter 19

Three Months Later….

"So, when do I meet Randolph and the little chocolate baby who's obviously turned your house into his little daycare?" Robbie asked as he picked over the fruit bowl while sitting at my kitchen island.

"Soon. And why my house gotta be a daycare, huh?"

Robbie didn't turn around, just pointed to the TV, while he eyed me.

"Bitch, you got a parking lot of Tunka Trucks, toy cars, and a blue dog under your 85-inch QLED TV. I bet you when I turn that shit on, it's on Gracie's Corner or that Rachel Lady. Next, you're about to have a personal art collection of his drawing on your walls and subzero refrigerator, it's giving luxury Toys R Us heifer."

We both laughed; it was true. Little Man had his personal section in my living room and at the office. When he came to either, he knew right where his toys were. I even had a little plush sofa and chair for him at my house to sit in while Dolph and I sat on the sofa. Dolph, too, told me I spoiled him, but I didn't care about anything but the best for my favorite little guy.

"At this rate, you need to sell this place to me. Move in with Big Daddy so you can be a full-time wife and mommy. So y'all can have some more chocolate babies. Just know I don't babysit, but I will contribute to their fashion and college fund as an honorary Godfather. I'd also like a blown-up picture of me draped in velvet in an antique gold frame with a crown in your foyer, with the title *Godfather* under it on a gold plate, thanks. I'm thinking a Sir Issac Newton motif, apple and all, please and thank you."

Robbie had a whole plan in his mind. I sipped my coffee and rolled my eyes at his exuberant request.

"Robbie…"

"Aht aht aht…"

"I'm sorry, Sir Godfather Robbie."

"Yes, please get it right, peasant…now carry on." Robbie waved his hand to grant me permission to continue.

I wanted to cuss his ass out, but I couldn't help but laugh. I missed him so much. He never came to visit like he promised a couple of months ago due to a schedule conflict. He was supposed to be at the wedding, couldn't make it. And whatever love affair he was chasing took him on a trip at the last minute, a few weeks ago, so he canceled again. This was unusual for Robbie, but we were also moving in two different spaces, so I had to get used to him not being so "available." It sucked.

"Well, first…you don't live here. So, RENTING the space to you is pointless."

"I could use a summer home, this little shack of yours would do, I suppose. I mean, after some major construction like the removal of the duckies around the bathtub, so cliché, Sasha, yuck. But I digress, continue."

Robbie always called my beautiful three-story townhome a shack. He said it would motivate me to upgrade us again. Keyword Us, since no matter where I went, he would always have a room. Or a suite, as he liked to call it. It was our thing, and I loved it.

"Second, it's too soon to even think about moving in with Dolph."

"And why not? His son has obviously moved in here. Hence, the traffic pattern rug that's rolled up in the corner. Don't think I didn't see that shit either. Hand me one of those fruit snacks and an apple juice. And don't think I didn't see the box of pullups and baby wardrobe in the closet of my suite. The outfits are approved, by the way."

Robbie acted as if he were waiting for me to deny the things he pointed out. However, I didn't just hand him the snacks and juice then continued.

"Third, even if we did move in together, we're not getting pregnant anytime soon."

"Girl, please, I bet that man has you climbing the walls like Spiderman. Swinging from ceiling to floor, wall to wall, while he's shooting his arrows all up and through your club or whatever walls you allow him to."

He was right. Once Dolph and I reconnected, intimacy was more than just a word; it was a lifestyle. When we were alone or Little Man was asleep, we'd find anywhere outta ear range to just let loose. As if it were our first time. We'd even done it in his laundry room. That went well until there was a baby on the move. We heard him going towards the basement door. We popped out and scared him. He cried for five minutes, then refused to let his father go. So yes, we were having fun, lots of it. However, that was it. Just some adulting release. Or at least that's what I allowed myself to think since things seemed to have shifted with us once again.

**Thanks for Reading! Part Two is
Coming Soon!
Peace. Love. Blessings.
~ A Lady on Her Way**

Author's Page

A Lady on Her Way (bankonyourselfllc@gmail.com)
A Lady on Her Way, affectionately known as **Dr. Shan** or **Doc,** is a proud native of the DMV. She's a true Aquarian with a creative mind and sarcastic humor, always keeping her loved ones on their toes.

She's an Amazon bestseller of the *Sharnel* series (Books 1-3 are available now). There's a calling on her life that contains multiple commas. While writing is her passion, she's also a certified life coach, a professional development facilitator and trainer, and a business owner. She holds a Doctorate in Philosophy and possesses extensive experience in professional development, higher education, and technology.

For more information about Sharnel or other projects, please visit the website or Instagram page.
https://mysharnel.com/sharnel (website)
https://www.instagram.com/sharneltheseries/ (Instagram)
bankonyourselfllc@gmail.com (email address)

Back Cover

Dr. Sasha Philips, 42, is a savvy licensed clinical mental health counselor who is currently single. While she exudes grace in public, she reveals a different side behind closed doors. Although she enjoys running her private practice and appreciates the support of her well-meaning but intrusive family and friends, she is still on the lookout for a love she can truly call her own.

In a chance meeting, Sasha encounters Randolph "Dolph" Carter, 45, a single father and entrepreneur who is open to love. From their initial interaction, he consistently proposes intriguing ideas for their future together. However, Sasha remains cautious, waiting for what she believes might be a hidden flaw in Dolph. Despite her antics, Dolph's desire for her only grows, leading him to question whether he has misjudged the woman he cares for deeply.

When Sasha finds herself in a precarious situation that jeopardizes her career and future, she must take a step back from everything to reconsider her future. Later, when she's confronted with an uncomfortable truth about Dolph, she must decide if their love or a future is worth pursuing. Will she finally take a leap of faith and embrace Dolph's vision of love? Or will Dolph become weary of trying to create that dream alone?